COSA NOSTRA II

EMMA NICHOLS

J'Adore Les Books

First published in 2020 by:

J'Adore Les Books

www.emmanicholsauthor.com

Copyright © 2020 by Emma Nichols

The moral right of Emma Nichols to be identified as the author of this work has been asserted by her in accordance with the Copyright, Designs and Patents Act 1988.

All rights reserved.

This book is licensed for your personal enjoyment only. This book may not be re-sold or given away to other people. Except as permitted under current legislation, no part of this work may be photocopied, stored in a retrieval system, published, performed in public, adapted, broadcast, transmitted, recorded or reproduced in any form or by any means, without the prior permission of the copyright owners.

This is a work of fiction. Names, characters, and incidents are either the products of the author's imagination or used in a fictitious manner. Any resemblance to actual persons, living or dead, or actual events is purely coincidental.

ISBN: 979-869-0319243

Also available in digital format.

Other books by Emma Nichols

The Vincenti Series:
Finding You (Book 1)
Remember Us (Book 2)
The Hangover (Book 3)

Duckton-by-Dale Series:
Summer Fate
Blind Faith
Christmas Bizarre

Ariana
Forbidden
Madeleine
This Is Me
Cosa Nostra

To keep in touch with the latest news from Emma Nichols and her writing please visit:

www.emmanicholsauthor.com

Facebook: @EmmaNicholsAuthor
Twitter: @ENichols_Author
Instagram: @enichols_author

Thanks

Without the assistance, advice, support and love of the following people, this book would not have reached your reading device, or your doorstep.

Bev. Thank you for slaving through my copious versions of this story with unfettered enthusiasm. You have been a great sounding board and your insight into the policing world in Sicily has ensured this story has remained true to reality. There's a job over there, in the sun, when you retire.

Kim and Doreen. Thank you for your candid feedback. I am delighted you enjoyed this story.

Mu. Thank you for your on-going support, creative ideas and nailing the toughest job of designing another brilliant cover. Awesome job, my love xx

Thank you to my amazing editor at Global Wordsmiths, Nicci Robinson. The first cut may be the deepest, but it is also the one that has made such a big difference. Thank you. I will be forever grateful for your expertise and honesty. Your input helped me transform this work into a truly gritty and exciting read. I take full responsibility for the final copy 😊

To my wonderful readers and avid followers. Thank you for continuing to read the stories I write. I have really loved writing this thrilling series and I hope you love the sequel as much as you did – if not more than – Cosa Nostra.

With love, Emma x

Dedication

To the women who have fought for love. Whether you won the battle or not, this book is especially for you.

1.

Simone's hand shook uncontrollably as she tried to insert the key card into the narrow slot and release the lock to *their* hotel room door. The heat from Maria's body pressed against her made the task even more challenging.

The five-hundred-yard walk back from the Palais Garnier to the Ritz couldn't have been more dissimilar to her stroll to the ballet less than four hours earlier when the world had looked an entirely different place. She'd been alone on the way to the theatre, dreaming, hoping, and wishing that Maria could be with her. All of that had somehow come true, and she had walked back with Maria's hand in hers. Maria, who Simone thought had died and been buried in Sicily, hadn't. Shock and elation had released suppressed grief and disbelief. The surrealness of the whole evening lingered in the ongoing battle between comprehension of the present and the kaleidoscope of mixed emotions imprinted in her consciousness from the past.

Inhaling Maria's perfume, with traces of vanilla and white musk, and the strength of her hand in the small of Simone's back was a potent reminder of all that she had missed in just over three months without her. She had stopped counting the days. Heartache for what had been lost thundered loudly beneath the veil of wanton desire. She hadn't done with grieving yet, but now she had to attune to this new reality. It was the best kind of adjustment to have to make, but elusive when the pain of loss still felt so raw.

She fiddled with the key card and no matter which way she turned, it refused to find the narrow slot. Her hands were trembling. Tears stood on guard behind her eyes, and she knew they were just a second from being deployed. And worse, she had no control over stopping them. The strong comforting hand that covered hers, and the soft whisper of support was all that was needed to set the emotional past free. Tears spilled onto her cheeks and her shoulders began to shake. She sniffed as she wiped her eyes with the back of her hand. "I'm sorry," she whispered.

"Hey." Maria's tone was quietly compassionate. She lifted Simone's chin, looked into her eyes, and wiped her cheeks. "Come here."

Simone pressed her head to Maria's chest and found comfort in the strong heartbeat that resounded in her ear. Raw hurt reared up in a wave then drew her down with more force than she had the courage to withstand. Maria felt good, so good. Too good to be true? *What if I lose you again?* She should feel joyful, excited, ecstatic. Another wave came, unease this time, something more akin to fear, and her knees buckled. She braced herself against Maria and clung to her, craving protection. *Protection* was where it had all started. Maria protecting her from the very person who tried to take Maria's life.

Maria's perfume became stronger, comforting, and reassuring. Simone held Maria tighter still, then worried she might break her. "Please don't leave me again." With the heat of Maria's breath touching the top of her head, she closed her stinging eyes and buried her face into Maria's white cotton shirt. She inhaled deeply, just to be sure that she wasn't dreaming. She thought she knew she wasn't, but doubt was sometimes easier to grab hold of than reality. *You're alive.*

"I'll never leave you," Maria whispered.

She felt better in Maria's arms. Time passed outside of her awareness, and her heart settled into a slow, easy rhythm. For a moment she dared to allow herself to enjoy the truth without fear of it being torn from her again. The hotel door was still locked, and light background music she hadn't noted before intruded. The footsteps were getting louder and the voices were deep. They were talking in French and laughing.

Then two men came into view, wearing evening suits, a bow tie hanging loosely around an open collar. They seemed to move swiftly; faster than expected for the time of day and state of their dress. Simone held her breath and felt Maria's grip tighten around her. Was that Maria's heart pounding or her own? A chill shot down Simone's spine. Maria was staring at the men with wide eyes and an unwavering gaze. Simone let the men pass before taking a breath. The paranoia, she knew it as such, didn't abate in the face of reasoning or logic. "I'm sorry, I didn't mean to—"

Maria's smile looked restrained as she nodded. She seemed distracted and watched the men until they disappeared out of sight and when she spoke her voice sounded affected. It was a moment later before she released Simone. "Shall we go in?"

Simone hesitated to touch Maria's cheek. *So soft. So real.* Her heart raced, her body ached and thrummed in all the right places, and her stomach twisted. Jumbled thoughts, some of them irrational, fuelled spiralling emotions: unresolved grief, fear, and uncertainty about the future. She had too many unanswered questions. Why hadn't Maria contacted her? What if she hadn't turned up at the ballet and Maria had? What happens now? Who else knows?

After hearing about her father's death, Simone's life had become simple. Go home, take care of Roberto, and get a job. And, of course, Patrina Amato had been there to help her with the latter. Maria's death *had* been simple too. Death is simple. It's clear cut; no going back. Painful, yes. It was excruciating to wonder how Maria had died and whether she suffered, to envision her body blown to pieces and strewn across the sea. She had never asked how, and no one had spoken of it in her presence either. Instead, she had focused on coming to terms with the finality of her loss. She'd started to adjust and think about the future.

And then this evening happened. She sounded ungrateful. What the hell was she thinking? Maria, the love of her life, was alive, and she was here. They were here together. The past she thought she knew didn't exist. The future was no longer what she had thought it might be as she headed to the ballet.

This was good, so unbelievably good...except for the lingering feeling of dread that Maria would be taken from her again.

She looked into Maria's eyes and traced her fingertips across the smooth skin of her cheek and along the sculptured line of her jaw. *Right now, right here. Here with me.* Delicately, she touched her thumb to Maria's mouth and her own lips tingled in response. She pressed her lips to Maria's in a lingering kiss that stilled her mind and sparked her desire. Maria tasted so good, so tender, so perfect. Another wave came, lighter this time, and she kissed Maria more firmly. The cool air on her lips stirred her, and she opened her eyes.

"Let's get into the room."

Maria's voice was hoarse, and her eyes shone. Simone turned swiftly and slotted the card on her first attempt. The door clicked and she shoved it open, releasing a pleasingly floral aroma into the corridor. She tugged Maria into the room and flicked the light switch, giving rise to subdued lighting from the tall light stands that snuggled into the corners of the deluxe bedroom. The light revealed a bottle of Veuve Clicquot champagne, a vase of red roses, and a box of truffles on the table. Light pink rose petals were strewn around the floor and across the bed. Her heart raced, light and flighty. Those things hadn't been in the room when she left it to go to the ballet.

Maria closed the door and Simone pushed her against the hard surface. Maria mumbled under her breath. She was waiting, wanting. God, she looked...so incredible. She leaned into Maria and slipped her hands around her waist, tugging her closer to feel the strength of her own craving. She kissed Maria, savouring every millimetre of her softness. "God, you feel so good to touch." Sensing Maria's urgency, she increased the firmness in her grip and sensually probed with her tongue.

Maria eased back and kissed Simone's cheek, her neck, her throat, and down to the top of her breasts, beautifully exposed by the cut of her gown, and Simone's skin felt caressed by the sun. Simone tugged the shirt free from Maria's waistband and gasped at the feel of hot skin and the shivers that danced at her fingertips as she explored Maria's body. She slid her hand up Maria's back. Simone gasped as the texture at her fingertips changed.

Maria jolted and released a soft sigh. Simone moved her fingers gingerly over the uneven surface at the back of Maria's ribs, watching as Maria tensed. Sadness welled at the blemished skin that she instinctively knew was a new scar. "Does it hurt?"

Maria took a deep breath and released it slowly. Her cheeks were flushed, and a light sheen of moisture coated them. "No, it's fine now."

"You were shot?"

"Yes."

"In the back?" She heard the rise in her voice and the incredulity in her tone. Of all the insults, that Maria had been shot in the back was pure cowardice typical of Alessandro. Maria shook her head, and Simone frowned. "Where?"

Maria undid her shirt to reveal the small, almost perfect circle of redder scarred skin just above her heart.

Simone swallowed, imagining the bullet ripping through Maria's flesh, crushing bones and muscles, splitting veins, and bursting free through her back. She let go of the exit wound as if it had stung her finger.

Maria took Simone's hand and placed it on the mark on her chest. "I want you to touch me, all of me. This is healed and I won't break. I need to feel you, Simone. Please don't be afraid."

Simone stared at her own hand, surprised to see it steady. This wound had a different quality to it, as if a fire still raged just beneath the surface of the scolded skin. Her fingers started to tremble. "I *am* afraid."

"It's a shock, I know. But it's okay."

But it wasn't okay, not entirely. She wasn't afraid of touching Maria, although there was a fine line between the excitement of being able to touch her and the anxiety that came with her thoughts of losing Maria again. She was petrified of experiencing another broken heart and *that* she couldn't even begin to contemplate, let alone handle. The thought made her feel feeble. She wished she were stronger. She wished she could just forget the mafia world in which they lived...in which Maria had lived. Maria had reacted to the two men in the corridor too. She had felt it. Maria was different, affected by what had happened. Of course she was. Who wouldn't be? She swallowed down the urge to scream. Maybe, time would heal the past.

She grazed her fingernail lightly over Maria's soft breast down to the line of her bra. Maria gasped a short breath as if the air was hard to find and impossible to hold onto. Simone flicked her thumb across the thin cotton that shielded Maria's nipple and she jerked. A rush of fire zipped through Simone. The feeling settled just below her ribs and radiated heat, connecting them.

Maria inhaled sharply. Simone looked into her teary eyes and swallowed hard.

"I don't ever want to lose you," Maria said.

Simone knew that heartache like an old friend. "Never going to happen," she said with the confidence she knew Maria needed to hear even though she was a quivering wreck inside.

Maria wouldn't be easily deceived but she'd given it her best shot.

Maria smiled and kissed her. Simone became consumed by soft textures, and salty sweetness, and comforting sensations that gently transfused into sweet and tender longing. She ran her hands through Maria's hair, held her head, and drew her closer and deeper into the kiss. She eased back. "I love you so much," she whispered and placed tender kisses on Maria's eyes and her cheeks. She stopped again at her mouth, nipped at her lip and savoured the taste of nectar.

Maria unhooked the buttons on Simone's red evening gown. The weight of the satin fabric slid the dress from her shoulders, and it pooled at her feet. Maria released the clasp of her bra easily. Simone wriggled, and it dropped to the floor. She moaned as Maria caressed her breast with kisses then blew air that felt cool against her nipple.

"I love you more than life," Maria whispered.

She stroked Simone's face slowly and delicately, then inched her fingertip across Simone's mouth as if admiring her for the very first time. Simone eased Maria's shirt from her shoulders, taking care not to hurt her, released her bra, and undid her trousers. She tried to appear unhurried even though she was desperate to touch her, to feel her, to reconnect; it was an internal struggle she was determined to win, to savour every second.

Maria kicked off her shoes and her clothes fell unhindered to the floor, exposing Maria's narrow hips and toned legs.

"You look...good," Simone said.

Maria tilted her head, her lips curled up just a fraction. "I've had time to work out."

Simone trailed her fingertips down the line of Maria's beautifully defined stomach. "Really good," she said, stroking Maria's thigh.

Maria gasped.

"You're so beautiful."

Simone's throat tightened. She eased Maria's underwear to the floor and smiled. The sweet scent aroused her. Maria's skin pimpled, and the tiny hairs on her forearms stood to attention.

"You're cold?" Simone asked, her question not serious.

Maria's sparkling eyes narrowed as she smiled. "No. Not even a little."

She lifted Simone into her arms and tumbled her onto the bed.

Simone leant on her side to face Maria and stroked the soft definitions of her arms. Shadows darkened the skin beneath Maria's heavily lidded eyes and her cheekbones appeared higher. Her ashen cheeks dipped where they would have previously been fuller and had a rosy complexion. She saw the pain of the recent past though Maria tried to mask it with the joy of the present. That agony tortured Simone's heart too.

Simone wanted to make love, but she wanted something else even more. She wanted to be held. She looked into Maria's eyes. "I need to feel your skin against mine, your heart beating next to mine. I need to know that you'll be here when I wake up."

Maria slowly smiled. She released a slow, easy breath. "I need that too."

Simone inhaled warm air infused with Maria's scent and rose. Maria looked tired. She felt more fragile than Simone had ever known, and her breathing seemed a little more laboured than normal. There would be time to talk about what had happened, but that time wasn't now. Simone closed her eyes and treasured the weight of Maria's head nestled into her, the comfort of Maria's arm wrapped around her waist, and the tenderness of Maria's fingers stroking her with lazy sweeping motions. *Please don't leave me.*

2.

"I need to stop," Simone said, puffing for breath. She straightened her back, rested her hands on her hips and inhaled deeply. "How many steps are there?"

"Three hundred and sixty to the first level, and three hundred and forty-four to the second level, give or take." Maria laughed with the joy of being close to Simone. Simone was incredible, and unfit, and she loved her with all her heart for being both things and more. The days Maria had spent in hospital and then in rehab wondering, and the time since, waiting to find out whether Simone would come to the ballet, to learn whether they had a chance of a future together, had felt like a lifetime of isolated imprisonment. Now, here in the most romantic city in the world, she wanted to treasure the intimacy of the moment for as long as possible. This was a dream on the verge of coming true and one that Maria had sketched out many years ago. Though, she had never envisaged anyone as wonderful as Simone. *No good girl wants to be associated with the business,* she had said to her mother. Well, she was out of the business now and she had a chance at true love, and the freedom to live life.

Simone groaned. "How many have we climbed?"

Maria laughed louder as Simone put on a defeated face. Maria had visited Paris before, but never with a lover and never had she climbed the tower. "About fifty."

Simone puffed deeply. "I am so unfit."

Maria took Simone's hand and squeezed. "A little, maybe, but you did burn at least five thousand calories before we came out, and you've only eaten a croissant."

Simone's cheeks flushed. "Remind me, why couldn't we have taken the lift?"

"We have to take the lift for the last bit, and we'll go down in the lift. I thought you would want the full Eiffel Tower experience." Maria tugged Simone to her and brushed the thin film of moisture from above her lip. Butterflies took flight in Maria's stomach with the love she saw in Simone's eyes. God how she ached for Simone. "You know, you look so sexy when you're all hot and sweaty."

Simone rolled her eyes. "That helps…not." She laughed as she wiped the beads of sweat from her brow and started to climb again.

"Apparently, it's really romantic at the top," Maria said, Simone's buttocks swaying in front of her with every step. "Views across the whole of Paris and beyond." She nearly choked on the words.

Simone turned to her with a grimace, as if to say, "you call hiking up a thousand steps romantic…seriously?"

"It's renowned. I've never been here before." Maria said and shrugged.

Simone stopped, touched Maria's cheek and smiled. "I'm sure it's stunning."

Heat blossomed across Maria's skin. "Did you know there are twenty-thousand lights on the tower, and it stands at over three-hundred metres. It's an amazing feat of design and ingenuity. Gustave Eiffel wanted to show that steel can be used for construction rather than stone. It's lighter and just as strong."

"It looks like giant Meccano," Simone said, looking up at yet more metal.

They alighted at the first floor, and Maria took Simone's hand. They strolled around the space to the transparent glass floor.

Simone leaned forward and peeked through the glass. "Oh, Jesus Christ, that's scary. My stomach just hit my throat." She swayed.

Maria laughed, wrapped her arms around Simone to steady her and tugged her backwards. "Come on, we'll step across together."

Simone hesitated. "I can't move. My legs won't work. I'm stuck."

"Close your eyes. It will help."

Simone closed her eyes and her breathing slowed. She grabbed blindly for Maria's hand.

Maria winced as the vice-like grip squeezed the blood from her fingers. She put her arm around Simone's waist and slowly encouraged her onto the transparent surface.

"Oh my God. Oh my God."

"You're safe." Maria hugged her closer. The height above the ground paled in comparison with the dizzying effect of Simone's body pressed to hers.

"I can't open my eyes."

Maria chuckled. "You aren't going to fall. It's solid."

Simone puffed out in short, sharp bursts, slowly blinking her eyes open, and keeping her head up. She dared to glance down and shut her eyes quickly, before she opened them again and exhaled a long slow breath. "I feel sick."

"Deep breaths."

"I am breathing deeply."

Maria stifled the bubbling in her chest. Simone was really freaked out and she still looked gorgeous. She had an overwhelming urge to protect her, hold her close and never let her out of sight. "On three, ready?"

"No."

"One, two, three." Maria tugged Simone.

Simone jolted forward onto the glass floor and stopped dead.

"See, you're stood on the glass now. You can open your eyes."

Simone blinked one eye open and hesitantly tilted her head down just a fraction. "Oh, holy fucking shit." She stepped tentatively across the glass floor and onto the metal floor at the other side then squealed, arms thrashing and jumping from foot to foot. "Oh my God, that was so exhilarating."

Maria stared at her with wonderment. "It is spectacular."

Simone's eyes sparkled as she smiled, and her cheeks were rosy pink. They continued to climb at a steady pace to the second level.

Simone pointed to the macaroon shop. "I love macaroons. Do you?"

Maria nodded. "The colours remind me of the corals and fish at the reef." Simone's soft, dreamy gaze reminded her of the time they had sat together on the beach at the villa, enjoying the tranquillity, with the sun caressing their faces. Their kisses had been tender, unhurried, and had touched Maria's heart deeply. Nothing in Maria's world had been the same after that moment. The only thing that had real meaning was Simone. She sighed.

Simone's smile faded and her focus became more intense. "Do you miss home?"

Maria sighed. "Some things, like the reef and my family, but not enough to want to go back. There are so many beautiful places I'd like to see and too much I'd have to give up. Besides, I don't exist anymore." She shrugged. Simone nodded, her focus still intense.

Maria had said she would have come for Simone if Simone hadn't turned up at the ballet when truthfully that may not have been possible. Maintaining her new identity as Mariella Sanchez was the difference between having a life and not. If Stefano discovered she was still alive he would ask questions, and when Stefano asked, there was always some scumbag willing to dig deeper to find out the truth. Her life would be under threat and so would Simone's. She couldn't risk that for Simone. She couldn't ever contemplate going back to Sicily.

She had seen flashes of concern in Simone's eyes, questions poised at the tip of her lips that she had refrained from asking the previous night. She had wanted to say, "Don't worry just come with me and we can live together in the Pyrenees or wherever you want. We will work it out. We can go anywhere, do anything, have children if you want. Anything is possible now." Well, almost anything, she would have had to say. The one thing you can't do is go home or see your brother again. To live with me you must live as Simonet Benoit. But she couldn't say those words, because Simone hadn't had the time to adjust to anything that had happened in her life since meeting Maria. Not even the fact that Maria had survived when Simone believed she was dead. Simone had never been a party to Maria's plan to change her identity. Even though they had talked briefly—well actually Maria had talked about the possibility of them living at the farmhouse in the Pyrenees— they had never discussed the ramifications of creating a new life away from Sicily. It was too much to ask of Simone to give up everything she had ever known just to be with her.

The dense feeling that had eclipsed Maria since recovering from the injury still cast a shadow. Would the oppressiveness ever lift? Freedom had appeared so clearly, in vivid and vibrant colour. Walking together through the meadows hand in hand, laughing and chattering about anything and everything. Savouring the balmy warm evenings with a chilled glass of wine and freshly prepared aperitifs while sitting at a table outside the local bar. Strolling *home* under clear starlit skies and listening to nocturnal life awakening.

Home.

She had taken the opportunity to escape Sicily not knowing whether she might live or die. The plan to create a new life she had put into place as many years ago as she could remember had been suddenly brought forward and with no notice or time to consider the impact, and no way to explain to those she loved, and to Simone in particular. She had accepted the risk, the price that she – and *they* – would need to pay for her freedom. For her life.

If she were honest with herself, a twinge of regret at having escaped from Sicily in the manner she did persisted. But being with Simone would make not seeing her family more bearable. That didn't stop the guilt, prickling her skin. Maybe it would always be this way.

Simone looked pensive as she ordered a selection of macaroons. Maria smiled at her as she walked toward her, and Simone's appearance softened. They ate the macaroons while waiting for the next available lift to take them to the top of the tower.

"I feel a bit seasick," Simone said, leaning against the metal frame.

"The tower sways."

"That's deeply reassuring."

Maria chuckled. She leaned toward Simone and kissed her tenderly.

Simone opened her eyes. She looked at the other visitors hogging the space around them as she cleared her throat and gave a sideways glance to Maria.

Simone was enthralling when slightly flustered, puffing air out in an upwards direction that fluttered her eyelids and sent loose strands of hair floating, and with deliciously rosy cheeks that developed a healthy glow. Maria's heart melted. This was what made everything right.

When the lift doors opened, they tumbled in after other visitors alighted, and Simone gasped. Surrounded by glass, with what looked like a thousand feet of fresh air between them and the ground, Simone froze, and the colour drained from her cheeks.

"This is scarier than the glass floor."

Maria moved closer and wrapped her arms around Simone from behind. She was trembling. In a whisper, she said, "It's spectacular. Look, you can see the Arc de Triomphe over there." She lifted her arm slowly from Simone's waist and pointed to the monument in the distance.

Simone leaned back into Maria and looked out. "Wow."

Maria touched her cheek to Simone's and embraced her. Heat pulsed at her core. "I would love to make love to you here," she whispered.

Simone turned her head and kissed Maria on the cheek. "Me too," she said.

"It's breathtaking, isn't it?" Maria asked.

The lift came to a halt and the doors opened to reveal a glassed-in viewing area and the serving hatch of the tower's iconic Champagne Bar.

Maria ordered for them, and Simone held the chilled flute to her lips. "This is going to go straight to my head."

Maria took a delicate sip. The single strawberry at the bottom of the glass complemented the flavour and the bubbles came alive on her tongue. The heady feeling of being suspended above Paris with a horizon that never ended, and the love of her life by her side, intensified. The pleasant giddy sensation fluttered in her stomach. She had never felt more alive. "Come, let's look through the telescope." She strode to the edge of the tower to claim a telescope that had just been freed up and watched Simone sway toward her.

"I feel like I'm floating," Simone said and stifled a champagne-induced giggle.

Maria held out her hand and Simone took it.

They exited the tower a few hours later and stood at the base of the mammoth metal structure looking upwards. Simone took a deep breath. "That was quite incredible, but I think I prefer my feet on the ground."

"Will you take a walk with me?" Maria offered her hand.

Simone took it, and they strolled along the bank of the Seine in contemplative silence. A gentle current moved the river and light danced like pearls, sparkling on its surface. Music boomed in waves from passing traffic interspersed with the harsh beep of car horns doing battle.

Thoughts of Simone's imminent return to Sicily landed like a boulder in Maria's chest. Simone hadn't come to the ballet with a view to staying permanently. The boulder plunged lower and her stomach turned over. Simone's soft, warm hand was suddenly the most precious thing connecting them, and the most vulnerable. If she let go, she might lose her forever.

Yes, she could dream of a future with Simone, but was she naïve to think that the future started here and now? Roberto would expect her back after the ballet. She couldn't just disappear from his life. She could stay a while, but even then, Roberto and Simone were very close and eventually he would ask questions and want to see her. The intimacy she had experienced between them in the tower shattered, and she stopped walking.

Her own pain reflected in Simone's eyes, she swallowed hard and pursed her lips. "I love you," she said.

A tear slipped onto Simone's cheek. "I need to go back," she said.

Her voice, barely above a whisper, could have easily got lost in the cacophony surrounding them but Maria didn't need to hear the words. She bit the inside of her mouth as she nodded, inhaled deeply, looked away and then back at Simone. "Will you come with me to St Lizier for a while first?"

Simone threw herself into Maria's arms and held her tightly. "I love you so much."

"I know there's a lot we need to talk about. I just need a few days with you. I want you to see the farmhouse. I'm buying the restaurant in the village. I thought we could make a home there together." Maria, eased from the hug, looked down at her feet.

Simone lifted her chin, leaned closer, and kissed her fervently. Her eyes shone with the moisture clinging to their surface.

The gentle pressure from the kiss and the hint of sugary sweetness from the macaroons earlier lingered on Maria's lips. She had the urge to kiss Simone again.

"I would love to see it," Simone said.

Maria brushed her thumb across Simone's lips to stem the quivering. "I love you, Simone. I know we can make this work."

"Yes," Simone said, though it came out like a croak.

Maria closed the space between them, her heart racing, and kissed Simone deeply. When she eased out of the kiss and opened her eyes, Simone was smiling. She looked beautiful. Tingling rippled across her skin.

"Come on. I want to take you to the artisan market. We can get a caricature drawn there and delicious street-food...if you'd like that?"

Simone held Maria's cheek. "I would love to."

Maria took Simone's hand and started toward the market.

The low-level vibration that came with feeling exposed to the world had become tangible in the last few hours in Paris. It had been acute at the hotel the previous evening with other guests moving around the corridor and she had worked hard to contain her anxiety throughout the day. One more person knowing of her existence increased the chances of her being discovered, but that was a risk she had to take or choose to live without Simone. Had she been selfish getting Simone involved in living in hiding without first asking her? Her throat ached at the thought. She cleared her throat. "It won't be easy," she said.

Simone looked at her quizzically.

"You can't tell anyone about me. You know that? Even Roberto."

Simone's hand became limp. A frown developed and deepened.

The tightness in Maria's throat made it painful to swallow. She was essentially asking Simone to lie, and Simone wasn't a liar. She was asking for the impossible, driven by her own fear. Maria had kept her working relationship with Roberto from Simone in Sicily and that had almost destroyed their relationship. She couldn't afford to lose her again—not to secrets, not to anything. But being discovered would lead to far more devastating consequences for them all than withholding the truth. "At least not yet...please." *Never.* She couldn't insist that Simone never speak to her brother again, though that would be the safest for them both, but they had to be cautious about him knowing where they were. It was for his protection too. There were so many details to sort out. *Fucking mafia.* "Does Roberto know about the farmhouse?"

Simone nodded. "He saw the paperwork in the case. Said I should leave Sicily and live there. He knew you wanted me to have a life."

"That's good." Maria smiled though her chest tightened. "Where is the case?"

"At home. In my wardrobe. I said I couldn't live there without you. It would be meaningless. He was trying to be supportive, I think."

"Ah... This is tough, but the more people who know I am alive, the greater the risk of Stefano finding out and coming after me."

Simone lowered her head.

Maria groped for something that would convince Simone that the risks were significant. Simone really didn't understand the ways of the mafia. "Stefano will think I killed Alessandro, Simone."

Simone released Maria's hand, stopped walking, and looked directly at her, a look that said she didn't want to know the truth but had to ask the question.

"Did you?"

Simone's tone shuddered through Maria. She shook her head, wishing that Simone wouldn't need to ask that question. "No."

Simone looked away. "It was the 'Ndrangheta, like they said then?"

"I don't remember what happened." A prickling sensation jabbed her conscience with the lie that tripped so easily from her lips. She cringed. The distance this conversation created between them expanded quickly.

Simone was staring at the road.

Simone didn't know what had taken place on the boat that night, and the less she knew the safer she would be. Some rules didn't change even if you weren't working inside the mafia. Maria wasn't deliberately protecting Patrina, who had killed Alessandro and in doing so, saved her life. It was just that some information didn't serve anyone by being shared.

"How did you get shot?" Simone asked softly, still staring at the road.

"Alessandro shot me. He was high, and unstable, and crazy. Fortunately, he was also a shit shot." Her dry humour didn't reach Simone. It was also a white lie. If he hadn't taken a bullet himself before he squeezed the trigger, he would have killed her even in his inebriated state. She was trying to add levity to the conversation, but Simone just continued looking at the road. She turned Simone toward her. She was teary-eyed. "Listen. I'm alive, and you're alive, and that's all that matters. We can be together. Patrina helped me escape from the boat, but I was badly hurt and, like you, she assumed I died. For her own safety, my mother doesn't even know I escaped. Giovanni and the doctor who treated me are the only people in Sicily who know, and neither of them is aware of where I am now. Rafael, in Spain, is the only person who can find me, as Mariella Sanchez should the need arise." Wearied with revisiting a past that still troubled her thoughts, she kissed Simone on the nose, brushed the tears from her cheeks, and swept the hair from her face. "Come with me tomorrow. Take a holiday, a few weeks in the Pyrenees. Call Roberto, he will understand. Then we can take the time to work out what we do next… Please?" Simone slowly nodded. Maria eased her gently into her arms, closed her eyes, and held her tightly. *Please, Simone, don't leave me now.*

3.

The farmhouse door squeaked as Maria closed it behind her. "I still need to look at that," she said, to remind herself of another little job that needed fixing. There was always something that demanded attention at the farmhouse. A hinge that squeaked, a bracket that needed securing, tiles that needed replacing. And since the purchase of the restaurant there was now the major project of gutting and redesigning it.

Her cheeks tingled from the change of temperature in the room. She plucked a log from the hearth and placed it carefully on the fading fire, poked at the embers, and watched the flames lick at the bark until it crackled and lit. Sap oozed from a crack in its skin and a sweet smell emanated from the smoke. "It's getting chillier out," she said. The nights seemed to close in faster now that autumn had arrived in earnest and the temperatures dropped sharply even before the sun dived behind the mountains. In Sicily the nights would be balmy at this time of year, the sun seeming to hold its heat for longer. St Lizier had a different smell about it too. Lush, damp, and earthy. Palermo would still be dry and taste of dust. She had thought about Palermo more since Paris, and particularly in the last couple of weeks, though she wasn't quite sure why.

She walked through the open plan living room into the kitchen and dining area, into the homely aroma of herbs and red wine. "Something smells good."

Simone was standing at the window overlooking the back of the farmhouse. She turned her head and smiled as Maria approached. "The henhouse looks amazing."

The shed that Maria had constructed and just painted sat pride of place in a corner of the meadow that was now fenced off with chicken wire. The hens would be free to roam, and each would have its own bed inside the house. It was perfect.

Simone's eyelashes delicately flickered, the tiny scar above her eye became more visible, and her mouth made tiny movements in silent speech as if she was self-conscious at being admired by Maria. It was deeply endearing. The urge to kiss Simone, to touch her, and to hold her tightly and never let her go was as agonisingly fierce as it had been that first night after the ballet in Paris. But there was something intangible restraining her. Maria inhaled deeply to release the other feeling, the one that haunted her, the tightness in her chest being a constant reminder of the wound that scarred her body. She knew her smile was a little lacklustre, affected by her thoughts of Palermo, but she hoped Simone didn't notice. She didn't want Simone to worry or think something was wrong. There really was nothing wrong. She blinked her eyes and focused on what was real, here and now.

Not all scars were visible or significant, were they? Sometimes the invisible wounds held the greatest meaning and had the deepest impact. The memories of a past Maria desperately wanted to forget were still lodged in every cell in her body. The flashbacks had been infrequent and lasted just a few seconds, although it often felt as though they went on for a lot longer. They took her into a place of never-ending darkness from which there was no escape. Mostly they happened during the day. There was a damp, chilled quality inside the black void, and she would rouse from the recollection shivering uncontrollably with her heart racing. There was never anyone else present and no sound to orientate by. It was just her, alone, lying prone and completely immobilised by an invisible force, and a searing pain that gripped her in waves of increasing intensity. The moment would pass, and then her point of focus would shift to the present as the residual effects leached through her body. In these moments she felt raw, exposed in a way that she had never felt before, and reduced to something she had never been before. Keeping busy with the farmhouse had kept the flashbacks at bay, though in the past week she had had two incidents. Thankfully, Simone hadn't been around to witness them. She saw someone she didn't recognise, and worried that Simone would see the changes in her and wouldn't love her.

She took another deep breath and her chest objected with a slight squeeze and a dull ache. It was nothing serious. It wasn't even real pain anymore, just a fading muscle memory. A trigger to that night on the boat. The night she had survived, and her life had changed forever.

Yes, we all have scars, Maria, and secrets. We all have a past. Patrina's words echoed from the time Maria had sought solace with her after Maria's first kill. That Maria had a past she detested was bad enough, but worse still was the deep-rooted feeling that her history didn't want to let her go, that in some way it hadn't finished with her yet. But *she* had finished with the past, and she had promised to never revisit it.

She wound her arms around Simone and kissed the back of her neck. Softness and warmth tingled her lips. "It's secure. The hens will be as safe as they can be." The tiny hairs on Simone's neck tickled her and a shiver passed through Maria that had nothing to do with the colder weather. "What are you cooking?"

"Beef bourguignon." Simone leant back into Maria and rocked in her arms.

"Smells almost as good as you."

They rocked in silence. Maria closed her eyes and took a long slow breath.

"Are you excited about going to look at the chicks tomorrow?" Simone asked.

Maria squeezed her tightly and kissed the top of her head. "It will be a hoot."

"Owls hoot. Chickens cluck."

Maria chuckled. She turned Simone toward her and lifted her chin. "I'll make you cluck or hoot, or squeal." She licked her lips seductively then kissed Simone firmly.

Simone moaned in pleasure, wrapped her arms around Maria's neck, slipped her leg between Maria's and leaned into her. She eased out of the kiss and cupped Maria's cheek. Her smile was inviting and exuded kindness and love.

"Are you hungry?"

Maria's stomach rumbled as if on cue. She shrugged. "Always."

Simone picked a fleck of paint from Maria's cheek. "You need a bath."

Maria sniffed close to her armpit. "I don't smell that bad."

"You have paint on your face and in your hair."

Maria lifted her hands. Her fingers were splattered with brown paint too. She rolled her shoulders. In truth, she was feeling the strain of having built the henhouse from scratch in just three days and then painting it. It had tested muscles she hadn't realised existed, muscles that hadn't felt the strain for a long while, though she felt better for having done the work herself. A bath would be relaxing.

"Wine?"

"Thanks."

Simone went to the stove and lifted the lid off the pot. Herbs, onions, beef, and red wine aromas filled the space. She stirred the contents and replaced the lid.

"I'm really starving," Maria said, inhaling the aromas.

"After you get cleaned up." Simone pointed in the direction of the stairs.

Maria screwed up her face.

"Did you speak to the carpenter?"

"Yes, he can start in a couple of weeks."

"That's good." Simone poured two glasses of red wine from the decanter and held one out to Maria.

Maria reached for it and stopped at her phone pinging. She plucked the mobile from her pocket and glanced at the screen. When she looked up, Simone was frowning at her.

"What is it?" Simone's pitch was higher than normal. She craned her neck to see the phone.

Maria pocketed the mobile slowly, staring at Simone, and she spoke quietly. "You remember Tommaso Vitale, the bent detective who covered up my father's murder."

Simone nodded. "Yes."

"He has been released. All charges dropped."

Simone put the drink down and went to Maria. She pulled her into her arms and held her tightly. "I'm so sorry," she whispered.

Simone's warmth didn't impact Maria. A chill stiffened her spine and her head filled with a pressure so tight that she couldn't think. The sound became muffled and incoherent. Then Simone was holding her shoulders and looking at her through wide eyes, her mouth moving. She looked like a puppet on strings.

"Are you okay?"

The words blasted through the ether even though they were spoken quietly. "Yes. I'm fine," she lied. "It happens all the time. Corrupt officers. Money changes hands. It all goes away."

"At least Alessandro got what he deserved," Simone said.

Maria nodded. "Yes," she said, aware that her tone lacked enthusiasm.

Alessandro Amato, Stefano's nephew, had died. And perhaps that was the best she could wish for. Justice for the cover-up the DIA had initiated, which resulted in the Amatos not being held to account for her father's death, was small scale by comparison. Yes, Alessandro Amato was dead and that was all that mattered. Or was it?

Why did this news now sit like an immovable rock in her stomach?

"I'll go and bathe," she said and stroked Simone's cheek. She kissed her on the lips and smiled. "I'm so hungry," she said, although her appetite had disappeared. She took her glass from the table and headed up the stairs, questions rolling through her mind. Who would have paid for Vitale's release? Why? What would happen next? Only one answer came to her. Stefano Amato. Had Stefano ordered Alessandro to take the hit on her father? Every cell in her body was screaming, yes. And, if Stefano had engineered Vitale's release, then Vitale would owe him. What the hell was Patrina doing in all this?

Vitale is a threat.

Vitale was an ex-DIA paper pusher who had been on Capitano Massina's team. Massina, she had trusted. Vitale was in Amato's pocket though, and therein lay the problem. *Giovanni can handle the situation.* She tried to breathe deeply, and her chest resisted. She was puffing before she reached the top of the stairs. She put her glass on the side of the bath and ran the water. Her head spun. She slumped down onto the toilet, bent her head over her knees and closed her eyes.

4.

The clanking of steel on steel rang loudly in Patrina's ears, and she winced as the prison guard closed the door behind them both and unlocked the second door in front of them. The harsh resonance trembled through her, and her heart thundered in her chest. It was an unnerving feeling, strong and persistent, and she felt debilitated by it. She was more on edge visiting Stefano today than she had been seeing him the first time after Alessandro's death. There was no explaining her disquiet, other than it was simply Stefano that affected her. He had frightened her for a long time now. Perhaps he always had, and she had been young and too arrogant, blinded by the thrill of marrying a man of his standing, to realise how aggressive and intimidating he was.

The prison had passed on the news to Stefano about his nephew's death. He had known for three days before she had managed to see him, and the rage in his eyes didn't shift in the time she had sat behind the screen. It had been present every time she had visited him since, like blackness covering darkness giving it a quality of richness and depth that only profound loss can create.

She had visited infrequently over the weeks following the funeral and she was only here now because Stefano had insisted that he talk to her about the business. Was she naïve to think he would let her run the Amato clan without his interference? Even in solitary confinement he had kept abreast of what was going on outside. He had eyes and ears willing to spy for him, and she would be hard-pressed to find out who those belonged to. One of the guards? An inmate? With the new regime asserting its authority, clamping down on mafia communication and activities, it should be harder for him to operate. But it didn't seem to be. There was always someone wanting to make a quick buck or find an easy route into a world of high wealth and power. *Fuck you all.*

She walked a pace behind the guard along the corridor and into the meeting room. She glanced up at the small window to the outside world as the door closed behind her. Sunlight, channelled by the bars that spanned its width, was the only indication of whether it was day or night inside the grey walled room. The familiar screen split the space in two with a telephone handset on either side, and there was the scent of a woman's perfume, presumably from whoever had recently sat in the same seat, visiting their man before her. Did they feel disgust toward their husbands and lovers as she did for Stefano? Her stomach churned. She hesitated to sit, resisted the urge to head back out the door, and stood frozen with fear and trepidation. Even though he couldn't reach or touch her, he did, and she would never be free of that feeling no matter what barriers stood between them.

She flinched as the door on the other side of the screen opened and Stefano entered the room. Her heart pounded though she sat and smiled as he approached. The look in his eyes was the same, darker if anything. *Fuck.* She swallowed and tried to smile through her eyes, but she felt tight and had probably grimaced.

His features remained still, finely chiselled by whatever it was that vexed him. There was no softness, no tenderness in his expression, and she wondered if there ever had been. He had a rugged, fierce look carved by a hard life, becoming an animal that protected himself by threatening those who approached him. He was no chameleon though. His appearance hadn't shifted from one of frustrated rage since his incarceration. He looked every bit the caged beast that he was, and it was from that fact alone that Patrina gleaned some comfort. He would spend the rest of his life behind bars. She continued to smile, her heart settling into a regular but quick beat as she waited for him to speak. His jaw remained rigid, giving his face an aesthetic, warrior-like appeal. He had become fitter in prison. A smile would make him exciting, dangerous, and irresistible. Instead, he looked crazed and threatening. She took a deep breath and pinched her lips between her teeth to wet them. He seemed to be enjoying the silence, assessing—no, interrogating her through his twisted perception.

He tilted his head toward the handset. She picked it up and held it at her ear. He waited before picking up the handset on his side. It was a power play she would afford him with amused pleasure. "Hello, darling," she said softly.

"Patrina."

He sounded gruff, distant, and distrusting of her. The latter was nothing new, but since Alessandro's death, she had taken care of business and things had run smoothly. He had no good reason to doubt her ability to take care of the clan. It was as if the Amatos were back to where they had been before Stefano's imprisonment, when the Amatos and the Lombardos benefited from a respectful working relationship with clearly defined boundaries.

She still grieved for Maria and always would. Patrina's emptiness had become a void that could never be filled in Maria's absence. Not only had Maria been a special lover like no other, she had also been an ally and friend.

With Giovanni as the Lombardos' don and the 'Ndrangheta occupied by events in Italy, they had easily re-established a solid working relationship, and without narcissistic egos like Alessandro exerting their ill-founded power, business was good. Beto was a perfect second to her leadership. He respected her, and respect was key.

Stefano had never respected her. That had always been clear. But since Alessandro's death he assumed an even greater lack of tolerance for what he perceived as ineffective and was quick to want to dispose of the problem. *If looks could kill.* If the screen wasn't there to separate them, she would be sure to feel his bare hands around her throat squeezing the life out of her. She could see his homicidal tendencies in the maniacal intensity in his eyes. His hatred was his most resilient quality and seemingly impervious to change.

She leaned her head forward a fraction and frowned, hoping to convey concern. "How are you, darling?"

Stefano's lips thinned, and his eyes became narrow slits. The whites of his knuckles showed around the handset and he clenched his other hand and pressed it down on the narrow table in front of him. His Adam's apple seemed to bob up and down in slow motion as it fought to flex through the tension in his neck. His head sat on a tilt and he leaned his chest toward her.

"What. Happened. To. The. Fucking. Casino?"

Ice crystallised along Patrina's spine. His tone sucked the air from her chest. Of course, he would have something to say about giving up the casino so the tech park could be built. She'd been on edge waiting for the news to drift through to him and avoided visiting in the last few weeks for exactly this reason. He looked as though he had been boiling for a while and despite her intense fear, a flurry of nervous amusement at his suffering lifted her.

She had made a promise to Maria that she intended to honour—to ensure the legacy of Don Calvino Lombardo, Maria's father and the man Stefano's nephew had assassinated. When she'd agreed to Maria's proposition, she hadn't considered how Stefano would take the news. She'd had only one thing in mind, getting rid of Alessandro. She was leading the business, despite what Stefano thought and, in any event, they couldn't afford to continue with the construction because Alessandro had bled their finances dry with his failed business interests.

She hadn't cared for the casino and giving it up had been a small price to pay to wipe out the Amatos' debt to Maria. In fact, the Lombardos had done her a favour in wanting the site back. It had become too much hassle without the funds to do the job. But Stefano was greedy, and now her decision was about to bite her where it hurt. He was clearly pissed and wanting answers she couldn't give him. How could she tell him that she had killed his nephew because he was destroying their business? Nervous laughter bubbled up in her chest and, maintaining eye contact with him, she cleared her throat.

"There was a change of plan," she said.

His chest expanded slowly, and he bared clenched teeth. "What the fuck do you mean a change of plan?"

There were some part-truths she could share. "Maria found out that Alessandro was responsible for Calvino's death. I, we, owed it to her to reinstate her father's legacy, or she would have taken matters into her own hands."

Stefano snapped his head to the side and his features looked even sharper in profile, the veins in his neck more pronounced. When he looked back at her, she saw something unfamiliar in his eyes. Pity?

"You fucking stupid bitch. I owe her nothing. You owe her nothing. The woman's fucking dead. Get the fucking casino fucking back."

He hesitated. Was he waiting for an agreement from her? She couldn't give it.

"Do you fucking understand what I'm fucking saying?"

She felt her head shaking of its own volition and wished she had taken conscious control of her response and forced herself to nod. His face turned crimson, and he looked as if he were about to implode. *Shit.* He ran his fingers firmly across his shaved head, leaving thick lines of red along his tightly shaved scalp. She watched them soften slowly but remain as a faint discolouring of his skin, an indication of his aging. His chest expanded and softened. He relaxed his jaw. His smile looked fake.

"I have interested parties, Patrina. They have expectations of me. You can't give up the casino. Get it reinstated."

The last three words bounced around her awareness with the image of Maria lying in Giovanni's arms bleeding to death. "No."

She stared at him feeling nothing other than contempt, and the voice in her head screamed, no. No, she wouldn't renege on her promise to Maria. No, she wouldn't allow him to take back control of the Amato business from inside these walls. No, she had had enough of Stefano Amato and the shit she had put up with from him over the years. "We don't have the money to invest in it."

"Find it, Patrina. If you don't sort this, I will find someone who will. Get the casino reinstated, or else."

He put the phone down. The chair tipped as he stood. He let it fall and walked out of the room.

Silence deafened the screaming in her head, and the walls closed in around her. She felt numb, diminutive, and out of control. She replaced the handset and slowly rose to her feet. The door behind her opened, and she walked through it. Blankness opened a door to nothingness and became a welcome abyss in which she wanted to disappear, and then she was standing on the outside of the prison and the air she breathed was humid.

How could she tell Beto this news? Any action to take back the site would kick off another war with the Lombardos, but if she didn't try to come to some arrangement with Giovanni, Stefano would find an alternative solution, and that would certainly result in unnecessary casualties. And, one thing she was sure of, she had no desire to become one of Stefano's victims. But more to the point...who the hell was feeding him information?

5.

Maria's sister's image, heavily pregnant and with a glowing smile, flashed across her mind. The jabbing sensation kicked hard into her chest, winding her. She could see herself reaching out, screaming to Catena, chasing the image of her and the baby as it faded to nothing. Darkness surrounded her. Darkness and silence, cold and piercing. Her eyes flew open as if outside of her control. Her heart raced. Her palms were damp, and she wiped away the moisture that had formed above her lip and across her cheeks. Simone's features looked sharper now. The colours in the room were vivid and vibrant, and the sounds of the birds, previously barely noticeable, were harmonic. An icy sensation crawled across her skin, with the thought that something terrible was going to happen. She took a deep breath and then another.

She must have moaned out loud because she opened her eyes at the sleepy mumbling sound to see Simone frowning at her. She smiled. "Morning," she said.

"You were thrashing and shouting and you're sweating," Simone said.

Maria couldn't deny the facts. The sheets clung to her, cool and damp against her skin. Her heart was racing from the effect of the dream and made worse by Simone's worried expression. She wanted to take away the pain revealed in Simone's beautiful, sad eyes. Pain she had caused. "Sorry."

Simone caressed her cheek and Maria's eyes closed briefly. "What was it?"

She didn't want to lie, but she had no choice. "I must have drifted." She smiled and kissed Simone on the nose. "Come here," she said, trying to distract Simone from any further questions. She pulled Simone to her.

Simone pushed back and stared at her. "Was it another nightmare?"

Maria sighed. She lay on her back, hands behind her head. "Must have been. I can't remember." She had promised not to hide things from Simone, but she didn't want Simone to worry unnecessarily. The nightmares would lessen in time. She wanted them to focus on the future, on building a life at St Lizier, and not feel trapped by a past she wanted to forget ever existed.

The lines deepened across Simone's forehead. Maria reached up and smoothed them. "You'll get stuck like that, you know?" she said softly.

"I don't like seeing you—"

"I'm fine. Honestly. It was just a dream."

"You're suffering." Simone spoke in a whisper.

"I'm not suffering. I'm very happy. I'm with the woman I love in a place I love. It doesn't get any better than that." Simone traced the shape of her face, her jaw and lips, and with the lightest touch the hairs on her neck rose. Tingling sensations slipped down her spine. "And, if you touch me like that we won't be going anywhere today."

A smile grew slowly on Simone's face then she pulled Maria to her and kissed her tenderly on the lips. "Oh, yes, we will. You've always wanted an orchid farm." She leapt out of the bed.

Maria had always wanted an orchid farm, but she wanted Simone more. She admired the curve of Simone's hips leading to the smooth skin that exposed her delicious sex. She could still taste Simone and the ache deep inside her started to pulse. She moaned as she stood from the bed. "I need you now," she whispered. Simone glanced over her shoulder and pursed her lips, eyeing Maria up and down. Her gaze stopped on Maria's breasts. The sparkle in Simone's eyes made them look bigger and more alluring.

"Is that so, Ms Sanchez."

She nodded and followed Simone into the shower. She wrapped her arms around Simone to reach for the tap. A spray of cold water stole her breath. Simone squealed and flapped her hands. The laughter felt liberating. Simone held her under the spray and giggled. It was delightful. The thrill reflected in Simone's eyes, and she gasped. Simone's lips came to hers with urgency clashing their teeth. She moaned at the feel of Simone's soft inner thigh, her silky wetness, and the folds that separated at her touch.

Simone moaned, then turned suddenly and spun Maria around. Aching, sweet, penetrating heat, and the desire to be fucked until her legs buckled consumed Maria. The feeling was like no other, pressing, and pure, and intoxicating. She clasped Simone's shoulders, dug into her flesh, and cried out as Simone brought her quickly to orgasm. "Oh God," she whispered, trembling, and Simone quieted her with her mouth.

She leaned against the cool tiles. Burning tears spilled onto her cheeks. Simone kissed her neck, her chest, the scar, and then the flesh of her breasts. She jerked involuntarily as Simone sucked and bit her nipple. Her legs trembled, and her heart raced. She watched Simone teasing her breast and a moan rose into her throat. "You're so perfect." An electric current sparked from her breast to her core and she moaned.

She took Simone's head in her hands and fought the urge to clamp her to her breast. She eased Simone from her and looked into her eyes. "God, I love you," she whispered, and Simone's answering smile was intensely sweet. Slowly, Simone inched closer, parted Maria's lips as their mouths came together and caressed her with kisses of silk that became a soothing wave.

Simone ran her fingers leisurely through Maria's hair. "I love you."

The kindness and sincerity in Simone's eyes rocked her to the core. And then Simone kissed her with such tenderness she had to fight to stop herself crying. When Simone eased out of the kiss, Maria's heart ached for the contact.

"Now, let's get going."

Maria smiled, still reeling from the effects of the orgasm and the profundity of the moment. She blew out a long breath before she spoke. "There's no rush." She ran her fingertip across Simone's nipple, eliciting a moan of pleasure. "So, what do you say?"

"If you go there—"

She silenced Simone with a deep kiss. Simone wrapped her arms around Maria's neck.

Simone moaned and pushed Maria gently away. "We have to source everything locally," she said and stepped out of the shower.

Maria chuckled at the sudden change in subject. Simone's attention was clearly on the restaurant and everything they needed to do to get it renovated and supplied. They would get a good feel for the local produce and make connections with potential suppliers at the food festival later that day. Everything was going perfectly. Why then was she feeling anxious about heading out of the village to look at land for an orchid farm? Why did her inner voice keep telling her that it could wait? Were her instincts playing tricks on her? She smiled to release the tension in her jaw.

Simone's enthusiasm was heart-warming. She looked gorgeous and very determined, dripping water onto the bathroom floor with her hands resting on her hips. And her forthright tone while standing stark naked made Maria's heart warm. "Of course."

"The local community is just like a big family." Simone huffed as if she had just expended a lot of energy pondering. "We need to support each other."

It was more about sound business principles; sustainability and the practicalities of sourcing products that had a shorter distance to travel made economic sense. Everyone was in it for themselves at the end of the day. If they could negotiate a good deal locally it would be good for business. If not, they might be better looking further afield for their suppliers, but she would cross that bridge with Simone if or when it arose. Simone was adamant and happy. "Yes," she said.

Simone picked up a towel and dried herself. She dressed quickly and paced the room while Maria dressed. "Come on, let's go."

Maria pulled a jumper over her head, trying not to give her racing heart any attention. "I'm ready," she said and chased Simone down the stairs. The burst of movement helped.

Walking to the car, the unsettled feeling simmered in her stomach. She looked across the meadow and tracked the boundary to the wooded area beyond the fields. There was nothing of note there, but the feeling bubbled irritatingly. She opened the door to the passenger side of the car and smiled at Simone as she got in. Quickly dropping her smile, she glanced around again, up the driveway to the main road and beyond as far as she could see. She walked to the driver's side, got into the car and turned the engine, her attention still fixed on seeing something that most likely didn't exist.

The feeling abated as she became aware of Simone saying something about the hens that they planned to buy later in the week. A question?

"Sure," she said, without knowing what she had agreed to.

"You're not listening, are you?"

Maria took Simone's hand and squeezed it. "Sorry, I was distracted thinking about turning the barn into an office and a gym." The lie caused her chest to squeeze. She scanned the road ahead, to her left and her right, and checked the rear-view mirror, her heart still pounding.

6.

Simone stirred beneath the downy quilt and opened her eyes. The heavy curtains that concealed the start of the day had been peeled back and dust particles danced on the rays of light entering the bedroom. Roberto's image was more vivid this morning and the burden seemed heavier than previously. Her return to Palermo had been a topic of conversation neither she nor Maria had voiced, but it was close to six weeks since she had left for Paris and the void in that aspect of her life seemed deeper and demanding of her attention. It wasn't that Maria wasn't enough for her. She couldn't bear to think of that. Maria was everything. But that didn't mean Roberto didn't matter to her. He was like a son and that was a bond like no other. He wouldn't ask her to return, but that didn't mean he didn't need her. The quality of his messages, brief and evasive, told her all she needed to know. She stretched and turned away from the window.

Maria, resting on her elbow and staring at her, took her breath away. The sunshine streaked her hair with lighter tones. The fine lines that fanned her eyes when she smiled were smooth and her gaze seemed to reach her soul. Her mouth was soft and enticing. She looked handsome. A smile developed slowly on her face and broke the spell.

"Morning," Simone said, and Maria leaned in and kissed her.

"Morning," Maria whispered.

Simone tugged Maria on top of her, pressed herself into Maria's thigh, and murmured into her ear.

"I know that feeling too, but we've got an appointment with the cheese man and can't be late," Maria said and jumped up from the bed.

"Cheese is not *that* exciting," Simone said. She could think of more enticing activities right now, such as Maria's hands exploring her body again. She sighed.

"Cheese is very exciting," Maria said, but she was chuckling.

Simone moaned and pulled the covers back over her. She inhaled Maria's scent in the warm space beneath the sheets, snuggled into a ball, and closed her eyes again. Suddenly, cold air flew across her skin and she screeched. Maria had yanked the covers from her, and her excited laughter echoed around the room. Simone laughed. The sun streamed brighter, and the earthy scent of trees and grass had a stimulating effect. A feeling of weightlessness lifted her from the bed. She stood naked and invincible, and wanted the euphoric feeling to last forever.

"Cheese is an essential component in French cuisine. You can't run a restaurant here without a decent selection." Maria's tone was light-hearted and sincere as she mimicked the cheesemonger they had met at the food festival.

Simone did know. They had sampled every variety of cheese on offer and she had had indigestion for the rest of the evening as a result. Each type of cheese had been accompanied by the wine that best suited it. *A restaurateur must know the appropriate wine,* the cheesemonger had said. It was like art and had to be taken seriously in the restaurant business. He had studied her and Maria quizzically, and she would bet critically, until Maria had asked him about supplying the restaurant. Then his demeanour softened, and he had talked animatedly, and for so long that she had switched off, about how the cheeses were made and their origins. Maria had listened intently and seemed to have remembered everything. Simone had favoured the Cabécou cheese with its creamy smooth texture and tangy taste together with a glass of chardonnay. Maria had been more impressed by the nutty flavour of the Briquette de Brebis and especially discovering they could make their own version in their cellar. She had cleared the cellar already; they would be making cheese.

"Come on." Maria kissed her firmly on the lips and hurried her to the bathroom. "We have to be there for eleven, and it's a good hour away. Plus, we can stop at the boulangerie on the way," she said and headed out of the bedroom and down the stairs.

Simone had fallen in love with the boulangerie. Everyone in St Lizier shopped there for fresh bread and pastries daily, for patisserie treats at the weekends, and for customised cakes on special occasions. It was one of the social hubs of the small community, along with the restaurant they had acquired and Madame Berger's health shop, and it was a place to go for friendly gossip. She had fallen in love with St Lizier and their life at the farmhouse, though a persistent voice reminded her that she had unfinished business in Palermo.

She stepped into the shower and allowed the warm water to soothe her worries. She lathered herself in the scented soap and luxuriated in the gently invigorating effects of the natural salts exfoliating her skin. Refreshed, she dressed quickly. By the time she headed down the stairs, a nutty coffee aroma filled the house.

"Here." Maria handed her a cup of coffee and ran upstairs.

Simone wandered onto the patio at the back of the farmhouse, looking across the meadow. The late autumn air was fast turning toward winter, cooler and more humid. The few remaining leaves on the trees were varied in colour—shades of yellow, rusty orange and red. Fallen leaves formed piles shaped by the wind and littered the ground. A refreshing breeze gusted, and the hairs on her arms rose. Familiar clucking noises from the meadow drew her attention. She smiled, put her cup on the table, and wandered across dewy grass to the henhouse.

They had selected six young Wyandottes from a local farmer—two silver-laced hens they named Kip and Kana who ran as if they had a limp; two buff-coloured hens named Frango and Kura who refused to venture too far from the henhouse; a golden fat hen called Pollo; and her favourite, a blue laced hen called Poulet, who always seemed to study Simone with its head on a tilt and a pecking motion. They all now made a chattering racket, with Kip and Kana sprinting from across the field to greet her. Pollo, the largest hen, was the first to arrive and jutted and flicked her head as she pecked at the ground around the shed. Poulet came to greet her and looked up at her quizzically.

"Hello, little one," she said and stroked the soft blue feathers on its back. The hen, seemingly satisfied, nipped at the grit around her boot and scuttled off into the shed. Simone scooped a large cup of grain from the bin in the shed and sprinkled it on the grass. The squawking became riotous, and the birds flapped their wings like whips as they fought each other for their breakfast. She went back into the shed, grabbed a bowl, and collected an egg from each bird's bed.

She watched the hens pecking and skittering around in the dirt, slowly venturing further into the meadow. She wandered back to the house with the eggs. She had never thought of chickens as pets but having had this gorgeous little flock for a couple of weeks now, who all knew their own and each other's names, she couldn't see herself eating them and would be devastated if anything untoward happened. Already, these clucky, feathery friends were her family, and she had become even more protective over them than Maria. She had worried about foxes getting to them, but the farmer assured her that they would be better egg layers if they were free to wander during the day. The birds naturally gravitated to the indoors at dusk, and Maria always locked them up at night.

The farmer had been right. The eggs tasted richer and creamier than those delivered to Café Tassimo in Sicily. Simone's skin crawled. She had no desire to think about the café, or the Amatos, and especially not Patrina. Roberto's image came to her as it had earlier, an itch she couldn't scratch. She didn't think he was being deliberately evasive—he had never been overly forthcoming about discussing his business with her—but she sensed a change in his tone that she couldn't identify. She couldn't talk to Maria about it because Maria would worry, and the stress might exacerbate her nightmares.

Perhaps it had been inevitable that her relationship with Roberto would become more distant even though he supported her, but her gut told her it wasn't just that. Maybe he was just giving her the space and freedom he thought she needed. He had been deeply engrossed in the tech park construction and out of harm's reach when she left, she was sure. If she could see him though, at least she would be reassured that everything was going well and that he was safe. Maybe there wasn't anything wrong at all. Maybe he was just busy living a young man's life. Until she could speak to him properly and look him in the eyes, she couldn't stop worrying, and the scenarios she had dreamed about weren't helping at all. They had become increasingly disturbing and vivid.

She missed him.

Last night she imagined she had discovered him badly beaten in a dark alley, though where they were in the world she couldn't tell, and before she had been able to identify whether he was alive, she'd been ripped from his side by a strong hand, accompanied by a stranger's voice she didn't recognise, and she had screamed for Roberto to wake up. But he wasn't responding to her. His body was limp, contorted, and bloody, and torturous pain filled her as she wailed. The dream had startled her awake, and she stared into the darkness while her consciousness caught up with reality. It had taken a while for her to settle and the unease returned now as her thoughts drifted to returning to Palermo.

The memory of Café Tassimo's eggs had resurrected an emotional scar. The tremor continued to quake in her chest as she picked up her cup. She sipped cold coffee and winced. She made her way back into the kitchen wrestling with the urge to go back to Sicily. She would have to go soon, stay a short time, collect her things, sort out the house and return to the farmhouse. Maybe it was just closure she needed with Roberto and with Sicily. After all, when she returned to St Lizier the next time, it would be for good and there was a chance she may never see her brother again. A sharp jab in her chest and a wave of sadness moved powerfully through her. She couldn't abandon Roberto as Maria had abandoned her family. She just couldn't do it. She wasn't like that; she wasn't like Maria. Maria had always wanted to leave Palermo. She hadn't considered life outside of Sicily an option since returning from university. Yes, maybe she would have moved out of the city at some point, but it hadn't occurred to her she would start a life in another country. She hadn't wanted a new identity. Another feeling shocked her: fear.

I need to go home.

Maria entered the kitchen, and Simone's thoughts stalled. Her hands were shaking, and she had an overwhelming sense of wanting to run. "Oh, hey," she said noting the stutter in her voice. She took a deep breath and forced a smile. As she took in Maria, her heart ached.

Faded blue jeans hung from Maria's hips, and a dark-blue woollen sweater accentuated her lean physique. She didn't look like a local farmer or the other folks from the village. There was no broad brimmed hat on her head or double-barrelled shotgun hanging from the crook in her arm. She didn't chew on a blade of straw. She looked sophisticated, elegant and classy. No matter what Maria wore, she looked handsome and beautiful, and Maria had such a big gorgeous heart. She didn't want to hurt Maria, but she was determined to fight for what she needed, if she had to.

Maria smiled as she closed the space between them.

Simone became lost in the sensation of softness as Maria kissed her tenderly, and the disconcerting feeling faded. Nothing except this moment, this taste, this feeling, and Maria's touch mattered. When Maria eased out of the kiss, longing gripped Simone and spun a weave to her core. "How do you do that to me?" she whispered.

Maria smiled. "Come on. The cheese man awaits us," she said and held out her hand.

Simone sighed. She would rather go back to the bedroom. Maria exuded passion when she was excited like this, and it was wonderfully infectious and deeply erotic, and in the moment, it made Simone forget that Sicily ever existed. She wanted to forget, but she couldn't. Not now she knew she needed to see Roberto. She walked to the car with a heavy heart.

Simone locked the seatbelt in place and smiled at Maria.

The light reflected in Maria's eyes and her soft smile caressed Simone with love. *Shit.* She studied Maria, her chest becoming tighter, her throat clamping the words she needed to say. "You are so handsome and wonderful," she said instead.

Maria blushed.

"And loving and kind." Simone held Maria's gaze, wanting her to feel every word she meant. "And honest and protective."

A frown appeared and deepened across Maria's brow. "What's happened?"

"You know I adore it here," Simone said. "I really do."

Maria's eyes narrowed and she leaned toward Simone. Shaking her head, she took Simone's hand. "What is it?"

"It's perfect here," Simone whispered and caressed Maria's cheek.

"What's wrong? Something's up."

Simone saw hurt and frustration in Maria's eyes. Maria was right. Something had changed. The joy of waking next to Maria, the laughter and promise of a future, seemed extravagant in the face of her concerns about Roberto. "I need to see Roberto."

Maria squeezed Simone's hand and leaned back against the driver's seat. She stared silently out the windscreen for what seemed like an eternity.

"I know you don't want me to go."

Maria turned to face Simone. Her lips were pursed, her features crafted by the tension that she couldn't conceal. "I don't. It's not safe for you."

"It's not safe for you. No one is interested in me. I will be fine." Simone hadn't intended to raise her voice.

"Call him. Talk to him."

"It's not the same. I have called him. He doesn't say anything. I need to... No, I want to see him. There are things I need to discuss with him."

"What things?"

Simone clenched her fists, stiffening her arms and shoulders. "You're being unreasonable."

"I'm not being unreasonable. I'm concerned about you going back."

"I know you are. But there's nothing to be worried about." Simone turned away and looked out the side window. She shouldn't need to justify her decision. Maria was being obstinate and irrational. Maria didn't trust her. The tightness in her throat burned.

"What about Vitale?"

"Who?"

Maria's shoulders rose. "The bent detective."

"What about him?"

"He will be working for Stefano."

"So?"

"Fucking hell, Simone. Something could happen to you. Why can't you deal with it from here?" Maria gripped the steering wheel, bracing her arms.

"You're being paranoid."

"I'm not."

"You are. You're getting worse. You need to see someone, but you're too stubborn."

Maria bit down hard on her lip. "I don't need to see anyone. I need you to stay here where you're safe."

Simone turned swiftly on a fit of frustration and bellowed, "I want to go and see my brother. I don't understand you not wanting to see your family, but I don't quiz you on it. I don't challenge you. That I want to see him should be enough. I don't need your permission."

"Shit. You have no idea how this works, do you? Every person you interact with is a direct route back to me. The chances of me being discovered increase with every conversation you have. The risks are too great."

Raw pain stabbed Simone's chest. "Fucking, fuck you."

Maria flashed Simone a look and Simone felt an insurmountable distance between them. They had been thrust apart though they hadn't moved an inch. The pressure at the back of her eyes affected her vision. She cursed her bottom lip for quivering and pinched the bridge of her nose.

Maria gritted her teeth and turned to look out the windscreen.

Simone inhaled deeply and swallowed hard. She spoke quietly. "You are overreacting. I can go back and see my brother, collect my things, and return here. Surely, it would be odd if I didn't go back? And what do we do when Roberto starts asking questions and wants to come and see me? You've never wanted to have this conversation, I know, and I'm sorry if it hurts."

Maria looked at Simone, her eyes wide, her focus intense. "He can't know I'm alive, Simone. It puts him at risk, and us."

"He's already at risk, Maria. He works for the fucking business. Your business. The one you dragged him into." The assault tripped effortlessly from the hurt that Maria had inflicted on Simone. They were hurting each other.

"He doesn't need to know. It's for his own good."

"Maybe. Or maybe it's easier for you to keep an emotional distance from those you love by having everyone think you're dead."

Maria shook her head. "No, that's not true."

"You've had years preparing for this and I'm not like you. Don't you miss your family, even a little bit? What about them? Don't you think their lives would be richer if they knew you were alive? Do they get the chance to choose? No. You can try and play God, my love, but you're not allowing others to live when you do."

Maria didn't respond.

Simone got out of the car, slammed the door behind her, and stormed toward the back garden. Her breath ringing in her ears, her heart pounding, she marched to the henhouse. Tears streamed down her cheeks. Rewind the clock; take it all back. She couldn't. She had blurted and the words that had come out had been uncensored, and it had come out all wrong and now she wanted to bury herself in a hole. But she was right, Maria was overreacting and becoming increasingly paranoid, and Maria needed help. And yes, Simone loved her with all her heart. But she wouldn't let her life be dictated by anyone ever again and especially not a woman with roots inside the mafia. Never.

7.

The systematic clicking of what sounded like a three-footed walk alerted Maria to the woman entering the restaurant. She stopped packing the cardboard box with the crystal glasses left by the previous owners of the Lizieria restaurant and smiled. She had only seen Madame Verdéaux once before, at a distance when they were at the food market, but through reputation and rumour, she knew of the woman's life almost intimately.

Maria had overheard the locals talking at the restaurant before it closed for refurbishment, sharing their stories. She had been part of an organisation working the secret escape routes over the central Pyrenees during World War II, securing safe passage for Frenchmen, Jews, American airmen, and RAF pilots needing to escape into northern Spain. She had been a heroine and saved many lives. She had that hardy look about her that told Maria she had seen things few people had. Without even speaking to the woman, Maria felt a strong affinity with her.

The tweed hunting jacket with soft leather patches across the shoulders, certainly gave her a presence befitting her designated authority and heavily disguised her petite frame. The classically shaped, dark olive-green hunting hat with its narrow rim and triple-roped design around the base looked as if it had been made to measure. She didn't use the walking cane because the deep crevices that marred her face dictated she should. Rather, it was an aesthetic feature that supported her image. Maria admired both her sense of style and her posture.

"Good day to you, Madame Verdéaux." Maria dipped her head just a fraction, not out of deference, but as a mark of sincere respect. Her greeting drew a smile from the woman who dipped her head in response though her gaze remained attentive and Maria felt assessed. Then Madame Verdéaux broke eye contact, as if she had taken in all she needed to, and Maria wondered what she had deduced. Maria watched as her guest scanned the room.

"I heard you bought the place." She had a gruff edge to her deep voice. She pulled out a pack of Gauloises Brun cigarettes and offered them to Maria.

Maria shook her head at the offer. "I don't, thanks."

"Probably for the best." She coughed, a rough sound, pulled out one of the filter-less cigarettes, lit it and inhaled deeply. She took in the walls with a deepening frown then raised her eyebrows at the boxes and piles of crockery littering the floor space. She stood in a stream of smoke as it drifted from her lips and blinked as it wafted across her eyes. "It's a big job, eh?"

Maria sighed. It wasn't the scale of the job that had her feeling the weight of the world on her shoulders; it was the fact that she had dropped Simone at the airport earlier and barely a word had passed between them in the past three days since the argument. "A big job, yes."

She and Simone had already spent a week clearing out the restaurant for reconstruction work to start, and it still didn't look anywhere close to being emptied. The job was made more challenging now by the dark cloud that overshadowed Maria. Simone's hurt had been clear, and Maria had been desperate to console her but had done and said nothing to alleviate it. She had come straight to the restaurant from the airport to immerse herself in hard physical labour and quiet her overactive mind. It wasn't working too well. She was still kicking herself.

The crevices on Madame Verdéaux's cheeks rose and fell as she finished her smoke. She stubbed the cigarette out on the dusty tiled floor and scanned the yellow-brown looking ceiling. She tapped her cane twice, perhaps testing the stone surface or as some kind of ritual to summon the dead to help. She held Maria in an effortlessly commanding stare, and the smoker's lines bunched around her thin lips.

Maria waited.

"Place needed it." She tapped the cane again.

Maria cleared her throat. "Can I offer you a drink?" It was only ten past eleven, but time was irrelevant to the rules of social etiquette in St Lizier and she could do with something to numb her own pain.

Madame Verdéaux's eyes shone as they narrowed, and her closed-lipped smile smoothed her cheeks to something resembling the wavy plains of a desert. One could imagine warmth and kindness behind the naturally austere appearance the woman had clearly crafted over the years.

"Did they leave any cognac?" she asked, looking over Maria's shoulder to the bar.

Maria smiled. She had bought the place all-in, so whilst there was a great deal of work to do to clear the restaurant, there were some items that were of small value. She turned to the packed box of spirits and whipped out an almost full bottle of cognac. "How about this?" she said and held it aloft and received an approving nod.

"A good one too. Jerome must be losing his marbles. Not like him to pass up a fine brandy."

Maria smiled. Jerome had seemed delighted and relieved to sell the place with all its contents as far as Maria could tell. The effort of removing any unwanted furniture, which translated to pretty much everything that could be removed from the restaurant, would have probably tipped him over the edge. And with the deal they had struck he would be able to afford plenty of cognac should he wish, but Maria had the impression that Jerome wasn't the man he had once been. He had allowed the place to deteriorate to a shell of what it was when he took it over. He had shown her a photograph. He wore a white shirt tucked neatly into black trousers, and the woman next to him, Maria assumed was his wife, was dressed in a floral print dress. They stood in the doorway, his arm around her waist, and they both had joyful smiles and rosy cheeks. The newly painted sign shone brightly above the door. It must have been early summer because they were squinting into the light, and large baskets filled with red and pink flowers hung from the walls on either side of the doorway. He didn't mention the woman in the photograph to Maria, but a tear slipped onto his cheek as he relived his memories and Maria had felt his loss as her own.

    Maria passed a large shot of cognac across the bar and raised her own glass.

    Madame Verdéaux lifted her drink to Maria's. "Santé."

    Maria slugged the cognac and winced as it burned her throat. "I'll go and make coffee," she said and headed into the kitchen. She returned with a tray with two small cups of espresso coffee, a bowl of sugar, and a jug of milk, and placed it on the bar. As she looked up, she jumped and grabbed her chest at the sight of a man with a heavy moustache and dark-rimmed glasses peering through the restaurant window. *Christ!* Her heart beat hard against her ribs.

    Madame Verdéaux looked over her shoulder. "Bonjour, Gerard," she said and waved. "Gerard's the butcher. His shop is at the other end of the village. Nosy parker but a heart of gold," she said to Maria, and chuckled.

    Gerard came to the open door and tipped his hat. He craned his neck to see inside. "Good day to you, ladies. Anything I can help you with?"

    "We're fine, thanks. I'm just packing up a few things," Maria said. She noted Madame Verdéaux give a half-smile and glance around the littered room with raised eyebrows. Okay, it was more than packing up a few things, but Maria didn't want to inconvenience the man. She didn't need any help. She didn't want strangers around her. She wanted Simone back.

"Très bien." Gerard doffed his cap again. "Bonne journée." He set off down the street.

"Bonne journée," Maria said.

Madame Verdéaux downed a second cognac in one hit, narrowed her eyes and studied Maria closely. "So, perhaps can I help you?"

Maria looked around the restaurant. "It's okay," she said. "I'm not in a rush."

"Who said anything about rushing. Just helping out a neighbour."

Maria nodded. "Right, of course," she said softly, feeling mildly chastised. She motioned to the tables and chairs and the knick-knacks that cluttered the space. "We're gutting it and extending out the back. I need to get rid of everything that's here."

Madame Verdéaux looked around as if searching for the other person Maria referred to.

"My partner, Simone and me. She…she's had to go back to Sicily…to visit her brother." She watched her guest light another cigarette, suck down hard on the tip and blow out a long stream of smoke.

"Not in trouble, is he?"

The words jolted Maria. "No, nothing like that."

"You look bothered."

Maria huffed off the truth and forced a smile. This was becoming a lot like an inquisition. It appeared, not much escaped Madame Verdéaux. "No. I'm good. I need to get this place ready for the builders."

"Without letting anyone help you."

"Um."

"It's all right. I'm teasing you. Anyway, good for you with this place." She scanned the room again. "It's needed a damn good makeover for years, since Katerina passed. Maybe I'll come and eat here again when you're finished. I would like to meet your partner, since you're both setting up to stay here."

She sounded reminiscent and a little remorseful. Katerina must have been Jerome's wife. Maybe she was reminded of a more pleasant time here in the past. Maybe she had dined here with her husband years ago. Maybe Maria would chat with her in the future. She would enjoy that more than she liked to admit. Even with the directness, she sensed a bond with Madame Verdéaux that came from a recognition of having lived with secrets that could not be shared. Had she taken someone's life during the war? Maria had the sense that she had, and she would never need to ask. There was comfort in knowing their worlds were connected beyond the decades that separated their lives, in a way that few people could comprehend; they were united by similar principles and values, and a cause greater than themselves. She didn't get the impression Madame Verdéaux was like Patrina either. She was astute and far more secure in her sense of self than Patrina. Maria didn't think Madame Verdéaux needed anyone either and that made her trustworthy. *Those who need others can be easily bought. They cannot be trusted to act rationally.* Her father's words, spoken to her at a time when Patrina had been one of *those* people in her life, rang in her ear. Yes, she trusted Madame Verdéaux.

"Right," Madame Verdéaux cleared her throat, squinting at Maria. "I'll go and get my trailer," she said. "What are we doing with this lot?" She pointed at the tables.

"Taking them to the dump."

She shook her head as if Maria had just levied an insult and although her features remained intensely concerned, her eyes still shone with excitement.

"I know just the place. Leave that with me."

"If you're sure?"

"Of course. I know excellent trade people too, if you are looking?"

"Thanks. A recommendation would be great."

"Of course." Madame Verdéaux plucked a cup from the tray, added two cubes of sugar, and stirred vigorously. She blew repeatedly on the surface then downed the coffee in one slug. "There, that hit the spot," she said. "I'll go and get the Rover."

She plonked her hat on her head and picked up her cane. She dipped her head to Maria and clicked her way out of the restaurant.

Maria smiled to herself. Yes, Madame Verdéaux would be a good friend. A feeling Maria knew well, the comfort that came from having a strong parent with the heart of a lion who protected you no matter what bad thing you had done, settled in her chest. She thought of her mother and her heart ached. She hadn't thought about her matri or her sister often in the last five months but every time she did the sense of loss seemed to become more evident. Simone had touched a nerve. She took a deep breath and thought about Madame Verdéaux and the restaurant, Simone and the life they were creating together. Was their future here in St Lizier? Then she thought about Simone travelling back to Sicily, the argument, and her increasing sense of unease and felt empty.

She walked outside and stacked the last box of crockery at the front of the restaurant and spotted Madame Verdéaux heading toward her in an ancient-looking Land Rover. The vehicle's distinctive rumbling sound, an apparent lack of suspension, and the rattling of a trailer as it bounced at the rear would alert the whole village. Maria smiled as she came to a swift landing at least half a metre from the curb.

Immediately, and almost before she'd halted the vehicle, she jumped out of the driver's seat, strode to the trailer and lowered the side closest to the curb. "Come on then, don't dawdle. We'll get this lot shifted in no time," she said and marched hastily into the restaurant.

Maria, almost jogging to keep up, smiled.

Madame Verdéaux made light work of moving the tables and chairs onto the trailer, and with barely a shift in her breathing. Maria enjoyed clearing the furniture with her. They filled the caged trailer to the brim, and the restaurant looked bare even though they were only half-way through disposing of the furniture.

Madame Verdéaux downed another brandy with ease. "I'll be back shortly," she said and marched out of the restaurant.

She crunched the gears, and the engine squealed and growled, and the Land Rover jerked as it moved slowly down the road.

Maria winced at the state of the overfilled trailer. Something about Madame Verdéaux was comforting and reassuring. She felt lifted by her company. She was a delightful combination of the nurturing, empathic mother figure and the independent spinster aunt who was blunt and who had probably broken more rules in a week than Maria would ever dare in her lifetime. When she sounded the vehicle horn and waved to acknowledge another villager, swerving the Rover and causing the trailer to wobble precariously, Maria smiled to herself. She was definitely closer to the independent spinster, she would guess.

She walked back into the restaurant thinking about Simone. She would be in Sicily now. The emptiness burrowed deeply in her stomach. She poured another shot of brandy and slugged it back, vowing not to worry. It didn't help. The negative thoughts kept coming. She picked up her phone and sent a text.

I love you x

8.

The black painted front door of the house Simone had lived in for as long as she could remember, barring her short time away at university, looked as it always had. The sash style windows and shutters would benefit from a coat of paint soon, ideally before the winter set in. There would be minor decorative details to address inside the house too, no doubt. She noted his old scooter parked on its stand in the small front courtyard to the left of the door and chained to a steel ring cemented into the ground, and thought with fondness about St Lizier and the fact that people often didn't bother to lock their front doors. She admired the exterior with a feeling she identified as an emotional distance. This wasn't her home anymore.

She had to force the key to get it to turn in the lock. She eased the creaking door open, and a cool damp texture with a strong whiff of mustiness crept across her skin. She couldn't detect Roberto's zesty deodorant or the residual smell of stale tobacco that he carried with him. He didn't smoke, but everyone around him did.

She dropped her case in the hall and wandered toward the light emanating from the kitchen. The sun exposed a thick layer of dust on the inside of the windows and across the kitchen surface. A coffee cup sat in the base of the sink with a spoon in it. A dark brown ring stained the inside of the cup where coffee had dried on its surface. She opened the fridge door and drew back instantly, gagging from the rancid smell of sour milk. She plucked the container of yogurt-like substance and squeezed it down the sink, trying not to choke. She ran the tap until the water was hot enough to disperse it more quickly. Roberto had clearly not lived here in a while. She opened the window and breathed in the fresh air before going into the living room.

There was a faint odour of something that was neither the unique musty damp smell belonging to the house nor the masculine scents she associated with her brother. She sniffed again. Maybe she was dreaming. Where was the old armchair her father used to sit in smoking of an evening while she sat on his knee reading as a child? She had had a fondness for the seat and argued with Roberto for its continued protection. He'd obviously taken the opportunity to get rid of it. *Little shit.*

She smiled softly. Roberto always had been a cheeky kid, and he, unlike her, had the patience to wait for the right moment to get his own way. She snapped her head around and stifled a gasp as the latch clicked and the front door squeaked open. She threw her hand to her pounding chest, staring at the broad grin on Roberto's face and cursed. "Oh my God, you scared the shit out of me."

"Hello, sis." He slammed the door shut and strode toward her. "Look at you, all rosy cheeked. You look healthy. The French air must suit you," he said and wrapped his arms around her.

She squeezed him tightly, reassured by the familiar tobacco smell that wafted from his suit, then she jolted at the solid object at the side of his chest. Had she been naïve to think he wouldn't be carrying a weapon? He was mafia now. She held him at arm's length and looked him up and down, hoping to hide her shock. He somehow looked older, which was ridiculous and a figment of her imagination. His eyes held the dark distance that they had when she had left for the ballet, though they still sparkled with his smile.

The ability to transform in appearance and conceal emotions seemed to go with the job. Maria had been the same when Simone first met her. Either she was less effective at concealing them now or Simone could read her better. She couldn't read Roberto's expression the way she had previously.

Soft lines spanned his eyes, and he looked at her intently. He looked well, although something about his demeanour was different. Maybe he was just growing up quickly, with the responsibility that went with his job.

"You look really great," he said. "You needed that break."

He brushed her cheek. He removed his hand quickly and tugged her into another swift embrace. It was the quality of his grip that gave him away. It was firmer, as though he was grateful for the child-like form of comfort. It was subtle but distinctive, as it had been when he was a child. It was his form of apology, as if he were saying, *Sorry I've done something I shouldn't have, please forgive me so I can forgive myself but don't make me talk about it.* A tear threatened, so she tried to smile it away. "I've missed you," she said. She gave him one last squeeze and pushed him away. "So, where have you been living? Because it sure hasn't been here."

He lowered his head, smiling demurely. "Sorry, I meant to get here yesterday to clean up a bit, but work got in the way." He shrugged. "I'll sort it out, I promise."

She shook her head. "It's okay. I have time to clean."

He beamed at her. "So, how was the ballet? I'm so glad you took a good long break. Have you had any thoughts about staying in France? Is it nice? Are the people friendly? Have you met any new friends?" He turned away and looked to the floor. "Sorry, I'm firing questions at you, and you've just stepped through the door."

"Come on. I'll make coffee, and you can tell me where you've been living," Simone said and wandered through to the kitchen to put the kettle on.

"There isn't any milk," Roberto said.

"I know, I just threw your homemade yogurt down the sink. So, where have you been sleeping?"

He shook his head. "You're sounding like mum."

She raised her eyebrows and stared at him with a half-smile. He started blushing. "And?"

"What?"

"You have a girlfriend, don't you?"

He huffed as his skin darkened further. "How did you know?"

"I can see it in your eyes," she said, pointing at him. It was a little white lie but worked to her advantage if he thought he couldn't hide anything from her.

His eyes widened, and he rubbed his chin. "Really."

"So, who is she?"

He shook his head. "No one you know. Anyway, it's early days." He waved his hand in the air as if to brush off the conversation. "So, tell me about your trip. It feels like you've been gone forever."

"You wish. It was only a month."

His smile faded. "Six weeks and two days, and I did miss you," he said.

Simone sighed. She avoided eye contact. She thought about the argument she had left behind, the mixed emotions that had travelled with her. She had felt dreadful leaving Maria at the airport, angry with her stubbornness and frustrated that they hadn't resolved their differences before she had left. Now, she felt hollow, alone, and her heart ached to feel the closeness they had enjoyed before the disagreement. She wished she hadn't opened her mouth, but if she hadn't, she wouldn't be here now. It was more than an argument though. It was a fundamental difference in their thinking and that worried her more than anything. She busied herself with the task of making coffee. She had an overwhelming need to share everything with Roberto, the good and the bad, to ask his advice and use him as a sounding board. She bit her tongue. Excitement, joy, and passion tugged against fear, sadness, and the need for discretion. She willed the fire in her belly to abate, swallowed hard, and moved slowly, lazily preparing their drinks as if her thoughts didn't exist, her body tense from holding in the negative energy. "It is lovely there," she said

"That's good. How was Paris? I'd love to go. It's supposed to be the most romantic city in the—uh…sorry."

His dreamy tone stalled, and she turned to look at him and saw remorse in his eyes.

"Sorry, I didn't mean to…"

He looked away, and she wanted to free him of his guilt. Maria was alive and if he knew that, they could talk openly and freely, and laugh and celebrate, and everything would be right with the world again. He could help Maria to stay safe. Everything would make sense. She bit her lip harder, kept her words as thoughts, and parked them in the back of her mind where they would stay locked away. "It's okay," she said and gave him a half-hearted smile. She turned back to the kitchen worktop and ran her finger along the dusty surface. "We have to continue to talk about her, you know," she said softly.

"Sure."

The void between them became cavernous. She knew he felt it too because his tone was subdued, and even though she had just said they should talk about Maria, she suspected he wouldn't. The closed topic wrenched her heart.

"I'll nip out and get some milk," he said.

He had made a swift exit before she could say she would drink it black. The coffee aroma soon wafted around the kitchen, but the place still didn't feel like home.

She picked up a cloth and some furniture polish and went through to the living room in time to see Roberto pull away from the drive in the black Maserati. *Maria's car.* Her heart skipped a beat. Melting warmth filled her and then a profound chill stilled her. She rested her hand on the window ledge and closed her eyes. Maria was safe and alive. It hadn't all been a dream. It was beautiful reality, and they were building a micro farm and a wonderful life in a small village deep in the Pyrenees. One week to sort things out here and she would go back and hold Maria in her arms and apologise for the hurt she had caused in her fit of anger. She gazed around the room.

Just hours back in Sicily, and she was doubting her sanity in choosing to return here. Maybe she'd discovered something better in St Lizier. Maybe the weeks away had given her a new perspective on life and this place had always been the same as it was now. Maybe she had tasted real freedom or grown up in some way. Whatever it was, she needed to trust her instincts. She needed to know that Roberto was safe too and if he had a girlfriend, Simone wanted to meet her. Determination stiffened her back, and she opened her eyes. She had time to clear up before they had one of Roberto's pizzas for tea. She laughed. Roberto hadn't worked at the pizzeria for a while now. Was it still the best in town? Would he eat with her or did he have somewhere better to be? The throaty roar rumbled outside the window signalling his return. She made her way through to the kitchen and poured their coffee.

She too had questions for him.

9.

The clanking of the fine metal ropes that marked the perimeter of the boat had a delicate ring to them as they swung on the light breeze. Clear blue skies and the large white ball of sun belied the cooler autumn temperature in this part of the world. The sand on the beaches here in Valencia, Spain, was coarser than at the beach villa, but the smells of the sea were similar. The afternoon spent diving and fishing had lifted Maria's spirits.

She had come to the Octavia to think clearly. Standing on the deck of the cruiser and being on the sea evoked a feeling of solitude of the quality she'd enjoyed at the cove of a night time, gazing up at the stars and wishing for a time when she wouldn't need to have eyes in the back of her head just to survive, or to carry a gun, or to take a decision that would end another human being's life in the name of honour. Fuck the code that meant the guilty never got called to justice. Fuck the mafia that had killed her father and stolen her life from her before she could walk. And fuck Palermo for having a hold over Simone. She had vowed never to go back to Sicily. Why then did the idea of returning torture her every waking hour? Simone had accused her of not giving her family a choice, of not allowing them to decide about her. She had removed herself from their lives, it was true. *I did it for their protection.* The words resonated as hollow now. She wrapped her arms around her body. The trembling came from deep inside and her tears tasted saltier than the sea.

It wasn't just the black hole in her world created by Simone's absence, it was the nature of the argument that haunted her. Reflecting on what Simone had said in a fit of anger made Maria feel enraged and she knew she was being defensive. Maria had turned her mind in circles trying to work out the real problem. The last time Simone had blown up at her and walked out, Maria had deserved it. She had omitted to tell Simone that Roberto worked for her. She had underestimated that, in Simone's world, being involved in the mafia's business was a big issue. Was it wrong to not want harm to come to the one you love? No. And she didn't entirely agree with Simone. She trusted her as much as she could. It was simply a fact that, even though Simone had worked for Patrina, she was naïve when it came to the workings of the mafia. Seriously, Simone hadn't even realised her own father had worked for Stefano Amato before being *accidentally* killed by him – collateral damage in the world of organised crime. The sick feeling that accompanied her instinctive sense of Simone's predicament hadn't abated. Even though Simone was blind, Maria wasn't. She had set an alarm at night to sleep in short bursts so as to avoid the nightmares. The tiredness didn't touch her nearly as profoundly as the sadness had.

The farmhouse seemed greyer and lifeless now. It had lost its homely appeal, quickly becoming just a space in which to eat and avoid sleep. Necessary to stay out of the elements, but not *home*. The classical background music they enjoyed together while they worked or relaxed, or made love, now stirred anger and frustration. The chickens did their best to ignore her and spent most of their day huddled in a cluster watching the house. They were waiting for Simone. They would peck at the grit around Simone's feet, stand on her shoulder and follow her across the meadow, and Simone's laughter would carry across the meadow. The silence, particularly at night, had a sinister quality to it with the absence of nocturnal life and the constant rush of a swirling wind. Maria had sat at the bedroom window the past two evenings during the moments when she should be sleeping and peered out…vigilant and waiting.

The not-so-small issue of the potential for her own exposure niggled. Maria didn't trust the bigger voices in

Palermo, the underground networks, the corrupt authorities, and the clans looking to assert themselves to get a bigger piece of the mafia pie. Nor did she trust the Amatos. Patrina was the exception, though Maria could only trust her to a point. Questions excited curiosity. And curiosity could get you or those you loved killed. Everyone had their price and while she knew Giovanni and Roberto would look out for Simone, Maria was better equipped than them both to take care of her. There was nothing irrational about her thinking.

She stepped off the Octavia and secured the rope to the mooring.

She turned toward the car as it pulled to a stop on the track behind her and smiled as Rafael approached. Her heart warmed to see the man who ran the Lombardos' business in Spain, the man who had supported her over the years and arranged her medical treatment and safety following the shooting. She trusted him with her life. He had a spring in his step today. Warmth expanded from her chest. She strode to meet him and hugged him tightly. "It's so good to see you, my friend."

"Good catch?" he asked, pointing to the sealed icebox on the deck.

"Fair. A couple of sea bass and three bream."

"Pretty good. You haven't lost your touch." He looked her up and down and smiled. "You look very well."

She tilted her head. "Better than the last time."

His smile was faint as he nodded. "Did you dive? I hear it's very pretty."

"Yes, it's very beautiful." She turned and looked out to sea. The sense of being under the water, in nature, compared to nothing. A state of blissful freedom.

"Well, it's good to see you, Maria."

She smiled. "You look...happy," she said and laughed as she patted his developing paunch. "Isla must be feeding you too well."

He chuckled. "She is an excellent cook." He looked Maria up and down again. "She's excited to see you again. She will have cooked a feast. I hope you are hungry."

"Always. Farming is hard work. You should try it." She patted him on the back. "I'm glad you're doing well. How are the boys?"

"Ah, they are boys. They play and fight together. They are happy, and they are sad. And now they are at school, so that is a new experience."

"Time passes..."

"Too quickly," Rafael said softly. "And you never know what is coming next."

They stood in reflective silence with the hush of the sea and clinking of ropes. Maria recalled Simone's bright eyes and her excitement when they bought the chickens and how she had snuggled Poulet in her lap in the car on the way home. *Family, their family.* She took a deep breath and turned her attention back to Rafael.

He waved his hand. "Come, Isla will be waiting for us and she will curse me if we are late."

She followed him up the track to his car. "How is the business?"

"Business is good. Cement is still in demand though not as high as when you were taking care of things." He chuckled.

She rubbed from her mouth to her chin with the palm of her hand. "You're sure everything is fine?"

He glanced at her and back to the road. "Yes. Why wouldn't it be?"

She tilted her head, averted his gaze, and pursed her lips. "That piece of shit, Vitale, for one."

He shook his head. "Nothing has come back to me. Perhaps—"

"People like him don't just disappear."

Rafael put his hand on her shoulder and looked into her eyes. "It's not your problem now, Maria. Your job there is done. Why are you worried?"

"Simone has gone home."

He lowered his hand and then his eyes and then she saw the same look her father had given her at times.

"And you think there will be trouble for her?" He frowned, and pressed his lips closed. "Do you think Giovanni, Angelo, and Roberto will not look after her?"

Maria shoved her hands in her pockets.

Rafael spoke softly. "Sometimes we see what we fear vividly. We may think that what we see is so obvious that we cannot be wrong. If this feeling you have is so compelling, then you need to trust your instincts. But if you do, everything you have worked for will be...for nothing."

"That's what worries me. I get the sense I have already been compromised."

Rafael shook his head. "How?"

Maria lowered her eyes. What she was about to say was as unbelievable to her as it would be to Rafael. "I think I'm being watched."

He looked around him, frowning. "Are you sure?"

She averted his gaze and, in a whisper, said, "No."

He wrapped his arm around her shoulder and continued to walk with her.

He thought she was crazy. She would think the same thing if she were listening to someone else. But he was right about the most important thing. She needed to trust her instincts. She would stay alert and talk Simone into coming home sooner rather than later. *Only let them see what you want them to see, Maria,* her father's voice echoed.

10.

The glint in Stefano's eyes was more disconcerting than the look of loathing he normally levied at Patrina when she visited him. He resembled the younger version of himself. Excited, alive, and virile. Except that he seemed to stare through her rather than look at her adoringly as he had done in the beginning. He indicated for her to pick up the phone. Resistance slowed her response. She lifted the handset and pressed it to her ear.

He leaned toward the screen. "You haven't dealt with the fucking casino, have you?"

She sat upright to ease the sharp pain in her chest. He knew. Lombardo construction was still progressing the tech park, albeit slowly. She had persuaded some of the suppliers to stall deliveries, but it was costing them money they didn't have. She hadn't taken the situation to the mayor to pull strings from that angle and didn't intend to. He probably wouldn't listen anyway since his loyalty was now to the Lombardo project. Heat imploded in her stomach; shock waves rippled across her skin. She tried to stop the trembling from affecting her voice. "It is in progress, Stefano," she said. There was weakness in her tone.

He noticed it too. He scowled at her, his jaw clenched, his rugged cheeks darkening by the second.

"Fucking sort the fucking problem," he said through gritted teeth.

She nodded. "I am working on it."

"Not. Fucking. Good. Enough."

Was he implying she should take a hit on Giovanni? She couldn't do that. She had a good working relationship with the Lombardos. Business was stable now and stability was strength in the changing climate; the authorities were taking decisive action against the mafia and more bosses were being incarcerated faster than ever before. She wasn't going to spend the rest of her life, however short that might be, in a prison cell, and she was not inclined to instigate a war with anyone. Her loyalty to Maria was her bond and nothing Stefano said was going to change that fact. The brave words clung to her dry mouth as if retreating. She couldn't speak her mind to Stefano. It would be akin to signing her own death warrant. It hurt her throat to swallow, and she wetted her lips with her tongue. "Darling, please. I am working on it."

He leaned closer to the screen, his eyes bright and his glare vacant, a look that showed no remorse and conveyed an unrelenting lust for power. She inhaled deeply, the hairs rose at her neck and a shiver ran down her spine.

"I want you to increase the distribution of merchandise across the city. Take control of *their* restaurants and the shops."

His quiet tone sucked the air from her. He was telling her to get into a turf war. Blood would be shed. "Is there anything else?"

"Find decent suppliers or get the fucking costs down. We are being ripped off."

"We have good relationships with our suppliers."

"Fucking relationship is not good when I'm being taken for a fucking ride. And get the fucking casino back on track." He leaned back, clasped his hands behind his head and puffed out his chest. His cheeks were darker with a strong ruddy complexion that made him look as though he might implode.

She stifled a sigh that expanded swiftly in her chest. "And how are you, darling?" She smiled sweetly. His impotence came through clearly in his frustration and she didn't need to exacerbate it by challenging him.

His eyes narrowed as he gritted his teeth and tapped his nose. "I can fucking smell it."

She frowned. "What?"

"Bull. Fucking. Shit."

"I don't understand." She really didn't have a clue what he was talking about.

"You think I don't know?"

"Know what?"

"That you've got more interest in playing happy fucking families with the Lombardos than making my business work." He pointed to his eyes and then his ears, as if his words needed a physical cue to be understood. "The Lombardos, all of them, are a threat, and I don't need fucking complications. This is all your fucking fault. So, *you're* responsible for eliminating the problem. Capisci?"

Patrina stared at him. There was no doubt, he was insane. The Lombardos weren't a threat. Giovanni wasn't a threat. Even Don Chico had gone quiet since assuming responsibility for Alessandro's death and receiving a substantial financial donation for his silence, not that Stefano would know about that transaction, of course. She had an agreement with them all that was working smoothly, for now. Was this really about the tech park, or did Stefano have other plans he wasn't inclined to share with her? The thud behind her ribs became heavier.

The glint in Stefano's eyes became brighter, and his lips curled into a disingenuous smile. "I'm going to become the king, Patrina. Alessandro's soul came to me. We talked."

Now he sounded deranged.

"We owe Alessandro, Patrina."

She didn't owe his pig of a nephew anything. He got what he deserved and not soon enough. As for Stefano becoming king, God help them all. "How?"

He tapped his nose and lifted his chin. "Big growth. We're going to take control of the supply of merchandise into Palermo. All of it."

He was referring to drugs, alcohol and tobacco. The Amato clan had been diminished as a result of Alessandro's failed efforts to grow the business, and they still hadn't recovered financially or in number. "We don't have the men or the money."

"I'm sending someone to you. He helped me. You will work with him to build the business." He leaned forward. "Capisci?"

She tightened her grip around the handset. "Who? How do you know this man?"

"He did a good job for me. He has useful contacts. He'll come to the café and introduce himself. Tommaso Vitale."

"Contacts where?"

"High up the chain. It doesn't matter. All you need to know is he gets things done."

Patrina swallowed. The name registered though she couldn't picture his face. The news regarding Vitale's arrest for tampering with police evidence had been overshadowed by the authorities' new plans to clamp down on mafia activities. The clear-up operation was expected to take two to three years, but they had promised Sicily would soon be free of the fear that had threatened hard working citizens for too many years. Vitale's release without charge hadn't made the headlines. So, this was the man feeding Stefano information.

The door opened behind Stefano. He returned the handset and stood. He stared at her for longer than would be normal and then smiled. He mouthed the words, "next week," then he turned and walked out of the room without a second glance in her direction.

Her stomach roiled. She rubbed her hands together to warm them. Stefano looked elated asserting his power again and it stuck in her throat. She wished she could change the course of time. She wished him dead. She clutched her arms to her chest. If Vitale had contacts, if Vitale dug deeper, if Vitale found out what she had done, she would be dead.

She exited the prison and strode toward her waiting car. She got in and looked across at Beto in the driving seat and released a long, slow breath. "He's sending Vitale to work with us."

Beto frowned.

"If we must, we'll take Vitale out. I will not go back on my promise to Maria." She turned and looked out the passenger window to hide her tears from Beto. He didn't question her about it and drove. She would win Vitale to her way of thinking and if that didn't work, she would happily dispose of him as she had done Alessandro.

11.

Bad men killed innocent people. Bad men needed to be stopped. Preparing to go back to Sicily wasn't as simple as getting back on the proverbial horse after a fall though. Maria had never wanted to be on this horse in the first place and having fallen and landed harder than most the idea of getting back on, of going back to Palermo, clouded her thinking and reinforced the nightmares. She might not get up from the next fall. The 637 Magnum lay in a leather holster in the box at the back of her wardrobe and although she had never intended to use it again, she knew she would if she had to.

A sheen of moisture formed on her skin as she punched the boxing bag erected in the barn at the farmhouse. It wasn't a full gym yet, but it was what she needed. The dense bag swayed reluctantly with every punch. She landed two jabs with her left and an upper cut with her right. Repeating the pattern, moving her feet swiftly in small steps, she puffed out short breaths with each punch. Six rounds, seven. She stopped punching, kept her feet dancing, and puffed out hard. The feeling of power and control was exhilarating. She started the routine again, punching harder, moving quicker, eight rounds and then nine. She let out a wild screech as she pushed to deliver the final punch of the tenth round. "Yes." She lowered her arms and, shaking the ache from her muscles, she continued to skip from foot to foot, looking to the roof of the barn and wincing. As she slowed her feet, she lowered her head and wiped the sweat from her brow with her forearm. Her chest expanded freely as she inhaled deeply. She pulled off her gloves and drank from the water bottle and stared out across the meadow.

Simone being in Sicily gnawed at her like a rat chewing the electrical cables in the roof. *If you don't catch the rat your house will burn down.* That Vitale had been allowed to walk free was indicative of everything that was wrong with the governing authorities in Sicily and despite their rhetoric about cleaning up the streets and ridding the mafia of its power and eventually, its existence, she wasn't swayed by the propaganda. That wasn't what was driving her to train harder than she ever had before; it was the thought, *I'm losing her.*

She had started a routine of vigorous exercise, boxing and running, on the back of her conversation with Rafael. He had been right; the anxiety had reduced significantly, and she had experienced a clarity of thought in the past week that she hadn't known since Sicily. Though that hadn't made conversation with Simone any easier. They had barely spoken and when she had asked Simone to come back sooner rather than later, Simone had become quickly irritated. Simone had administration, *and things,* that she needed to sort out. Maria wasn't trying to control Simone as Simone thought, but Simone had been evasive and the distance between them had become palpable. The idea of losing Simone inflicted a pain so deep and enduring that it drowned her in emptiness and despondency. She had no life without Simone. If Simone didn't come back to the farmhouse, then what would be the point of living? The *truth* was driven by Maria's instincts combined with a sharp intellect. And on both fronts, she had never been wrong before.

And her instincts were telling her, she had to go back to Palermo.

The desire for revenge caused men to do vile and crazy things. Alessandro was proof that man's insanity was more dangerous than any physical weapon. Her father had said that Stefano had lost his way after his conviction for the deaths that included Simone's family. She didn't doubt Stefano's crazed state of mind, and if he had Vitale feeding his ego, he was capable of anything. He could take a hit out on Simone without giving it a second thought. Roberto too. Was Stefano intent on finishing the job he started when he killed Simone's father, mother, and brother? Debt closed, finally. What if the Di Salvo deaths weren't an accident? And what about Maria's mother, sister, and baby nephew? There was no telling what Stefano would do to get what he wanted.

Men like Stefano didn't take a back seat. She had hoped Patrina would have handled the Amato business, but Stefano was clearly a law unto himself. Would he go after the 'Ndrangheta for his nephew's death? That would be a brave and stupid move. Don Chico's crew were bigger and more powerful than the dwindling Amatos and any hit taken out on Chico would be Stefano signing his own death warrant. The only way Stefano could challenge Chico would be to recruit, to expand, which would likely mean bringing in thugs willing to do the dirty work or take over existing clans. Or both.

Fucking hell. Was Stefano stupid enough to think he could pull it off? Giovanni needed to stay vigilant. Vitale could be watching the Lombardo crew too.

Simone, please come home. Why did this pain not go away? Suppressing the desire to scream, she slumped to her knees, hugged herself tightly and sobbed. No, she wouldn't lose the love of her life, even if it cost her everything she had worked to achieve.

She couldn't say how long she had been crouched. Her knees were sore, and her skin was dry and cold. The dark, damp void had claimed her, immobilised her, and silenced her thoughts. Now, bright light brought vivid contrast to the autumn landscape, the shades of auburn and gold were sharper and clearer, and the chickens' squawks were ear-splittingly annoying. Slowly, she eased herself up and stretched her legs. She rubbed her hands vigorously up and down her arms, her teeth chattering. She blinked her eyes, narrowing her gaze to the gate of a bridle path at the far side of the meadow, and started to run.

12.

Simone hadn't been snooping to overhear her brother's phone conversation. It had happened because Roberto's tone had changed during the call, and his responses had become monosyllabic. He'd got up and gone outside. She had watched him striding purposefully up and down the street, running his fingers tightly through his hair. He stopped, looked skyward as if seeking guidance, or despairing and looking for an answer.

Based on his hesitant manner with her now, he hadn't found those answers.

"Is everything okay?"

"Sure," he said too quickly.

"You seem on edge."

"It's just business. Nothing you need to worry about, sis."

His smile fell short of convincing her, and he didn't seem to take her concerns seriously. Maria used to say something similar, and while it didn't feel any more dismissive coming from him, she wasn't going to tolerate his flippancy. "Is it about the tech park?"

He glanced up at her, shifting his attention from the message he was typing into his phone. "The tech park is moving along."

"Is there a problem, Roberto?" She *did* sound like their mother. She waited in silence for him to look at her and remind her of that fact.

He gave her a fleeting smile as he pocketed his phone. "Materials are delayed again. Nothing we can't get sorted." He took in a sharp breath. "Anyway, Noella can't wait to meet you."

He grinned broadly, and there was a faint lightness that appeared in his eyes, but the muscles in his neck twitched, and the feeling of being cleverly dismissed came through loud and clear. He was hiding something, though now was not the time to push it with him. She had enough problems of her own to deal with. Problems she couldn't share with him. Maria was obstinate and frustrating, and she missed her desperately. She missed the old Maria too, especially the version of Maria she had first met. Maria had changed. It was inevitable given what she had been through. Maria needed help. Now, they were at an impasse and neither of them would budge. Stupid, yes, but she wasn't going to back down. She hadn't, and wouldn't, reveal Maria's whereabouts to anyone. Not even Roberto. There was no rush to return. Maria was safe at the farmhouse.

She had talked briefly to Roberto about going back to the Pyrenees but hadn't offered key information like when, where, and for how long and he hadn't pressed her. She didn't have those answers. Decorating the house had become a good excuse to stay a little longer, though she couldn't say why she felt a strong sense of obligation to stay. It didn't make sense. Roberto had already been looking at buying his own place, a villa closer to the coast since Noella liked to be near the sea. He had moved on and was growing up quickly. She enjoyed his company when he was there. Except when he was distracted by work, when he became distant and evasive and she felt the same niggle that she had when she arrived at the house.

She looked into his eyes and smiled. "That's good. When, where?"

"I thought she could come here one evening. I'll get pizza." His phone buzzed, but he dismissed it with a finger swipe. "Sis, I'm really busy. I have to go."

"I'll see you later?" she asked.

He put his hand in the air, palm down and rocked it, before making another call as he left. *That would be a no then.*

She decided to take a walk around the city in a while and eat lunch at Lo Scoglio's, one of the Lombardos' smaller restaurants on the main plaza. She recalled the lunch she had taken there with Maria in the summer, the fresh lemonade, and the waiter who reminded her that she was trapped spending all her time inside the boundaries of the villa while hiding from the Amatos. She had talked to Maria about her need to get out and Maria had reluctantly agreed.

Palermo was beautiful in the autumn and even though it was a similar temperature to St Lizier, the air felt degrees warmer. Its uniquely fragrant signature ran through her veins: grapes and honey, and herbs, and salt from the sea air. That she could not deny. *Familiarity operates on the psyche to create the illusion of comfort,* Maria had said. She was right. It was like a drug that called to you and kept you within its grasp. She had never fallen out of love with the city, just some of the people who inhabited it. Palermo would be a delightful place to live if she didn't have to negotiate the mafia.

She went upstairs, pulled the case from her wardrobe, and lifted it onto the bed, craving seeing the passport-sized photograph of Maria. Craving the feeling of closeness that they had shared in Paris. Why was Maria so stubborn? She clicked the case open and unzipped the lid. A flurry of butterflies took off inside her. She picked up Maria's T-shirt, brought it to her nose and inhaled the residual perfume that clung to it. Her vision blurred. She straightened the slightly creased letter Maria had written to her when she knew she might die. Maria had tried to take care of everything. Maria was still trying to take care of everything. *I do love you, so much.*

The small photo of Maria was nowhere to be found. She couldn't recall taking it with her, but maybe it had slipped into the envelope with the tickets for the ballet and was still in the case back at the farmhouse. Or maybe it got lost somewhere on route. She suddenly felt listless and had desperate need for Maria to hold her. Even though it was just a passport photograph and Maria looked serious and honestly not much like Maria looked, the tiny memento occupied a special place in her heart. *Damn it. Damn you, Maria.*

Black blouses, skirts, and trousers hung in the wardrobe. Work clothes. She didn't care for them. The clothes she had collected from the villa after she thought Maria had died remained untouched in the large suitcase on top of the wardrobe. She had taken just a few essentials and her red gown to Paris for the ballet. *We can buy new clothes,* Maria had said. And they had. She had no interest in taking any of these garments back to St Lizier with her. She would rather burn them as a symbol of letting go, a final farewell to Patrina Amato who had effectively bought her silence to save her own sorry arse. Patrina may have played some part in saving Maria's life, but that didn't mean Simone trusted her. She looked up and around the room and wished she was sitting in the living room in the farmhouse.

Light had to work hard to create any positive effect within the bedroom. The dark shadows occupied too much space and made the room feel even smaller. She'd been spoiled living at Maria's villa and the farmhouse. Maria wouldn't judge her for the state of this house, and she wouldn't want to live here with her. It was damp and dull. As a child, it had afforded security and comfort, but that feeling died when her parents did. She didn't feel a sense of safety or cosiness here. There was no solid reasoning for her complete change of heart. The explosions at the port that night, that had resulted in Simone moving into Maria's villa, seemed to have triggered every bad thing that had followed. They'd changed everything.

She rose swiftly, the overwhelming sense of having to get out of the house overcoming her. She returned the case to the wardrobe, changed into trousers and a blouse, and headed downstairs. Obscurity would afford her privacy, and she didn't want Palermo to see her. She wanted to see it, one last time.

13.

The door to Café Tassimo clicked shut and the steady, unhurried clip of heels on the tiled floor drew Patrina's eyes from her laptop. She had never taken much note of Tommaso Vitale, Capitano Massina's sidekick and looking at him now, she questioned why he hadn't attracted her interest. He had been insignificant in the scheme of things, an invisible administrator. What he lacked in width he made up for in height. His dark grey designer jacket complemented the skinny charcoal jeans that clung to muscular legs and his leather shoes looked handmade and highly polished. A man with an aesthetic eye, pride in his appearance, and the physique to carry it too. *Nice.* She smiled as he approached. She inhaled his body lotion, woody and warm, and swallowed back the stirrings of desire that sparked inside her. Without thought, she stood and held out her hand. Eyes of the lightest blue held her mesmerised and sparks flamed in her core. She withdrew her hand as it became clammy and hoped she hadn't revealed her sensitivity to him.

She cleared her throat to prevent a tremor in her voice. "Tommaso Vitale," she said.

He dipped his head, though his eyes never shifted from her face. "Lady Patrina. At last, we meet in person." He looked around the restaurant and nodded. "Nice place you have here."

His smile disarmed her. She motioned for him to sit and took her seat opposite him. Frankly, she hated the seventies dated décor. It had been Stefano's choice, and at some point, she would change it. "What can I get you to drink?"

"Whatever you're having. Thank you." He relaxed back in the chair and ran his fingers lightly across the surface of the table.

She indicated for the bartender to bring wine and turned her attention to Tomasso. He didn't strike her as a man who would be willing to get his hands dirty. His features were fine, his hands narrow with the long fingers of a pianist. He had a thick crop of dark hair parted at the side, a short sharply cut goatee, and smooth skin. Everything about him was neatly designed. He reminded her of Maria. Precise, orderly, and alluring. She wetted her dry lips and cleared her throat again.

"How can I help you, Tommaso?" She smiled. His eyes looked darker from this angle, his skin too. She inhaled the scent of him, comforted in the knowledge they shared a mutual attraction. That was always helpful in her line of business.

"I'm here to help you, Patrina, to look after your needs." His gaze drifted easily across her chest and back to her mouth, then he looked her directly in the eye and his smile seemed sincere.

The bartender came to the table and set a carafe of wine and basket of bread on the table.

"Thank you."

A man with manners. That *was* refreshing. "So, I understand you are no longer with the DIA?"

"With the speed the authorities wash their hands in this city, it's a wonder the soap manufacturers can keep up with demand. Injustice is rife, Patrina. You understand how these things work."

She saw something in his smile. Cunning? He came across as highly intelligent. That would have appealed to Stefano. It would balance her husband's stupidity. Intelligence fascinated her. Maria was brilliantly astute, and they had worked very well together. "You are in the cosmetics business now?" She smiled. She was teasing him lightly based on his polished appearance. The resulting shading in his cheeks told her it affected him.

He laughed. "No. I'm in the storage business, containers and warehousing and the like."

She frowned.

"I know, it's not as sexy as cosmetics, but it's a good business. People always need space. We make good money."

The large solid gold band with an insignia pressed into its surface on his little finger hinted at his association with the mafia. Alessandro wore an identical one. And the diamond-encrusted Rolex watch hanging loosely from his wrist implied wealth, and it sure as hell didn't come from the storage business or his previous work at the DIA. She looked into his eyes.

"It's my father's business. Or was." He lowered his gaze a fraction.

"I'm sorry." She frowned at his genuine grief.

The sparkle returned to his eyes. "He was suffering for a long time, so his passing was a blessing. We have several large warehouses on the industrial estate and further afield. I'll take you to see them sometime and give you a guided tour."

She shivered. He must have sensed her desire because he leaned forward and smiled.

"I have a very private space," he said in a softer tone.

She picked up her glass of wine and took a sip. She hoped he hadn't noticed the slight tremble in her fingers as she placed the glass back on the table. "You have spoken to my husband?"

He nodded and glanced around the room, before breaking a piece of bread to dip into his wine.

Methodical, considered movements defined his character. She noticed the smoothness of his hands. He'd clearly never seen the graft her husband had, and he operated with the grace and charm of an aristocrat whose power came as their right. Effortless and deeply seductive. Again, he reminded her of Maria, except for one thing...trust. She trusted

Maria with her life. She didn't trust him...yet, although he exuded charm. At least he was going to be interesting to work with and possibly good for a bit of sport on the side.

"How is business?"

"Business is growing."

He nodded. "Stefano will be pleased."

Mention of her husband's name numbed the pleasant sensations instantly. "The tech park is stalling."

"Not quickly enough, apparently. I'm here to help you with that." He dipped another piece of bread and took a small bite. "Is this your best wine?"

Heat spread to her chest. She had tasted good wine; Maria's wines were excellent. She knew what they offered at the café was poor by those standards, but the punters didn't seem to care, and the margins on cheaper wines were good. She smiled thinly. "Not the best, no."

"You save the best for special occasions?"

She chuckled. "Yes," she said, feeling the hoarseness in her throat.

He tilted his head. "Well, let's hope we have a special occasion to celebrate at some point soon." He dipped another chunk of bread and ate it. "The bread is very tasty."

"Freshly baked." She dipped a piece of bread and, pushed the thought to the back of her mind. She would fuck him. That was about need and desire, about power and control. Men were easier to read once that wall had been pulled down.

"Simone Di Salvo was seen in the plaza."

She tilted her head and waited for him to continue.

"She looks good. Well rested. I understand France is a beautiful country, especially as one heads south and into the mountains. It has such a diverse landscape, don't you think?" He didn't pause for her to answer. "Paris with its structural beauty, allegedly the most romantic city in the world. And then there's the rural magnificence. Do you know grape vines dominate much of the countryside? It's an incredible sight. Thousands of vines sprawled across the terrain for as far as the eye can see, and even crawling up the sides of the mountains. Quite spectacular. I sampled one of the best wines I've ever tasted in a small vineyard in the Bordeaux region. Can't remember for the life of me what it was called now. That was a long time ago though. Have you ever been to France? It's a lot bigger than Sicily, of course. I think you would appreciate the art and culture there."

He stopped for air, and she noted a shift in his eyes. What was he trying to say? He knew where Simone had been, what she had been up to? Who cared? Was this some veiled threat she should take note of? That he knew things she didn't, and she should have better control of matters. "No, I haven't been to France." She had only ever thought of leaving Sicily with Maria. Now, she was too tied into her life and without a lover's support, she had no desire to go anywhere else. If she hadn't had the balls to do it with Maria, she sure as hell wasn't going to do it alone or with a stranger she'd just met. Not that he had been asking her to go with him.

"I think you would enjoy the Pyrenees. There are many beautiful villages set in the mountains."

She rubbed her forehead, confused and pressured by the coded messages that she didn't know how to read. This was unexpected discourse and for a reason she couldn't define, unwelcome. She had no interest or desire to talk about the ex-employee who stole Maria from her.

"Autumn is stunning there. The air is clean and fresh, free from the pollution we find in our decaying city."

She had never considered Palermo as rotting. "Maybe I'll go sometime." She had no intention of doing so. Where was he going with this conversation?

"Simone Di Salvo has just returned from there, Patrina."

She narrowed her eyes though she hadn't intended to show such interest in his reverie. He seemed determined to talk about Simone though.

"One can't help but wonder what would keep her there so long. I mean, most people taking a holiday for that length of time at this time of year might go and see the sights or even travel more widely." He turned the glass in his hand.

"What are you saying?"

He leaned forward. "Motivation drives behaviour, Patrina. Love is powerful, no?" He eased back slowly. "Thank you for the hospitality. We should do this again. Perhaps somewhere more private next time?"

She didn't try to stand. He placed his hand gently on her shoulder and told her not to get up. She didn't look around as the door clicked quietly as he left. She was trying to make sense of his coded messages. So what if Simone stayed two months in a tent in the middle of the Sahara? She didn't give a shit. She had no desire to visit Paris, and if Simone had decided to stay in France, good riddance to her.

The door clanged, and she turned her head toward it. "Beto," she said and smiled as he approached the table.

The waitress poured him a glass of wine and he sat opposite Patrina.

"All good?"

"We just had a visit."

"Vitale?"

"Yes."

"And?"

"He's..." She huffed at the irony of what she wanted to say: that she could see something in Tommaso that she had seen in Stefano, and that Tommaso had class and was a learned man, rather than the ignorant pig her husband was. He talked in riddles as Maria sometimes had done. She poured herself a glass of wine and sipped. "He's going to take care of the tech park."

Beto closed his eyes briefly. "He's going to start a bloody war."

Patrina was reeling from the effect of being in his presence. He had charisma and manners and she couldn't think clearly in his presence. "I have no choice but to go with him, at the moment. Stefano has sent him. Resisting isn't an option unless we have a death wish."

Beto leaned toward her. "Giovanni and Roberto are as good as friends get in this business. We made a promise to Maria that you and I both know was sweet justice for that pig's indiscretion."

"I know. I will get Tommaso onside with us. If he is as good as Stefano thinks he is, then we need him with us, not against us."

Beto slugged his wine back in one hit. "I look forward to meeting him." His tone lacked sincerity.

"How is recruitment going?" she asked.

"The brothers I told you about, Alfonzo and Franco Puglisi. Twins, sixteen, live with their mother who works at the dry cleaners on the estate. Father died before they were born. She's done her best, but they need strong guidance and focus. I will get them collecting rent."

"Why haven't we approached them before?"

"The Romano brothers did not like them."

"Yes, well I didn't much like the Romanos either. So, since they're no longer with us, get the boys working quickly." She didn't hide her distaste for the two Romano thugs Alessandro had employed who had allegedly met their end at the hand of Don Chico. She smiled. "And, let Tommaso know about them. It's important he understands we're moving the business forward. We need Stefano to settle."

"They will be loyal. They are puppy dogs for cash."

"Keep them keen and get them up to speed." Tommaso could be a strong ally if she played him the right way, and she needed allies like him. Stefano would rot in prison thinking he still ran the Amatos. Tommaso could feed him what they wanted him to know. And she would enjoy having a confident man at her side once again. Yes, she liked that plan very much.

She slipped out of the light-headed daze and smiled. She looked forward to seeing how Tommaso handled the tech park situation, though she wouldn't help him in his endeavours. If he was sent to take it back, then that duty was his alone. The mild prickling sensation shifted quickly. Yes, she felt closer to Giovanni because he had tried to save Maria. And yes, she would do her best to honour the promise she had made to Maria. But she would be a fool to not realise that business was business at the end of the day, and it was her fear of her husband that kept her awake at night. Never knowing whether Stefano had taken a hit out on her was exhausting. If Tommaso was responsible for the Amatos' reclamation of the tech park, she might look weak, but everyone would know it was Stefano undermining her and she might still be able to save face with Giovanni and maybe even preserve something of the relationship between the two families.

Maria would have understood. And Stefano would settle down again.

14.

The unexpected knock at the door jolted the knife in Simone's hand. Her hand felt unsteady as she put the knife down on the surface. She wiped the blood off her fingers from holding the meat. Dinner could wait. Her heart slowed as she made her way to the front of the house. The pounding on the door came again and her heart raced.

"Roberto, are you in there?"

She hesitated, went into the living room and looked out of the window. *Giovanni.* She puffed out a long breath and strode to the front door.

"Giovanni."

His smile was brief. "Hello, Simone."

She saw a flash of excitement cross his eyes and then his brows furrowed. "Come in." She ushered him through to the kitchen. "How are you?"

"Good, thanks." He looked beyond her, and his curiosity became an unarticulated question that she expected he needed an answer to.

"I'm good." Thoughts of Maria warmed her. "We're both good."

He smiled, inhaling deeply.

She sensed his relief and then he looked over her shoulder again.

"That's great. We should have lunch sometime and catch up. Sorry, is Roberto not here?"

She stood taller. "Is there trouble, Giovanni?"

"It's just business."

A deep sigh gave way to a surge of frustration that expanded quickly inside her head. "Will you all stop evading the question? I'm not stupid. I've worked alongside these people for the best part of my life. First Roberto and now you. I can see something's not right. I can take the truth, you know. I might even be able to help you." His eyes widened just enough for her to know her words had hit the spot. "He's not here. I don't know where he is. Now please tell me what's going on?"

The creases spanning his forehead softened. "The Amatos are trespassing."

"Which means what?"

"Taking rent from our tenants. Moving gear around on our turf. Patrina's gone quiet. I can't get a meeting with her."

The sound of that woman's name sent shivers down her spine.

"We had an agreement, but something's shifted. Any ideas where Roberto might be? He said he was spending more time with you."

"At his girlfriend's?"

Giovanni's lips formed a thin line as he nodded.

Simone raised her eyebrows. "You don't like her?"

He looked skyward, seemingly searching for an appropriate response.

"Let's just say, I'm not as convinced as he is. She has no background, but that can mean very little these days. She's young, pretty, and keen on him, and he seems besotted with her. But they've not known each other long."

He sounded like a father would. It was heartening to know that Roberto had someone like Giovanni looking out for him. "I haven't met her yet, but it's clear he would rather be with her than his big sister." She chuckled.

"I'm sure you'll like her."

"Have you tried his mobile?"

"He's not picking up."

She didn't need to say that her brother was most likely in bed with the love of his life. She saw the same recognition in Giovanni's smile too. "Can I get you a drink?"

Giovanni hesitated, then nodded. "Sure, I'll catch him later."

She flicked the kettle on. The silence between them became prickly and when she turned and looked into his eyes, the damp shine across their surface gripped her chest. "Maria is good," she whispered. "Actually, she's bloody infuriating beyond belief." She laughed and felt relieved from sharing her frustrations with him.

He chuckled. "She can be very determined."

She crossed the floor and pulled him into a hug. "It's so good to be able to talk to you about her." He stiffened in her arms then eased away from her.

"I'm happy she's well," he said with a croak in his voice.

The kettle boiled and she turned and made coffee.

"How are you, really?" she asked. "I mean, how are things going? You can talk to me, Giovanni. We have secrets in common, remember. I can keep a secret." She had sensed all wasn't well, but Roberto hadn't been forthcoming with any details. Giovanni didn't look like a completely broken man, but he looked more troubled than he had done under Maria's leadership.

He took a deep breath and released it slowly, though his demeanour didn't give anything away that she hadn't already picked up.

"If you had asked me that question a week ago, I would have said they were going well."

She poured milk into the cups and handed a drink to him.

"Thank you." He sipped. "Vitale, you know the—"

"Yes, I know who he is."

"He's working for Stefano and is hiding behind a storage business his father owned. I'm not sure what he is capable of. There's been an escalation in activities. Petty stuff at the moment, but it could be he's just finding his feet. His talents are more aligned with the tactical and intellectual stuff. He's a tech whizz, not really a gunman. That doesn't mean he wouldn't kill. You never know whether someone will pull the trigger or not until the moment. But even if killing isn't his strength, he seems to have the authority to get others to do it for him."

"What does he want?"

"Power and control. Stefano has always been second to us. He wants to expand the business again. It's the only thing Stefano knows how to do... If he got Vitale's case dropped, Stefano must have been behind Don Calvino's death, or he sees something in Vitale that he can make use of. Vitale will get Patrina to grow the business quickly, which means taking what they don't own, and he will become Stefano's voice if he isn't already. It was Alessandro before him. Stefano can't trust his wife and doesn't like women in positions of power. He hated Maria because she had power." He half smiled. "It's always the same thing, eh?"

She didn't smile. "Is Vitale...like Alessandro?"

"He's not crazy or volatile like Alessandro. He's calculated and stable and gets results quickly, which makes him even more dangerous. He has connections high up, inside the authorities somewhere, and that means he has access to information, surveillance data, records. If he has the will and digs deep enough, he could find out about Maria. And men like him do what they need to, to influence men like Stefano."

"No." The word flew from her mouth. "No, he can't find out. No one can find out. I need to protect Maria."

"I know. There is no reason for him to start looking. But if he does, then having you here could be a blessing. If they thought Maria was alive and wanted to find her, they would trace her through you. You still need to be careful."

He was right. "I shouldn't have come here, should I?"

He lowered his eyes. "No one else knows she's alive, Simone. We need to keep it that way."

"What about the doctor?"

"I promise, he will never talk."

Simone put her cup on the surface and turned to Giovanni. "Is the villa still—"

"Empty? Yes. Would you like to spend some time there? It could do with an airing and the beach is—"

"Wonderful. I know." She hesitated. She hadn't seen what happened that night on the boat, but her imagination had done a good job of providing her with hideous video footage of Maria being rushed across the beach bleeding to death. She blinked and fond memories of her time there with Maria brought a smile. "That would be nice. I will cook us something one evening."

He put his cup on the surface. "I'm sorry. I need to track down Roberto. Angelo is waiting in the car."

"He'll be with his girlfriend still."

Giovanni laughed.

"He's young," she said and shrugged.

Giovanni gave her a look of appreciation. "Thank you," he said.

She saw his love for Maria in the quiet tenderness in his expression. "We have to keep her safe," she whispered.

His smile faded, and his face became serious again. "Yes, we must."

She stared out the kitchen window for a time after the front door clicked shut, comforted by being able to share Maria with Giovanni. And he, who was well regarded for his silence, had talked openly with her about the business as if he were talking to Maria. Did he love her as much as she did? Maria was their beautiful secret and she would do whatever was necessary to protect her. She would kill if she had to.

15.

The giant white ball that turned the blue expanse surrounding it into shades of silver did little to warm her skin. Its heat was cooled dramatically by the north-easterly breeze that whipped across the mountains and down through the valley. Maria split the last log with the long-handled axe and stacked the small pieces for a fire later in the evening.

Kana and Kip had roamed to the far side of the meadow. Their heads bobbed and their tails flicked as they pecked the ground close to the hedgerow. Frango, Kura, and Pollo explored the earth closest to the henhouse. Poulet stood by the fence staring at her. The blue-laced chicken was still waiting for Simone. *I miss her too.* She sighed and wandered toward Poulet who started clucking. The three large hens loitering around the henhouse joined in the chant, and Kana and Kip started running across the meadow toward her, their spindly legs barely able to keep up with their intentions. Their progress looked precarious, as if they might trip over their own feet. She laughed, headed into the henhouse, and came out with a cup of grain which she threw across the ground. The routine was habitual and satisfying. The clucking became riotous, and the hens pecked fervently as they squawked.

Movement in the woods bounding the meadow caught her eye, and she tried to locate the exact spot. Maybe it was someone walking along the path she had run earlier in the day. Her heart raced. A gust of wind kicked up dust, and the trees swayed in unison like giant talons reaching out. Ground level foliage trembled, and the long grass in the meadow bowed. It was impossible to define exactly where the movement had come from. An uneasy sense lingered in the persistent, grumbling thought.

She scanned the line of trees up to the road and studied the house window by window, despite knowing that there would be no unwelcome visitors inside the farmhouse. The chickens, oblivious to her concerns, pecked the ground around her feet, except for Poulet, who seemed to be watching her with her head tilted. She looked again to the point close to the track that had first attracted her attention. She narrowed her focus. Nothing. A shiver cascaded across her shoulders and down her spine. She rolled her shoulders, released a long breath, and made her way to the farmhouse, collecting the box of chopped wood as she passed.

Inside the living room, her pulse slowed. She stoked the fire, made a coffee, and moved the armchair to the window so she could sit and keep watch across the meadow. Her hand trembled as she stared at the blank screen of her phone. She didn't want to worry Simone or hassle her about staying safe. She had prepared to go to Palermo. Her instincts were still calling her to go. But Simone had made it very clear that she could take care of herself and that Maria needed to give her the space to do so. The last time she had tried to protect Simone, while at the villa, Simone had felt claustrophobic, and she didn't want Simone to feel she didn't trust her.

Simone's earlier text had been long, saying she had talked with Giovanni and how wonderful it was and how happy he was that Maria was safe. Angelo and Roberto were looking after her. She'd cleaned the house, which hadn't been touched in her time away because her brother had effectively moved in with his girlfriend, who she was meeting at dinner later. She'd enjoyed lunch at Lo Scoglio. The lemonade was sweet and delicious, and the plaza was busy with tourists. She was going to spend time at the beach villa. She had asked whether Maria thought Octavia would still be at the reef. Maria didn't know whether the octopus she had befriended and named her cruiser after would still be there, but it consoled her to think that she was. Simone seemed happy, and busy and she had felt the urge to call her and talk. Recalling the last time when she had called and tried to persuade Simone to come back to the farmhouse had stopped her.

Maria sat and watched the shadows form across the meadow as the wind died down. The chickens slowly made their way into the henhouse. Burning wood crackled and spat. Warmth suffused the room, but she didn't let drowsiness into her mind. She watched, her eyes becoming sore as the encroaching darkness strained them. She plucked her phone from her pocket and sent Simone a text. *Poulet was looking for you today. She misses you. I'm pleased you're having a good time. Love you.* She went back into the meadow and locked the henhouse for the night.

The nagging feeling seemed to amplify as night fell. A ball of elastic twisted and tensed in her stomach, so she slid the uneaten lamb and vegetables from her dinnerplate into the bin. She switched off the lights and went upstairs. Leaving the room in darkness, she approached the bedroom window and looked out. She leaned closer and squinted. How the hell was the henhouse door open? She was sure she had locked it properly. Frantically, she scanned the meadow as far as she could see. Nothing.

She reached into the wardrobe, pulled out the box, and opened it. She hesitated. The black handle of her gun reflected ominously in the ambient light. She pulled it from the holster, slotted six rounds into the weapon, and thumbed the chamber. Silently, gun in hand, she went down the stairs and into the garden. She stood for a moment on the patio, looking across the meadow. A gentle swoosh and frantic squabbling from inside the henhouse interrupted the stillness. She tucked the gun into her waistband and slowly made her way toward the hens. A crackling sound stopped her and drew her eyes. Foxes? Rustling faded to silence. She went into the henhouse and settled the chickens who hadn't moved from their beds, locked the door firmly, and made her way back into the house.

Her chest pounded as she leaned against the door and breathed deeply. She went to the kitchen sink and dry-wretched. When she stood, weakness moved through her body. She removed the gun, her hands trembling, and placed it on the kitchen surface. *Am I losing my mind?*

BANG, BANG.

The booming sound jolted her, and she grabbed for the gun, gasping for breath. The darkness blinded her quickly, and she was immobilised inside the void again. She willed herself to move but her body wouldn't respond. Then, she watched herself lying with eyes wide open on the concrete surface, a dark patch spreading across her white shirt.

She choked and flashed her eyes open. She stood, sighting the barrel of the 637 toward the front door of the farmhouse. She could distinguish the grain of the wood. The door was closed, but there was someone there. *Vitale?*

Slowly, she applied pressure to the trigger and waited.

Click. Click.

Knock, knock, knock.

"Maria."

She stared at the door and the weapon in her hand as her mind located the voice, and reality dawned. She tucked the barrel of the gun into the back of her trouser waistband, opened the door, and looked down into the heavily creviced face of her neighbour.

"Bon soir, Maria. I thought you could put these vegetables and cake to good use. Here."

Maria inhaled deeply and breathed out slowly, dispelling the image of having shot the old woman at the other side of the door. Her heart was still racing, and trembling waves flowed from her stomach. "Madame Verdéaux."

The woman gripped a crate-like box filled to the brim with vegetables: carrots, potatoes, leeks, onions, beans, and artichokes. A bulging paper bag balanced precariously on top, and she manoeuvred the box as if it were as light as a feather and without any sign of encumbrance.

Maria rushed forward and took the container from her hands. "Please do come in." Maria carried the box into the kitchen and spotted the six live cartridges sprawled across the table. She put the box down, swiped the bullets quickly into her hand and shoved them into her pocket. She had emptied the chamber before squeezing the trigger, though she had no recollection of having done so.

Madame Verdéaux peered at Maria over the top of her glasses and her broad grin revealed tobacco stained teeth. "My husband used to like hunting."

Maria smiled. Madame Verdéaux would know the difference between shotgun pellets and bullets. Was this a way of saying she had Maria's back? "Can I get you a drink? I have cognac?"

"You are too kind." She took a seat at the table, pulled out a pack of cigarettes and lit one. She offered the pack to Maria.

"I don't, thanks." She had already told Madame Verdéaux she didn't smoke. Maybe she was being tested. Consistency of behaviour was a good indicator of honesty. She put a saucer on the table. "Ashtray."

"Pheasant."

Maria poured two drinks and sat.

"He used to hunt pheasant, and rabbit."

Maria sipped her drink and savoured the warmth of the drink soothing the back of her throat. "He shot rabbits?"

"No. Snared them. Shoot rabbit, and you will have nothing left to eat." She rasped a deep, gravelly chuckle and started to cough. "You got hens then?" She sipped her drink again.

"We got six to start us off. Would you like some eggs?" Maria began to stand, but Madame Verdéaux's grip around her arm was steely. It softened immediately, so she stayed seated.

"I have chickens, and plenty of eggs. Are you going to eat them?"

Simone's love of the birds came to mind, and Maria shook her head. "No, they're just laying hens."

"Shame. You don't know good food unless you take it from the land."

Maria nodded. "You're right."

"There's been a vicious wind these last days."

"Is that normal?"

"It can be." She sucked hard on the cigarette and exhaled streams of bluish grey. "I remember nineteen-fifty-two, or was it four? The storm lasted three days in that November. We lost the trees and fences, and the village hall roof collapsed. My husband helped rebuild it, you know?"

She emptied her glass and looked to Maria, indicating with her eyes for a refill.

Maria poured her another drink. "How long were you married?"

"Nineteen-fifty to fifty-six. Married at thirty and a widow at thirty-six."

"I'm sorry to hear that."

Madame Verdéaux lifted her arm in a dismissive gesture. "It was a long time ago. He died with a heart valve condition. It would have been cured if he had been alive at this time. Medicine moves on quickly. We are lucky like that. He was twenty years older than me. We had a few good years, and I discovered a lot."

Maria didn't know what to say. She hadn't thought of her as the marrying kind, but things were different back then and finding a husband was what most women did. "You never found anyone since?" she asked, hoping the question wouldn't be perceived as intrusive. It was nice to have someone to talk to.

"There was someone else, yes. We first met before I was married." Her eyes glassed over, and the lines slipped from her brow. She smiled softly as if enjoying reminiscing. "I met a woman during the war. I was only young then, sixteen and helping to organise the routes across the Pyrenees. She was older than me." She took a slow drag on her cigarette. "She had a fire in her belly, and I loved her dearly. She taught me to have a passion for justice and for life. To stand up for what is right." Her eyes sparkled and she became silent. "It was only after my husband died that I had the courage to go and find her. She was married, and we saw each other when we could until she died a few years back."

Maria couldn't imagine the pain of loving someone and not being able to be with them. To not see them, not touch them, not wake up next to them in the mornings and walk down the street hand in hand. It was heartbreaking. She was glad she hadn't lived back then. "I'm so sorry," she said, her voice barely above a whisper.

"Ah, I was one of the lucky ones. To know love is the greatest gift we can receive." Madame Verdéaux tapped the table with her index finger.

Maria sipped her drink and thought about Simone. "Yes, it is."

Madame Verdéaux glanced around the house. "You have done this place up nicely. Houses are always happier being lived in."

Maria smiled. "Thank you."

"Are you and Simone going to manage the restaurant by yourselves?"

"Yes, we intend to."

"That is good. Folks like things kept local. They feel safer that way. You know what you are getting if it comes from friends and family."

Maria nodded. Simone had insisted they source everything locally. She had been right. It wasn't just about getting the best deal. It was about supporting each other.

"You will never get any trouble in these parts, you know?"

Except trouble might travel to these parts to find her. Madame Verdéaux stared at her. It was like she could see the movie of her own life in Maria's eyes. She knew how the plot played out, predicted the happy ending, and didn't bat an eyelid about the past.

Maria smiled, finished her drink, and poured them both another. What would Madame Verdéaux do in her circumstances? "Sometimes trouble comes calling, though, doesn't it?"

"Is that so?" She lit another cigarette and leaned back in the chair.

Maria thinned her lips. Madame Verdéaux was a trustworthy confidant. "I got shot once."

Madame Verdéaux winced. "Me too. It burns right through you."

"Yes, it does."

"Do you want to see my scar?" Madame Verdéaux said and smiled. She reached across the table and squeezed Maria's arm. "Listen, I suffered too. The mind plays tricks on you. Telling you this, telling you that. At a point, I didn't know the right thing to think. But your instincts come back, and you trust yourself again. Are you through the worst yet?"

Maria shook her head. "I don't know. I still get nightmares. And I think someone's watching me."

"You are from the mafia?"

Maria nodded.

"You know, you can run but you cannot hide."

"I thought I could escape."

"The mafia is a very different war, Maria. Maybe it never ends. Cut off the snake's head and it spawns another. In the Resistance, it was a moment in time. My enemy does not exist anymore. I do not need to look over my shoulder wondering if the Germans are pointing a gun at my back."

"Do you think I'm being watched?"

"I don't know the answer to that. But the fact you think you are, you might as well be. It is easier to deal with the enemy when you know where they are."

"This enemy is incarcerated."

Madame Verdéaux sucked hard on her cigarette. "Anyone can be reached, Maria, no matter where they are. If you have the will."

Maria sipped her cognac. Would she always be looking over her shoulder, wondering whether a gun was pointed at her back? That was no way to live. This wasn't the way she had planned a new life. But her plan had been put in place before she had fallen in love with Simone. Being with Simone changed everything. There was only one way they could have a life together and that was to take out the enemy. Stefano Amato. But how?

16.

The clip of Patrina's heels purposefully striking the concrete floor as she walked the long corridor between the two rows of industrial containers echoed her arrival long before she reached the concealed room at the far end of the warehouse. The familiar sound together with her lengthened stride was a mark of confidence and one that she had used her whole life to ensure her presence was noted, though in this place the further she went inside the building the lighter her steps became, until eventually she couldn't hear them above the voice inside her head. *Was she a fool to come here?* Cool air grazed her skin as she waited outside the fire door leading to the inner sanctum of Vitale's storage empire. Silence, eerily pervasive, enveloped her. Visiting her husband in prison had a similar effect, except she felt a modicum of protection in the screen that separated her from Stefano. Although Beto was waiting in the car for her, she felt subtly exposed. With her husband, such exposure would be terrifying. With Tommaso, it was closer to thrilling.

The door opened, and Tommaso smiled at her. "Welcome." He stepped back from the door, indicated with his hand for her to enter and bowed his head as she passed.

She slowed her pace. "Nice place," she said, with no intention of hiding the hint of sarcasm that caused his smile to broaden.

He breezed past her. She followed him into the bowels of the building. Doors led to mysterious rooms filled with who knew what. It was a rabbit warren. He held a door open, and she entered the room ahead of him. She stared at the four-poster bed in the right-hand corner, with red and black silken sheets. The memory of soft textures against her skin stirred her.

"Would you like a drink?"

Without waiting for her answer, he poured them both a shot of clear liquid and sat at the table on the other side of the room. He beckoned her to sit.

She sat and sipped the drink. "You wanted to see me?"

He cleared his throat, leaned forward, and sipped his drink. He looked into her eyes, his gaze narrowing as he smiled. "You look good, Patrina."

His scent was intoxicating, and he spoke with his eyes. He wanted her... Or he wanted something from her.

He topped up her glass and then his.

"You are an attractive woman, Patrina."

"Are you scared of my husband, Tommaso?"

"No."

His arrogant confidence amused and excited her. "Do you not think you should fear him?" His eyes, like Maria's, gave away nothing.

"No."

She smiled.

"What do you want, Tomasso?"

"I want to work with you, Patrina, not against you. I know your husband sent me, but I noticed you before. You need someone at your side you can trust. You can rely on me. We can build the business together. I can help you and treat you as you deserve."

"Have you sorted the tech park problem?"

"Of course."

She lifted her head up. As far as she was aware nothing had happened. "How?"

"Let's not spoil the brief time we have with redundant conversation. We have a common interest aside from the business. You are a beautiful woman. You know, I used to admire you from a distance, at the opera and official events. I never imagined this time would come for me, but I am very happy that it has." He stood and removed his jacket then placed it neatly over the back of the chair.

He had been spying on her, watching her silently, secretly, sitting in the shadows biding his time. "Tell me, why did you get released?"

He sat and pulled his chair into the table. "Because I did not tamper with the evidence, Patrina. I swear on my life."

She studied him. Despite his apparent sincerity, she had her doubts. Every man in the city proclaimed their innocence when caught and especially if those charges related to mafia activities. "You expect me to believe you?"

He tilted his head. "No. I will prove it to you."

"How?"

"With my loyalty." His tone was earnest.

"I made an agreement with Maria Lombardo, that the tech park would be built in the name of her father."

He looked away, biting his lip. "I did not know that."

"This is about honour, Tommaso. Something my husband lacks when it comes to business."

"I understand Stefano. His reputation is well…documented." He expanded his chest and held her in his gaze.

She stared into his eyes, looking for a flicker of something with which she could trust him. "I need to honour my word to Maria Lombardo." He gave nothing away.

"I need to manage Stefano's expectations, if *we* are going to be able to work together. If I don't make him happy, he will replace me and maybe the next man won't be as understanding as I am."

He was right about that. She didn't want to think about who Stefano might send her way next, and this man seemed genuinely interested in her as well as the business. She turned away.

He turned her to face him and lifted her chin. His touch was gentle, and she saw affection in his smile and when he leaned down and kissed her briefly, she didn't resist.

"I know you have no reason to trust me, but it would help if you can let me prove myself to you."

With the taste of salt and alcohol on her lips, she nodded.

*

Simone stared at the television screen. She cupped her mouth with her hand as the news flash revealed the latest incident. The front door slammed open, jolting her, and she turned to see Roberto stumble hurriedly into the hallway.

"What the hell?" she said.

She jumped to her feet and met him before his legs gave way, then helped him into the living room. He had blood crusted around his nose and a faint discolouring of the skin around his left eye that was sure to darken in the coming hours. A small cut on his temple trickled blood down the side of his face. It didn't look serious, but it would leave a scar.

"God, Roberto. What happened?"

He winced as he tried to move and cradled his ribs. "I got jumped."

She swallowed a gasp. Her throat burned. "Did you have anything to do with the shooting?" she asked, pointing to the television where the news continued to drone out the recent events.

He frowned at her. "What shooting?"

"Lo Scoglio. It's on the news." She paced back and forth in front of him, running her hands through her hair. If this had happened before, she could have been caught up in it while eating lunch there. *Christ.*

"Shit." Distracted by the images flicking past on the television—the restaurant's windows smashed, men's cut and bloody faces—he recognised one of the men and the black estate car with a faded-out number plate. "There's nothing for you to worry about," he said. Each word was punctuated by a pause for him to gather his breath.

"Nothing for me to worry about?"

He lifted his hand swiftly and winced. She cowered and jolted backwards. He held his palm up to her. "Don't shout at me, Simone."

She gathered herself from the shock of thinking he was going to strike her and held back a second outburst. She wanted to scream, slam him against the wall, and knock some sense into him. She turned away and stormed into the kitchen. "I'll get antiseptic wipes."

Roberto didn't respond.

He complained as she dabbed the wipe on his cut. "You know something about this?"

He didn't answer.

"Do you?"

He shook his head.

"Were they Amato's men?"

She prodded the cut. He groaned and pulled away.

"I don't know anything about it. I was at the port dealing with supplies coming in."

"More trouble?"

"Will you stop asking bloody questions? You're not my mother."

She closed her eyes and took a deep breath. "Does Giovanni know?"

"How do I know? He's at an inspection at the tech park and not answering."

She shook her head. "This is bad."

"Fucking hell, Simone." He snatched the cloth from her hand and groaned as he stood. Clutching his ribs, he scrambled up the stairs.

She heard the bedroom door slam and turned to the television as a new headline came up.

An accident at the tech park construction site has just been reported. The cause is thought to be health and safety related. It is understood that there have been fatalities though at this point, we cannot say how many. We will bring you more...

Simone tuned out and silently processed the report. God forbid anything had happened to Giovanni. What if? She couldn't bring herself to think of him being one of the victims. Was it a coordinated attack or was it just coincidental? Roberto needed to see a doctor, but she bet he wouldn't be interested. What an unholy mess. She desperately wanted to talk to Maria but what would she say? She couldn't tell her anything because if Giovanni was hurt Maria would be compelled to come. And if she came, *they* would get to her...and *they* would kill her this time. She couldn't speak to Maria about anything now because Maria would pick up on the concern in her tone. The last thing either of them wanted was for her to return to this life. She'd given up everything for a fresh start in France and Simone wasn't going to let her down by calling her at the first sign of trouble. Giovanni had insisted, they had to protect Maria's identity.

She headed toward the stairs, her heart in her mouth, as Roberto clambered down them.

"There's been an accident at the tech park," she said.

He rushed past her. "I know. Angelo has just texted. Giovanni is on the way to the hospital. He's alive but it's serious."

She clasped her hand to her mouth. She definitely wouldn't tell Maria.

"I've got to go."

"You need to see a doctor."

He took a slow breath, cupped her face, and stared into her eyes with concern and tenderness. "I need to find out what's happened. I'm going to the hospital to check on Giovanni. I can get seen there. You stay here. Promise me you won't go anywhere."

She shook her head, fighting back the tears. She needed to be strong for Maria's sake. Much as it pained her to keep anything from Maria, she resolved not to tell her anything about it.

*

Patrina waited until Tommaso lifted his head. He had been looking down for a while and it didn't take much to work out that he was contemplating something. He rolled the shot glass around in the palm of his hand and released a long breath. She waited, her heart racing. It was the feeling of being out of control that didn't sit well. Stefano often made her wait before he spoke and when Stefano spoke there was never anything good to come of it.

"I need to be honest with you."

Patrina raised her eyebrows, slightly taken aback by the comment and intrigued by what he had to say. "Go ahead." His eyes were lighter when he smiled as he did now.

"Maria is alive."

Patrina lit a cigarette and took a long drag. "Maria?"

He waited for a beat.

"Yes, Maria Lombardo."

She started to laugh. If this was the best he had to offer, to win her trust, it was a low blow. He remained unmoved by her response and the intensity in his eyes spoke to her. She struggled to swallow, moved back from him, and pressed her hands to her stomach. Pressure formed at the back of her eyes and she fought to not let the tears form. "You've been too long in Stefano's company. You must be mistaken." Her tone was accusatory. "We buried her months ago."

"There was no body, Patrina. You didn't bury Maria Lombardo."

She couldn't tell if he looked smug or he was assessing her reaction to the news. "You're lying."

He shook his head and frowned. "Why would I lie to you? I want to stand at your side."

"Because..." She couldn't think of a solid reason. If he wanted to lie to her, there were plenty of other things he could focus on. He didn't need to make false claims about Maria unless he intended to cause distress.

"Where do you think Simone has been all this time?"

"You told me she'd been in the Pyrenees. So what? That doesn't mean anything." The conversation at the café, when he talked in riddles about Paris and the south of France came back to her. He had talked about the Pyrenees as if he had seen them with his own eyes, or as if someone had told him about them. It was too much to take in. She resisted the truth and a lump formed in her throat. Her heart would break again if he was lying to her. That would be a cruel thing to do.

"Maria is alive, Patrina."

She was still shaking her head, her brain working hard to find a logical reason. *No.*

"Yes, Patrina." He reached across the table, swept the hair from her face, and traced a line down her cheek. His touch was tender and despite the conversation, she felt his compassion.

"How do you know?"

He took her hand and ran his thumb across her knuckles. "I have access to information, Patrina. And I need to know that I have your trust. I thought you would be pleased to know she survived."

She shivered and when she looked into his eyes, she saw something more disconcertingly familiar. Power.

"Is something wrong?"

He revealed his teeth as he smiled, but he looked at her as if from a distance and when he pulled her into a kiss, it tasted of bitterness.

"Nothing." This was too much to process. Too inconceivable to be true. Maria had been close to death when they had lifted her onto the beach. It had come as no surprise to know that she hadn't made it. But she had made it. Maria had survived. Maria had escaped Sicily. And now this man, who professed to be Patrina's ally, said he knew exactly where Maria was. She stood swiftly, acutely aware that he was watching her closely.

"Please, don't be in a hurry. I was hoping we could spend more time together."

"I'm not, I just have work to do."

He grabbed her by the wrist, tugged her to him, and covered her mouth with his. He sniffed her hair as he whispered into her ear. "We have something good, Patrina. Don't go spoiling it."

She smiled. "We can talk later. I need to go. Beto is waiting for me," she said.

He released her. "I want to go over the business plans in more detail with you," he said. "We need to increase our presence. Stefano expects quick results."

She smiled. "Of course." She unlocked the door.

"I won't tell Stefano about Maria," he said. "I promise. She is of no concern to me. To be honest, if Stefano knows and wants her dealt with it would be a distraction we could do without."

She wanted to take his word, but the niggling thought that he would tell Stefano in a heartbeat if it got him what he wanted wouldn't shift. She stepped into the corridor leading to the warehouse, her head in a spin. Maria was alive. She was compromised. Disbelief warred in her mind with the excited joyful feelings in her chest and relief, and...warmth. Such warmth. And then a cold chill accompanied the truth. If Tommaso had located Maria, what else might he discover? Panic gripped and threatened to crush her. Maria was in danger. Simone. Patrina's only connection to Maria was the woman who had stolen Maria from her. Bitterness filled her mouth, but she had to overcome that. Maria's safety was all that mattered.

17.

The tap on the front door was gentle. Simone looked up from her mobile phone, a chill moving down her spine. She'd had no update from Roberto and part of her didn't want to know if there was more bad news. Giovanni had been Maria's right-hand man and Maria loved him like a brother. Not knowing whether he was alive or dead affected her more than she anticipated. It was the affinity they shared for Maria that had drawn her to caring about him. She felt a strong sense of loyal protectiveness toward him, partly because he had talked to her about the business when her brother wouldn't, and mostly because he cared deeply about Maria. She wondered what would happen if Giovanni died and her chest tightened. Would Maria come back into the business? Would Roberto be next?

She stood from the couch and glanced out of the living room window to see who was knocking on the door, her heartbeat heavy and sluggish. Pressure filled her head. How dare Patrina come here? The gentle tap irritated her further, and she strode to the door with gritted teeth.

The door complained as it always did when stopped half-open. Simone lifted her chin and inhaled through her nose, on the verge of hurling a tirade of abuse at her former employer. The verbal assault died on her tongue. Patrina didn't look like Patrina. Her eyes were downcast, and she moved her head skittishly as if she was worried about being discovered. Her skin lacked vibrancy, the lines that shaped her smile ran deeper than Simone had remembered, and her lips were fixed in a taut straight line. She didn't look well, not that Simone cared. Still, a twinge of compassion pricked her conscience.

Patrina looked over her shoulder again. "Can I come in, please?"

Simone moved to one side to allow her entry. She closed the door behind them, and Patrina followed her into the living room in silence.

"I'm sorry," Patrina said as Simone turned to face her.

Simone crossed her arms. She had nothing to say. She saw pain in Patrina's eyes, deep and enduring, and there was something she hadn't seen before. Fear. Patrina looked vulnerable, wringing her hands together repeatedly, and couldn't hide her apprehension.

Simone tilted her head. "Are you responsible for the attack on my brother?"

Patrina squeezed her fingers in her hand, turning the skin white. "I don't know anything about that. I was at a meeting. I've come straight here."

Simone lifted her chin. "What about the accident today at the tech park?" They had said it was an accident, but the news always erred on the side of what would be perceived as normality. Nothing was ever as it seemed when it came to *accidents* in Palermo. Patrina's cheeks coloured and she broke eye contact. "So, you do know about that?" She rested her hands on her hips.

"I..."

"Don't waste your breath denying it, you fucking bitch." The crack of her palm against Patrina's cheek was briefly satisfying before the sting rippled through her fingers. She rubbed her hand.

Patrina barely flinched, though her cheek flared red and her eyes watered. "You think I deserve that, and you're probably right, but I didn't know about an accident at the tech park. What happened?"

Heat invaded Simone's skin, and an apology lingered on the tip of her tongue. Patrina seemed genuinely uninformed. "Giovanni has been taken to hospital. He's badly hurt. I don't have any more details."

Patrina pursed her lips and looked toward the window. She took a deep breath and pinched the bridge of her nose. "Fucking hell."

"They were doing an inspection. That's all I know. And Roberto got jumped earlier too." Her voice broke. "He'd better not die, or I'll kill you myself." Brave words spoken in the heat of anger, but she meant the essence of the message. *Maria will kill you if Giovanni dies.* "This is all your doing, Patrina. It's like Alessandro all over again."

Patrina straightened and raised her eyebrow. "I didn't come here to talk about this."

"Then why are you here?" Patrina was staring at her, unnervingly.

"She's alive, isn't she?" she asked softly.

Simone opened her mouth, but the words stuck in her throat. *Deny it.* Ice shivered down her spine, and she lowered her head. The words pulsed like a ticking clock, deafening and distracting. Every second that passed made the possibility of lying more absurd.

Patrina nodded.

The tension Simone had been holding for the past hour melted, and weakness crept insidiously into every muscle in her body until her legs trembled beneath her.

"He was right."

"Who?" Her voice crumbled.

"Tommaso Vitale."

Simone blinked. Dizziness threatened her balance and she supported herself against the window ledge.

Patrina took her arm and guided her deeper into the room. "Don't stand too close to the window."

Simone's knees gave way, and Patrina helped her to the sofa. She pressed her hands over her ears to drown out the sound, but the voices were coming from within. *Maria is in terrible danger.* She lowered her hands to hear Patrina saying the same thing. Tears burned at the back of her eyes, but she would not let them fall. Her hands trembled, and she clenched her fists tightly.

"You were at a farmhouse in the Pyrenees, right?"

Simone nodded.

"Simone…that means he can get to her. He has said she is not of interest to him, but I'm not sure that I trust him, yet. She needs to know she's been compromised. Can you get a message to her?"

Simone looked at Patrina with the sound of the woman's voice swimming incoherently in the space between her ears. "Sorry?"

"Can you get a message to Maria? She needs to know she has been compromised."

"Compromised. Yes. Message. Yes." Simone repeated the words absent-mindedly. She shook her head and regained her focus. "Sorry. Yes." She sent a text message.

"Simone. I don't think Stefano knows yet. Tommaso has said he won't say anything to anyone, but if he does… If Stefano finds out, he will put two and two together and think Maria killed Alessandro and ran. He will take a hit out on her."

"She didn't kill him though, did she? You did."

Patrina pressed her lips together. She hesitated as if deciding whether to continue. "I saved Maria from Alessandro. I will not let my husband get to her now. We need to keep Maria safe. She needs to move from the Pyrenees."

Simone felt the air being sucked sharply from her lungs. *Patrina had saved Maria.* If she had doubted Patrina was telling the truth, mentioning the Pyrenees was all the evidence she needed. It didn't mean she trusted the woman. A dull pain squeezed her chest. "She will come here, to the house. You know that?" As soon as Maria found out that Giovanni was down and the Lombardo business was under threat, she would be compelled to return.

Patrina nodded. "I know. I can help you both." She paused and looked away, and then held Simone in her gaze and her expression conveyed tenderness tinged with remorse. "She loves you, and she'll want to rescue you. Don't let her weakness be her downfall. If they want to get to her, you'll lead them."

The colour drained from Patrina's face and tears filled her eyes. "You really loved her, didn't you?" Simone asked softly.

Patrina smiled, but it looked forced, and a tear slipped onto her cheek. She brushed it away. "Yes. Very much. Sometimes you don't know what you have until you lose it. You should leave here tonight. Go to the villa. It's safer there."

Simone stiffened. She wasn't going to jump into following Patrina's advice even though she knew it was right. Patrina always put Patrina's interests first and this was no different, no matter how genuine her concern for Maria might appear. Vitale worked for the Amatos and Patrina was one of them. The woman might have saved Maria, but she was also responsible for the events of that afternoon. "Don't you think you should go and sort your own people out? The guys who jumped Roberto work for you. The *accident* is down to you. Vitale works for you… Or are you working for him now?"

Patrina lowered her head.

Simone walked to the door. "You can leave now."

Patrina nodded as she walked toward her. She stopped and faced Simone. "I wish you no harm, Simone."

Simone closed the door behind her. She leant against the hard wood, her heart racing, her hands clammy. She checked her phone to find the message to Maria hadn't been sent. Her mobile signal had dropped out. That wasn't an unusual occurrence…but, please, why now? She pressed send again, even though it was futile. She wandered from room to room, pressing the buttons on her phone in the vain hope that it might trigger the signal to return.

There was only one way Vitale could have known about the house in the Pyrenees. The case Giovanni had handed her at Maria's funeral that she'd left in her wardrobe when she went to Paris. She had fully expected to return home after the ballet and then consider what to do about the farmhouse Maria had gifted her. The missing photograph. The case had been tampered with. Icicles trickled in waves down her spine. Her throat clamped as she swallowed hard.

That's how Vitale knew. He had broken into the house and searched through her belongings. No, Vitale's word couldn't be trusted. The signal flashed a single bar. She pressed send.

18.

Maria held the phone close to her ear and put her finger in her other ear so she could hear him above the din in the airport lounge. "Rafael."

"Maria, there was an *accident* at the tech park earlier this afternoon."

She closed her eyes. The gravity in his tone and his cynical inflection at the word accident sapped her. She took in a deep breath, squeezed her eyes shut, and asked the question she didn't want to hear the answer to. "Who?"

"Giovanni...and two site workers."

"Shit." Relief flashed through her mind. Simone would have no reason to be near the construction project, but still. Anger flared in her chest and rage filled her head. "Fucking bastards."

"Maria."

She braced herself for the worst possible news. "How is he?" she asked.

"He is in theatre. It is very serious."

"How bad?" Another question she didn't want the answer to.

"He was crushed. His spine is broken."

She stood and paced up and down the aisle between the lounge seats. "I'm at the airport now, heading to Sicily." *Too fucking late.*

He didn't respond.

"I need to finish what I should have done already, Rafael."

"What can I do to help?"

"Can you get a crew to sail the Octavia to Palermo and arrange a heli-lift in the name of Sanchez from Catania to the airfield? I'm booked on flight CTA 257."

"Consider it done. The Octavia will reach the port in ten days."

She eased her grip on the phone. "Any news from Palermo comes to you, let me know."

"Of course."

"Rafael... Thank you."

"Please be careful, Maria."

She ended the call and pocketed her phone, her attention triggered by the final announcement for her departure. She moved swiftly, grabbed her rucksack, and headed toward the departure gate. It was seven forty p.m. If Simone knew about the accident and hadn't let her know, it was because she was trying to protect Maria. Simone wasn't going to be happy that Maria had chosen to return, but she would deal with that problem face-to-face when she was back in Palermo. Travelling into Sicily as Mariella Sanchez should afford her a bit of time to get organised. But it wouldn't take long before whoever was watching her discovered she was back in the country.

She made her way through the gate, onto the aircraft, and took her seat. Large raindrops flicked at the small oval window. They joined forces and in formation trickled in competing streams downwards. Just as quickly as the shower had started, it stopped. Single drops of water clung to the window until the aircraft moved. There was power in cohesion and in Giovanni's absence, she would lead the Lombardos and deal with the situation with the Amatos before it got completely out of control. *Fucking hell, Patrina, what is going on?* She cursed her inability to let go, but how could she? Loyalty was like blood. She hadn't planned for this scenario. Giovanni was supposed to lead the clan and Roberto after him. She had expected Giovanni to be around to help bring down Stefano. Now, the situation seemed to be spiralling downwards. *Fucking hell, Giovanni.*

The villa nestled in the cove, enveloped in security lights, revealed itself as a black hole in the centre of a star filled sky. The trip into Catania had gone smoothly, and the transfer to the chopper was seamless. As the helicopter approached the cove, the outline of surrounding scrubland, low-level rocky formations, and web of dirt tracks that Maria had once jogged expanded then slipped slowly beneath her, disappearing. Bittersweet melancholy moved like treacle through her veins.

The chopper tilted and dropped, orientating to the bare ground at the end of the private runway. Her stomach roiled. The helicopter made its final descent softly, and Maria wiped the moisture from her brow. She'd never been a fan of flying. She preferred being in control. She'd never had the desire to learn to fly either, never liked the idea of crashing. Helicopters were the worst feeling of all.

The blades quieted. She unbuckled her safety belt and reached for her rucksack. The pilot climbed out of her seat and opened the door. The woman's smile was perfunctory, and she closed the door quickly behind Maria.

Maria stepped into the darkness, slung the bag on her back and dipped her head as she ran away from the slowly rotating blades. The engines whirred loudly before she had reached the grassed area and a strong gust of wind from the spinning blades shoved her in the back. She cut swiftly across to the wooded perimeter, the chuffing and clacking of the rotor blades behind her becoming distant, and the runway falling swiftly into darkness.

Rustling and humming sounds disguised the scrunching at her feet as she jogged along the track through the forest. Her heart reminded her to stay alert, so she stopped before crossing the open rocky terrain, carefully scanning for movement or shadows that didn't belong. When the trees closed in on her again as the path joined the lane, her breath flowed more easily. Perspiration blossomed on her skin, though the climate didn't warrant the intensity of her response, and she slowed her pace. She joined the quiet main road that led to the villa and her heart slowed, and her breathing became a gentle ebb and flow. The statuesque iron gates stood proudly in defence of her private estate. There was no sign of anyone.

She approached the entrance with butterflies taking flight in her stomach. Light cast shadows of increasing blackness over the road leading up from the entrance toward the house. She keyed in the security number to the pedestrian gate. A green light flashed, and the lock released. She entered the grounds and breathed a sigh of relief when the clunk of the catch locked behind her. Slowly, she made her way up the long drive, scanning the shrubbed and wooded areas to her right and left. She stopped fifty metres short of the villa, crouched, and observed, orientating to the sounds and shadows. From this distance, the villa remained an almost featureless, irregular shape, in silhouette against the dark sky, and yet every detail of its character imprinted on her evoking fondness.

She headed to the side of the villa where her boxing bag hung. The whispers of crickets turned her attention to the shrubbery and rocks. Her heart thundered. The Alfa Romeo abandoned in the drive next to the villa reflected light from its silver sheen. The villa looked every bit as deserted as it had been these past months in her absence. She had run from this place and now she stood before it, expecting it to defend and protect her once again. A chill brushed her skin as she approached the boxing bag and caught sight of the dark sea beyond, and the cliffs set against the sea. The emotional memory of *that night* increased her pulse. Her gut twisted and she looked quickly to the other side of the cove.

Waves lapped idly in a low, swooshing rhythm. She became entranced and drifted for a moment with fonder memories, running along the beach with Pesto at her side, and enjoying Simone's company on the beach, and diving to the reef. The cove was as beautiful and serene as it had always been. A sigh fell from her lips. She nudged the bag softly and smiled, reminded of teaching Simone how to spar and Simone complaining bitterly while secretly enjoying the challenge. Simone had been tentative, and reluctant to hit the bag at first but she had quickly gained in strength and confidence and she had fire in her belly. It was that fire that attracted Maria to her. Simone was a gentle soul, but she also had more guts than Maria had anticipated. She had underestimated Simone and that was a mistake she vowed not to make again. Maria patted the bag with the palm of her hand, and dust plumed from its surface like confetti. She tugged at the adhesive tape gripping the leather surface at the top of the bag, and eventually revealed a perfectly cut line in the leather. She shifted the sand from the inner wall and pulled away another strip of tape. The key was safely stuck to it, and she clasped it in her hand. She stepped onto the veranda and let herself into the living room.

Simone's perfume still hung in the air, or was it her imagination playing tricks on her? The villa's unique charm, the aged leather couch, rustic wood furniture, porcelain tiled floors, and a blend of smells mingled with a consoling familiarity. She removed her rucksack and placed it next to the couch, flicked the light switch on and took a pace toward the open-plan kitchen.

A violent scream assaulted her ears, and she screamed back, startled. She lifted her hands up and turned her head away from the ear-splitting noise.

19.

"What the fuck are you doing here?" Simone yelled, wielding a block-heeled shoe above her head.

"Jesus Christ, you scared the shit out of me." Maria lowered her arms. She blew out a short sharp breath. Simone hovered the shoe menacingly above her head, staring at Maria with wide eyes and her mouth open. "Please, will you put the shoe down?"

Simone threw the block heel to the floor and launched herself into Maria's arms.

Maria kissed her and Simone felt intense relief. Maria tasted so good. Then she broke away and glared at her. "You're not supposed to be here. Why did you come back?"

"So that we can have a life together."

Simone looked away. They had become trapped because of Simone's bloody-mindedness. She had thought she was protecting Maria by not returning to France, that Maria was safe at the farmhouse, when Vitale had known Maria was there all along. Maybe it had only been a matter of time before they had both been taken out. But what would happen now? Her mind raced with concern and her heart ached with want, and she had the urge to both slap Maria and take her to bed. "What are we going to do?" Maria had an intense look in her eyes, focused and determined, of the kind Simone had seen before when they had stood in a similar spot in this kitchen. It was sexy and wonderful, even though she was angry with Maria, and shaken from being freaked out by her.

"Rafael told me about the accident. I was already on my way here. I must face the problem, Simone. It's not going away."

Simone touched Maria's face as she had done after the ballet, as if testing that she really existed. "They know you're alive, Maria."

Maria took Simone's hand and pressed it to her lips. "I know. I think I was being watched at the farmhouse."

Simone pulled away. She paced around the room. "You're not safe here either."

Maria went to her, cupped her cheeks softly, and waited until Simone looked into her eyes. "I'm safer here. Listen, if Vitale or Stefano wanted me dead, I'd already be gone. I'm not sure what game they're playing but I intend to stop it once and for all."

Simone lifted her chin and looked away. "Will this ever go away?"

Maria sighed. "I don't know, but I have to try."

"How? How exactly will you do that? Last time it was Alessandro and he nearly killed you. Now it's Vitale. You can get rid of him and Stefano will still send someone else. It will never end. Patrina is worse than pathetic." She wrapped her arms around herself to restrain from slapping some sense into Maria.

Maria went to the window and stared out. "I'm going to take out Stefano."

Simone shook her head. Her heart rose swiftly into her throat. "You're delusional. How the hell will you get to him behind bars? He'll have you killed first."

Maria turned her head and Simone released a soft gasp. Maria was deadly serious. She was going to get herself killed.

"I have nothing without you. We'll end up living our lives on the run. I should have taken care of Stefano before, rather than trying to escape. I can't spend my life looking over my shoulder, Simone, and neither can you. It will kill *us*." She turned back to the window, leaned forward, and pressed her head to the glass pane. Ripples, blackened by the absence of light, danced on the surface of the sea. "We will be as safe here as anywhere in Palermo. I'll deploy a team to watch from the cliffs. I'll increase the security at the front of the house to get better visibility down the road. When I move around the city, I'll go by scooter. It's easy to stay out of sight with a helmet on and I can move quickly."

The fluttering in Simone's chest increased. She expected Maria to protest what she was going to say next, but she was ready to challenge Maria's objections. They needed to do this as a team. She wasn't going to be bullied into staying at home like the good little housewife. She puffed out her chest and spoke with authority. "I'm going to help you."

Maria turned and walked up to Simone. "I've been exposed. You're in danger by association with me, and my family is under increasing threat. I don't want any harm to come to you or to them."

"I am going to help, Maria. You're not going to stop me, so you'd better get that into your stubborn head. I'm not going to take no for an answer." She hesitated and puffed out her chest again, just a little further. "I want you to teach me to shoot."

Maria closed her eyes and took a deep breath, released it slowly and opened them. Simone straightened her back and stared at her as if to say, don't you dare object. "You don't know what—"

Simone reached up and stroked Maria's cheek. Maria relaxed her jaw. "I told you, don't bother arguing with me. Like it or not, I'm already involved and I'm not backing down. We are in this together and I'd rather we die together than I am left alone without you."

Maria lifted her hands in the air. "You're right, and you can help. Does Roberto still have his old scooter?"

"Yes."

"Can you tell him to bring it here tomorrow for seven a.m.? I need a pizza delivery bag as well."

"He will want an explanation."

"Tell him something has come up and you'll explain in person when he shows up."

Simone made the call as Maria went to the kitchen.

"Is he okay with that?"

"Yes. He'll be here for seven."

"Good. Do you want a coffee?"

Simone nodded.

Maria put the coffee on to brew with one eye on Simone as she paced up and down.

"One thing I don't understand is why they haven't killed us already."

Maria pursed her lips. "I've asked that question a lot while wondering if I was being paranoid. The only thing I came up with is that I don't think Stefano knows I'm alive yet."

"Patrina said Vitale promised not to tell Stefano."

"If Vitale is the one controlling things, then he is closer to Stefano than Patrina. I need to talk to her."

"Do you believe him? That he won't tell Stefano."

"Not for a second."

Simone huffed. "Patrina's the one being played." Simone didn't know whether Patrina was being used by Vitale or Stefano, but Patrina hadn't denied the accusation that she wasn't in control of her own business and the woman clearly hadn't known anything about the attacks or the accident that had been carried out by her own men. "Patrina came to the house to tell me that Vitale knew you were alive and said to warn you not to come back. I think he broke into my house and found the case you gave me. That's how he knew where to find you." Her eyes burned. She held her head in her hand. "I'm so sorry. It was all my fault."

Maria reached out and thumbed the tear from her cheek. "Neither of us can change the past. If I had died you would have come back here after the ballet and none of this would have happened. It isn't your fault, it's mine."

"I don't want you to die."

"I'm not going to."

Maria couldn't say that with certainty, but Simone welcomed the words because she wanted them to be true. "I missed you so much, and I'm sorry we argued. I should have listened to you."

"I'm sorry too. Hey..." She waited until Simone looked at her. "Whether you came back here or not, this isn't going to go away unless I do something about it. I'll teach you how to shoot so you can protect yourself." She kissed Simone with tenderness.

Simone eased out of the kiss and looked into Maria's eyes. She had expected more of a fight. It was nice not arguing but she couldn't help thinking the resistance would come. She would be ready when it did. "You never wanted to kill again."

A soft smile crept across Maria's face. "Remember the first time I took you to the farmhouse and you said you thought there was a right time to take another person's life. You were right. I must stop Stefano, or this will never end. He's greedy, and he's insane. Whatever he acquires, it will never be enough for him. My father saw changes in his personality years before he was convicted, and I should have dealt with it rather than running away."

Simone recalled their time at the farmhouse, sitting at the table on the patio overlooking the meadow and drinking wine. Maria had confessed and Simone had seen the pain in her eyes, felt it move through her soul as if she'd been the one who had pulled the trigger. Maria wasn't a killer, not like Alessandro or others like him who took pleasure in the act of taking another man's life. Maria had needed to defend herself and in doing so she had rid the world of scum. Simone would pull the trigger herself if the gun pointed at Stefano Amato. Maria was staring intently at her. Simone couldn't read her expression. Maria seemed resolute and clear-minded. She was back to her old self, except that she wasn't that person anymore either. She had changed. She was resolute and driven, and it was enthralling, and Simone was finding it hard to control the urge building. She didn't want to stop it. Heat rose to her cheeks with the thought of making love to Maria, right here, right now.

"You can carry a gun. But when it comes to dealing with the business, you need to trust me to protect you. There are some things I can't get you involved in. If I give you an instruction, you need to follow it without question."

Simone closed the space between them, pressed her lips to Maria's and tugged her breast to breast. She was done with listening; she would address the rules later. "Fuck the gun. I want you. Now."

She ripped the jacket from Maria's shoulders and thrust her hand beneath the waistband of her trousers. Maria silenced her moans of delight with a deep kiss that clashed their teeth and as Simone touched the silky warmth between Maria's legs, Maria moaned into her mouth.

Maria eased back, a moan still rumbling from her lips, and her eyes were darker. Simone shivered with the intensity in her gaze. Maria had something else to say and didn't know where to start. Simone could take it, whatever it was, though her heart raced, and her stomach fluttered. They had talked and resolved things together, and that was the most important thing. They could face anything *together*. She was adamant. "What is it?"

Maria traced the shape of Simone's mouth and when she spoke her voice was affected by emotion. "I've been thinking."

Simone tensed. Her desire turned to worry, and she felt as if her stomach was on fire. "What about?"

Maria looked into Simone's eyes. She motioned to speak, hesitated, then took a deep breath. "I was thinking…when this is all over, will you marry me?"

Simone couldn't breathe. Her heart stopped. She felt the weight drain through her instantly and then she was floating in pure joy.

"Please, say you will?"

She tried to stifle the squeal that bubbled up into her throat and failed. Her insides were vibrating and it felt like nothing she had ever experienced before. She yanked Maria to her, lifted her and swung her around, and kissed her firmly. She loved the feel of Maria's strong arms around her, and the heat from Maria's body. Yes, she felt protected. But more than that, she felt loved. "Yes, Maria Lombardo. It would be an honour to be your wife."

Maria smiled broadly. "Really?"

"Yes, really." Her fingers trembled as she stroked Maria's cheek, then her lips, then her neck. "Now, stop talking and take me to bed."

20.

Patrina didn't look up from her laptop screen as the bartender approached with her coffee. She continued to scroll through the press releases dating back to Vitale's arrest and subsequent release. The coverage lacked detail. Vitale hadn't been found not guilty of tampering with evidence. The case had been dropped because there was insufficient evidence with which to charge him. He hadn't been reinstated by the DIA, though that fact spoke more about the DIA's desire to clean up their image and dissociate with any negative press than it did about any crime he may have committed. And, he had promised not to tell anyone about Maria. Patrina didn't know what to think. No one was entirely innocent in this country, and evading conviction when guilty of the offence was the currency upon which a man's reputation was based. She looked up and closed the laptop as he entered the café and walked toward her. She would judge him based on her experience of him.

"Good morning, Patrina."

"Tommaso. Good morning." She indicated to the bartender to bring more coffee as he took the seat opposite her. It was the seat Alessandro had sat in before him. Fortunately, that was the only thing that linked the two men.

"It's a beautiful day. Maybe we could take lunch somewhere later?"

Maybe. She smiled at him and watched his response carefully. He smiled back at her. She noted the sparkle in his eyes, the softness of his gaze. "Tell me, how exactly did you know about Maria?" His demeanour didn't change but for a small shrug of his shoulders.

"I had the Di Salvos' house bugged—"

The bartender came to the table with a pot of coffee and a cup. He smiled at her in acknowledgement and turned his attention swiftly back to Patrina once she had moved out of earshot.

"It was while Simone was away. I intended to get information about the Lombardo business through Roberto. I promised Stefano I would let him know every move they were making. I needed to build trust with him."

"But Simone wasn't—"

"She had a case in her wardrobe. Maria had gifted the farmhouse to her. There was a letter. I didn't know Maria was alive then. When Simone didn't come back, I had a hunch something was keeping her away, but it was only when she came back, I knew for sure. Simone called Maria from the house."

The coffee stuck in Patrina's throat. The conversation she had had with Simone had been captured on tape. He acknowledged her awareness of her predicament through a lowering of his eyes.

"Yes, I know that you killed Alessandro." He sipped his coffee. "The bastard deserved to die, so congratulations." He lifted his cup in a toast.

Nausea turned the coffee in her empty stomach.

"And, yes, I know about your...affection for Maria. I can appreciate that. Maria was an attractive woman with an acute mind and a strong sense of justice. Those are very appealing qualities to most of us."

"Is."

"Is?"

"She is alive."

"Of course. She was very well liked and I'm sure she will be again, when people come to know that she didn't die." He poured another coffee and sipped.

Patrina rolled her tongue around her dry mouth and struggled to swallow.

He reached below the table.

She tensed.

His hand appeared and he passed an SD card across the table to her. "This is the recording, Patrina. It is yours now. There are no other copies, I promise you."

She grabbed the small card containing secrets she didn't want revealed to anyone. He put his hand over hers.

"Your secrets are safe with me."

He squeezed her hand before letting her go. She took the card from the table and pocketed it. "Thank you."

"Now, shall we get down to the real business?"

One more thing was pressing her. "Did you set up the accident at the tech park?"

He shook his head. "No. That must have been a genuine accident." He bit down on his lip as he continued to shake his head.

She wanted to believe him, but something twinged in her gut. She was oversensitive. He had given her the card and she was erring on the side of believing him.

"I sent a condolence card to Giovanni. Poor bastard. Broken back apparently. I'm not sure what could have gone wrong, but it's a good example of the fact that the Lombardos aren't taking care of construction. There will be an investigation of course, with such a serious incident. I understand that two workers died. Dreadful for their families. Perhaps we should send their families a gift. What do you think?"

Patrina was still with her thoughts of the SD card in her pocket. How long had Tommaso been operating on Stefano's behalf before she was made aware of the arrangement they had? Was this just another example of her husband's disregard for her? Her hatred for Stefano flared in a ball in the pit of her stomach.

"How long have you worked for my husband?"

"Not very long. I have a contact within the prison. It was easy to get to him. You know how it is; there are means and ways. You have to trust me." He reached across the table and took her hand. "I went to him to get closer to you."

"You helped him. He told me."

"Yes, recently, with information he wanted. Because I needed him to trust me, to be able to work with you."

He had sent a condolence card to Giovanni. He would send gifts to the families who had lost a loved one in the accident. He wanted to get closer to her. His touch was warm and gently pleading. She held his gaze and his smile touched her.

"So, business?" he asked.

She nodded. He let go of her hand and sat back in the seat.

"I've been looking through the invoices. The cost of alcohol and tobacco has increased in the past twelve months. It's ridiculous. I think the Spanish are overpriced. And the wine they are sending us isn't good value. I've got contacts in Chile and Argentina I would like us to work with. We can buy wine at half the price and tobacco at a third of what we are paying the Spanish. What do you think?"

Patrina had never been asked what she thought before. "I... You think they can supply what we need?"

"I'm sure we can triple demand and they would be able to cope. The business you have here isn't that big." He looked at her with apology. "We can store stock at the warehouse. There are no limits to what we can achieve now, Patrina."

The café door opened, and two men entered. They glanced around the restaurant. Tommaso acknowledged them and waved them to come to the table.

"Patrina, I want to introduce you." He stood and shook hands firmly with each of the men. "Lady Patrina, this is

Davide, and this is Leo. These are men I would trust with my life. Gentlemen, this is Lady Patrina."

Davide immediately turned to her and smiled. He had steely eyes and a smile that conveyed sincerity. He held out his hand and she took it. It was warm.

"It's an honour to meet you, Lady Patrina." He dipped his head.

A gentle heat flowed to Patrina's cheeks. She felt courted in a way she never had before and uplifted by his display of respect for her, and when he let go of her hand, she lowered both hands beneath the table and touched the warmth in her palm. "It's a pleasure to meet you."

"Lady Patrina," Leo said and dipped his head. "Whatever you need, we are here to serve you."

Patrina glanced at Tommaso. He was smiling at her. It wasn't the self-satisfied, smug look she would have seen in Alessandro's features. His was a warm, reassuring look that said, you deserve this regard.

"Lady Patrina, I hope you don't mind. Davide and Leo will be looking after distribution for you. They know the systems and channels well. They will set up additional supply points around the city to give us a broader reach. Street trade will boom. With their help we will double demand in three months, maybe sooner."

Patrina looked from one man to the other. They both wore blue jeans and black shoes. One wore a yellow crew neck T-shirt, the other a grey shirt with white buttons. Neither wore gawdy jewellery around their neck or piercings. Davide had a narrow band on his ring finger even though he looked to be the younger of the two men. They presented themselves as businessmen rather than the thugs that had previously worked for Alessandro. They made the Puglisi brothers that Beto had recently employed look like amateurs. She couldn't deny, they needed more men of quality and standing around them. Men with a reputation. "Well, it's my pleasure to have you both taking care of our interests," she said, and smiled from one man to the other.

21.

She stood on the veranda in her black leather jacket and trousers, waiting for Roberto though he wasn't late, watching the driveway that led from the villa to the front gates. There was false security in the solid steel lump at her side, digging unforgivingly into the raw memory held in her ribs. Nonetheless, she needed the butt-nosed Smith and Wesson 637 now more than ever. She would rather have the gun she had taken to the farmhouse, but she would have had a hard time explaining that when going through international customs. This version had been her first-ever weapon and the one she had taken her first life with. Stefano would be her last kill. Maybe it would be a fitting end to the cycle, to use the same gun. She would drop the Smith and Wesson in the sea once this was over. It would mark the end.

Storm water dripped rhythmically through the thin canopy the trees afforded. The latest downpour had stopped, though the winding and narrow roads would be treacherous. And, especially on a scooter. The last thing she needed was a stupid accident to get in the way, to incapacitate one of her crew or herself. Every detail of the plan needed considered thought now. She had to be one step ahead of Vitale, to read the mind of this man she had barely met. Simone was right. Patrina could be weak and if Vitale was her latest weakness... If she had to, though she hoped it wouldn't come to it, she would take out Patrina too.

Simone had studied the security footage since they had woken and hadn't seen anything suspicious. Not a single vehicle had passed the villa's gates, which was normal, but until Maria had the place under permanent observation, she wouldn't rest.

The elevated pitch of the spluttering exhaust of the 125cc scooter didn't resonate as a trustworthy machine. She missed the throaty roar of the Maserati and the confidence that came with being able to accelerate quickly whilst being protected inside the car's metal armour. But the scooter was the best way to travel undetected. It would blend in easily with the hundreds of other scooters that darted through the city streets on a daily basis, and wearing a helmet, she would never be spotted. She watched closely under the cover of the veranda until Roberto stood the bike on its stand next to the Alfa Romeo and removed his black helmet. He turned off the engine and stood for a moment, looking around him, then he started toward the front door.

Maria stepped out from the side of the villa and greeted him. "Roberto."

His eyes met hers long before reality registered through the softening of his features. He grew in stature, the whites of his eyes appearing like beacons and then a smile slowly formed. Hardly surprising, since he probably thought he was seeing a ghost.

He scanned over his shoulder down the driveway toward the main entrance and then to the cove. He craned his neck as he looked at her through a frown. "Donna Maria." He moved closer.

"Roberto, come in." She opened the door and he followed her.

Simone was still watching live footage of the main gates.

"Anything?" Maria asked, checking that Roberto hadn't been followed.

"Nothing."

"Good." Maria turned to Roberto. "I need you to do something for me."

"You're…"

He was staring at her, clearly stunned. "Yes. It's a long story, and we don't have time right now."

"You know about Giovanni?" he asked.

"Yes."

"The Amatos are poaching. It's getting worse." He stared at her with a look of concern that shifted suddenly, and he smiled the broadest grin his face could carry. "It's so good to see you."

Warmth nudged her to hug him, but she held back. She put her hand on his arm instead. "Vitale set up the incident at the tech park, which means the orders are coming directly from Stefano again."

He gripped the helmet, raised his fist and punched it. "That's why Patrina's avoiding us. She stopped communicating."

"Roberto."

"Yes, Donna Maria."

The title rattled, but she let it ride. "There's going to be trouble. He has been inside your house." Simone's focus shifted from the CCTV screen and she lowered her head.

Roberto looked in the direction of his sister. "Fucking bastard." He gritted his teeth and looked back at Maria.

"We're going to stay here." Maria lifted her hand when Roberto frowned. "The villa is easier to defend. I need you to get men out here. I want eyes on both sides of the cliffs." She indicated through the living room window, to where she wanted them positioned. "And get someone down both ends of the road at the front of the villa. Capisci?"

He nodded.

"Good." She moved closer to him. "I'm going to stay under cover for as long as I can. I'll use the scooter. I have people I need to talk to."

"I'll get the men out here right away."

"Good men, Roberto, the best we have."

"I understand, Donna Maria."

He seemed to be grasping her plan, but there was clearly something else he needed to share. "What is it?"

"There are new faces. The Puglisi brothers."

She shook her head. She didn't know of them.

"Alfonzo and Franco. They're young, keen, and stupid. There are others too, street kids they are training up, but these two are the busiest." He lifted his hand to the faint bruising under his eye. He pulled out his mobile, pressed the keys and presented the screen to her.

She studied the images. They looked like many of the young men in town, styled dark brown hair, cleanly shaven tanned skin, and broad white smiles. "You need to keep your eyes open. These guys play in the gutter. I don't want you joining them. We don't fight that way. You see what you see, hear what you hear, and report back to me, capisci? Don't get involved."

"Capisci."

She went to Simone and kissed her. "If anything happens, you contact me straight away. I'll call if I need anything." She looked from Simone to Roberto. They both nodded.

She took her helmet from the table and put it on and zipped up her leather jacket. Simone followed her to the door and watched as she climbed on the scooter and turned the engine. The bike threw out its high-pitched splutter and demonstrated a poor excuse for power as she opened the throttle as wide as it would go. She smiled in the hope that her eyes would convey love to Simone. Simone smiled faintly. She steered the bike down the drive and the gates opened as she reached them. She looked into the CCTV camera and dipped her head. She hoped Simone had seen her, just in case it was the last time. She flicked rainwater from her visor with her finger, turned her attention to the road ahead, and attuned to the handling of the scooter. Its tyres felt sloppy, the road greasy, and with the box on the back, it was unstable. It had brakes made of dough. She chuckled at the thought that

Roberto had delivered pizza on the death trap for years before she spotted him. Give me the Maserati any day. At the main road she took a left and followed the road that led to Capitano Massina's house.

22.

Maria cruised slowly past the detached house, noting the familiar saloon car in the driveway. Black metal shutters remained closed around the six first-level windows and if there were signs of life on the ground floor, they weren't visible from a fleeting glance at this distance from the property. She continued along the coastal road, swung the scooter around the painted roundabout that led into the village centre and came to a halt on the other side of the road, directly opposite the house. Two tall palm trees guarded either side of the entrance to the stone and gravel driveway, giving a majestic appearance to the property.

She rested the scooter on its stand, turned off the engine and sat on the low brick wall with her back to the sea, facing the house. She took out her mobile phone. Eight thirty. Massina would be leaving for work within the next half hour or so. She pocketed her phone.

The buzzing sensation in her pocket caught her attention.

Patrina can meet you at the penthouse suite at three on Wednesday.

Two days was two days too long to wait and felt like an itch she couldn't scratch. Each hour that passed was a moment closer to Stefano discovering she was back in Palermo. And then, life would become trickier. She had hoped for a more immediate response from Patrina. Patrina would have her reasons. She considered calling her and stopped. All their significant meetings in the past had taken place at the penthouse suite, and this was one conversation that needed to happen face to face. She needed to look into Patrina's eyes, to know the truth.

She would take a ride around the city after catching up with Massina, out to Café Tassimo to get a feel for what was happening on the ground. She trusted her instincts and could balance the views of her men if she had some idea of what was going on. Which old faces were talking to which new faces? Which people stood in which corners of which plaza? The signs of business being transacted were often subtle, but she knew how to read them. It was like tasting a fine wine yourself rather than buying based on the word of the seller. It needed to be done.

She caught the door of the house opening and stood swiftly. She looked up and down the road and crossed hurriedly. Massina stepped out of the house and turned to shut the door. In an instant, Maria pulled the gun from her side, ran to the door and pressed the end of the barrel against Massina's head. "Stop." Massina froze. "Is there anyone inside the house?" Massina shook her head. Maria prodded Massina's head with the gun. "Get inside, quickly." Massina held her ground. "Don't make me pull the fucking trigger. Get inside the house, now."

Massina pushed the door open and stepped over the threshold, creating a space between her head and the gun. She turned sharply and faced Maria. "Do you know who I am?"

Maria held the gun in the air and kicked the door closed behind them. "Yes. I do. Wait." She slipped the gun back in its holster and went to undo the clip to her helmet. When she looked up, she was staring down the barrel of Massina's gun. She raised her hands. "Wait. I need to—"

"Who the fuck are you? What the fuck do you want?" Massina pressed the gun firmly against Maria's helmet.

Panic surged through Maria and the darkness started to encroach on her vision. She blinked repeatedly, fighting the feeling of being sucked into the void. Her heart raced and sweat coated her skin as she lifted her arms higher above her head.

Massina plucked her mobile phone from her pocket. She swiped her thumb across the screen, her eyes flicking from Maria to the phone.

Maria could barely breathe, let alone speak. She widened her eyes and puffed out short breaths. "Rocca. It's me. Maria Lombardo."

Massina jolted. She stared at Maria and something registered in her eyes and then Massina lowered the barrel and Maria took another deeper breath.

"Can I take the helmet off, please?"

Massina lifted the gun again. "Slowly."

Maria unclipped the strap and lifted the helmet from her head. She wiped her forearm across her face and hoped Massina didn't notice she was shaking. Massina lowered the gun and holstered it. "What the fuck are you doing here? Alive?"

"I'm sorry; I can explain."

"I'm sure you can. I've never seen a dead person looking as good as you." Massina seemed to stagger slightly as she turned and walked down the corridor shaking her head. "Come in. Jesus, you know how to make an entrance."

"I'm sorry about that."

"You could have just knocked."

"I didn't know if you were alone."

"Well, next time, please just knock on the door and find out. You could get yourself killed." She indicated the table and chairs in the kitchen. "Please, take a seat. Do you want a drink?"

"No. I'm fine."

"Mind if I get one?"

"No. Of course not." Maria set her helmet on the table and paced the room, watching Massina make coffee, and when the Capitano took her phone from her pocket and flicked the screen, Maria tensed.

"I need to stay under cover."

"Well, that doesn't surprise me. I was due at a meeting at nine. I need to tell them I'm going to be an hour late." She looked up. "Unless this will take longer?"

Maria shook her head. She hadn't seen this side of Massina before. She talked more as a friend and she had a dry sense of humour. "No."

Massina brought them both coffee and sat opposite her. "Maria Lombardo." She smiled, shaking her head. "How in God's name did you escape?"

Maria averted her gaze. "That's a long story. Maybe one we can have over a drink sometime."

Massina frowned. "You know I will have one hell of a lot of paperwork to fill out to explain this, don't you?"

Maria sipped the coffee. "Well maybe you should wait a bit and you might not need to. I need your help."

Massina shifted in the seat. "What do you want?"

"I need to get to Stefano Amato."

Massina straightened in the chair. "Whoa. Do you know what you are you asking me?" She shook her head and frowned at Maria with a look that suggested Maria had taken a knock to her head in whatever had caused her to fake her death, and that had seriously affected her mental faculties.

"I need access to him. Just for a short time."

"Maria, you know I can't arrange that."

"I know you're not bent like Vitale is. I know you serve justice. I know Stefano Amato has caused this city, and my family and Simone's family, immense suffering. And I know that no matter how long he spends behind bars, he will continue to inflict pain on us all. He will have me killed and you won't be able to stop him. There is only one way to end this. Anything. A moment alone in prison with him. Anything."

"I can't. You'll go down for murder and since you clearly survived whatever happened that night on the boat, that would be a waste of a second chance at life."

Maria lowered her head. Simone would never forgive her if she ended up in prison but at least the people she loved would be safe. "I know. I don't want that either, but what other way is there? There isn't any way of getting him out of the place." Something registered in Massina's eyes and then the Capitano broke eye contact. "Off the record, is there a way of getting him out of the prison? A visit to a sick relative. Patrina for example. What if something happened to Patrina?" She couldn't think of any other reason the authorities would agree to letting Stefano out of prison. Not even for one minute.

Massina sipped her coffee. "There is one possibility."

Maria sat up. "What is it?"

"This is so off the record, Maria." She looked at Maria.

Maria nodded. "Of course."

Massina inhaled deeply. "If he is giving evidence to the police, he would need to be moved for his own safety."

"Breaking the omerta, you mean?"

"Yes."

The omerta was the code of silence that prohibited anyone inside the mafia from speaking to the police about mafia-related activities and business. Talking to the police would make him a grass. "He may be many things, but he's not a grass. He would never do that."

Massina shrugged. "He doesn't have to actually give evidence. It would need a letter to the prison governor to say that he is, though. The governor would then need to arrange for him to be moved within forty-eight hours. I haven't said what I am about to say, but there are certainly people at the DIA who would be happy to have the problem go away."

"Can you arrange this for me?"

Massina looked down and shook her head. "You know I have always been loyal to you and your family. And, I want to help you. But I cannot get involved in what you are proposing. I have already said too much."

Maria swallowed. Massina looked as deflated as Maria felt. "Sorry, I shouldn't have asked you."

"If there's any other way I can help, I will. You need to stay safe. I can have the villa guarded, if that helps?"

Maria clasped her hands together and squeezed them tightly. That wouldn't help. It would draw even more attention. "My men are protecting the villa. But thank you." She stood. "I'm sorry, I shouldn't have come here."

Massina stood. "It's good to know you are alive, Maria. If I can help in any other way, call me. But I will say this conversation never happened. You understand?"

Maria turned at the door. "One last thing."

Massina nodded.

"Tell me about Vitale."

She took a deep breath and looked away from Maria. "He's in deeper than you think. He was an astute detective, articulate and persuasive. He was a deputy on my team for a short time and we worked well together. I trusted his judgment, and his intellect was an asset. I'm sorry, I failed you and your father." She thinned her lips and swallowed. "He has powerful people in his circle, though I don't know who they are." She stared into space. "It's not easy breaking into these cliques, but as a force we are trying."

"I know." Maria reached out and softly clasped Massina's arm. "And thank you." She turned and walked toward the scooter. The helmet felt tighter around her head, her vision fogged, and the sea was as vast as the void inside her. Maybe, Patrina would be willing to help her get to Stefano. Though her instinct told her that Patrina was already too close to Vitale. The one thing that might persuade Patrina to help was the fact that she hated her husband as much as Maria had come to detest him. Possibly more. Patrina would want him dead, wouldn't she? But what about Vitale?

23.

Simone turned in the bed and blinked her eyes open. Maria's eyelashes flickered delicately. She looked at peace and Simone wished she could capture the dreamlike state for her and rid her of the nightmares forever. It was still dark outside, but she was wide awake and couldn't resist the urge to touch. She weaved her fingers gently through Maria's hair. Maria stirred and mumbled. She trailed her fingertip along Maria's jawline. Maria's skin was soft and warm and tiny vibrations shot up Simone's arm and into her neck. Maria took Simone's hand and pressed it to her lips and the tingling sensations moved through Simone in pleasantly intoxicating waves.

"Morning."

Maria sounded deliciously groggy. Simone's core tightened and the pulse between her legs intensified. Maria opened her eyes and tugged Simone into a kiss. Simone moved on top of her and eased her leg between Maria's and felt her wet heat. The salty-sweet taste stayed on her tongue as she kissed Maria's neck and then her breast. Maria arched against her. She took Maria's nipple into her mouth. The skin puckered at the whip of her tongue and when she grazed it gently with her teeth, Maria bucked and moaned. She teased the hardened nipple with her tongue before lifting her head and smiling. "Good morning."

"I have missed this."

Simone pressed her lips to Maria's with a featherlike touch.

"And that," Maria whispered.

Simone traced Maria's eyebrow and down the outside of her cheekbone and across to her lips. "You're so beautiful." She placed light kisses where her fingers had touched, and Maria's arm tightened around her waist. She licked around the shape of Maria's ear and sucked the soft lobe into her mouth.

"Every part of you. So delicious." Maria's hand moved to her buttock and the pulsing intensified between her legs.

"You feel so perfect."

Simone took Maria's hand from her buttock and held it against the bed. Maria moaned though she didn't resist. She slid lower, placing kisses down the outside of Maria's breast and across her stomach. As she went lower, Maria murmured. The pressure from Maria's hand in hers increased as she kissed the sensitive skin inside her hip. Maria jolted as if a bolt of electricity shocked her. She interlocked their fingers and lowered her head to the scent of Maria. "So soft, so wet."

Maria cried out as Simone took her into her mouth.

Maria tasted of nectar and the essence of the sea when it moves on a gentle breeze. The soft fleshy folds that protected Maria's sex parted with ease, and her clit became firm with the circling motion of her tongue. "So delicious."

"So good." Maria rocked her hips in a gentle motion. "You feel so fucking good. Don't stop."

Simone kissed Maria's clit, then licked lower and as Maria bucked her hips, Simone slipped her tongue inside her. With silk on her tongue, and seized by the fire that moved through her, Simone located Maria's clit and sucked it into her mouth. She pressed her thumb against Maria's entrance and when Maria bucked, she eased her fingers inside.

Maria moaned louder and arched higher.

Simone kept a leisurely rhythm with her fingers, her thumb moving tenderly over and around Maria's clit, Maria's movement guiding her. She found the slippery softness at the deepest point inside Maria and felt her expand at her gentle caress. She changed the pace of her thrusts until Maria bucked hard. She kissed her tenderly as the quakes moved through her then rested her head on Maria.

Maria lifted up from the pillow, tugged Simone to her and kissed her firmly. "I love you."

Simone knew that love in the longing in Maria's eyes. She had always seen it, though she hadn't known to label it back then. And, no matter what happened over the coming days, *this*, having shared these moments of bliss, *this* would be enough.

Maria eased out of the kiss, and she watched the familiar concern return to her eyes. The urge to sweep her away from it all, what had happened and what was yet to come, was intense. But they were locked inside a world that they couldn't escape from. Without Maria, she would have nothing to live for. They either had to live together or die together.

Maria took her hand and pressed it to her lips. A shiver brushed across Simone's skin. "I love you with all my heart."

"I know." Her heartbeat stalled at the distance that appeared suddenly in Maria's eyes. She brushed it away with a tender stroke that ended at Maria's lips. "We will get through this."

Maria turned away from the touch. "And if we don't?" she said, her tone quiet.

"Then we will have loved and lived. I don't want to be alive without you." Simone took a deep breath and turned Maria to face her. "I want to kill the bastard. And I'm not afraid to." Maria's smile was reserved and her gaze became increasingly more distant, no doubt driven by her understanding of the mammoth task they faced. Maria had hoped that Massina could help her and although she hadn't shown her disappointment, Simone felt it. "So, are you going to teach me to shoot, or do I have to work it out for myself?" She was trying to add levity, to lift Maria from the disquiet that perplexed her.

Maria chuckled. "There are rules with guns."

"Of course there are," Simone said as she got out of the bed. In Maria's world there were rules for everything; rules saved your life. She was partly right, because some rules were definitely designed to be broken. They would find a way to get to Stefano, without the help of Capitano Massina. "Shower, then shoot." She raised her eyebrows and grinned. Maria leapt from the bed.

Maria loaded the Smith and Wesson and held the gun with the chamber in her palm. "This is the safety catch. You keep that on at all times unless you intend to pull the trigger."

"Right."

"When you squeeze the trigger, do it slowly. The gun will kick back a bit when it fires."

"Okay."

Maria held the gun toward Simone. Simone took it. She turned toward Maria, admiring the weapon.

"And don't point the gun at anyone unless you mean to shoot them." Maria turned the barrel of the gun downwards so that Simone was pointing it at the ground.

"Any more rules?" Simone asked. She gesticulated with her hand holding the gun.

"Not that I can think of." Maria lowered the weapon again.

"It's heavier than I expected."

Maria smiled. "That one's light. Some are really heavy and have the kick of a horse."

Simone could see Maria's man on the cliff top on the right of the cove carrying a rifle. The man on the left was out of view, as were the guys monitoring the road. "How far will this shoot?"

"This is for close targets. The further away you are, the harder it will be to hit anything. Here, you see that tree?" She pointed in the direction.

Simone nodded. It was about twenty metres away.

"Take a shot at it. Focus a line down the barrel. Want me to show you?"

Simone drew the gun closer to her. "No. I can follow instructions." She grinned, lifted the weapon, and pointed it. Remembering to squeeze slowly, she increased the pressure on the trigger. It seemed to lock, and she wondered if there was something wrong.

"Keep squeezing."

The gun felt heavy and was becoming harder to hold in position. Her vision blurred. She blinked and squeezed. The crack, like thunder, echoed around the cove, and a ringing sound reverberated in her ears. It was exhilarating though she didn't have a clue if she had hit the target. Maria was smiling at her.

"Not bad. You hit the rock, the one about two feet to the right of the tree."

"No." How could she miss by that much?

"It's harder the further away it is." She pointed to the man on the cliff. "He has a sniper rifle with a telescopic sight on it. He can take out you or me in the blink of an eye. We can't reach him from here."

Simone stared at the man on the cliff. "He'd better be on our side." She was joking.

"He is. Now, take a shot at that wooden box."

Maria had set out a range of targets. This one was about five metres away. It looked big enough to hit, until Simone looked down the barrel of the gun and her arm started to shake. She lowered her arm.

"Try to find your aim quickly, settle on it, and then squeeze steadily. The longer you wait the harder it can get."

Simone lifted her arm, sighted the box and squeezed. The crack came and she saw something fly from the top right corner. "Did I hit it?"

Maria's eyes had a sparkle in them. "You caught the right edge. Have another go. Aim for a very specific point in the middle of the box."

"You should have painted Alessandro's face on it," Simone said and lifted the gun, sighted it, and squeezed. The shot split the box just right of centre. "Well, that thought worked."

Maria nodded. "Keeping that thought in mind, hit the plastic bucket over there."

Simone took a deep breath and stared at the small plastic bucket, imagining Alessandro's pig ugly face, and felt thrilled. When she pointed the gun, she could see the point between his eyes above the bridge of his fat nose, the tiny hairs that linked his eyebrows. Squeezing the trigger, it was as if time slowed down. She remained still and the crack of thunder didn't seem anywhere near as loud as it had done the first time. Splinters of plastic propelled in all directions as the broken bucket spun into the air.

"Very good." Maria went to her and took the weapon from her hand. She kissed her softly on the lips. "I didn't think you could get any sexier, but I was wrong." She kissed her again.

Exhilarated from hitting the target, she clasped Maria's head in her hands and pulled her to her, deepening the kiss. "Fuck me. Here. Now."

Maria applied the safety catch, allowed the gun to fall from her hand and wrapped her arm around Simone's waist.

Simone felt the weakness hit her knees when Maria's hand came between her legs. And when Maria entered her, she lost control of her balance. Maria guided her to the ground. Her kisses were fierce, and the world was spinning in glorious technicolour. Yes, she would die for Maria.

24.

Maria hadn't expected to feel sick.

She stood at the front door to her mother's house for what felt like an eternity, forcing her tongue around a dry mouth with anxious anticipation of a moment that should be filled with unbridled joy. Her heart thudded behind her stiff leather jacket. She wrestled with the strap beneath her chin and removed the helmet, her hands trembling. As she reached up, hovering her finger over the doorbell, the door opened.

Her mother stared at her for a time, a vacant coldness in her eyes creating a fissure in Maria's heart. She watched her mother's eyes slowly slip into awareness and her right hand, the one holding the Beretta .357 Magnum behind her back, slumped limply at her side.

"Matri," she said, her heart bursting with remorse at what she'd had to put her mother through.

"*Tesoro*...tesoro...tesoro. Oh, Mary, mother of Jesus and Joseph. I knew it. I knew it."

Her mother tugged her swiftly across the threshold, glanced around the garden, and slammed the door shut behind them.

Pesto bounded toward them from the kitchen and jumped up at Maria.

"Hey, Pesto." She knelt and allowed him to lick her enthusiastically. His nose tickled her ear and her neck. He jumped on her and clawed at her arm. She took his head into her hands and looked into his eyes. "I missed you too, boy." She ruffled the scruff of his neck. He continued to jump and sniff at her and mouth her hand playfully. "Good boy."

"Pesto, away." Her mother clicked her fingers and Pesto sat, though he continued to wag his tail, making sweeping motions across the floor.

Tears glassed her mother's eyes as she wrapped her arms around Maria and squeezed the life out of her.

"I knew. I knew. In my heart. You never left me, tesoro." Her mother stepped back and patted her hand on her own chest repeatedly, tears sliding down the centre of her cheeks. "I knew as only a mother can know." She wiped her face with the back of her hand, sniffed, and grabbed Maria's shoulders. She looked at her intently. "You are too thin. This is not good."

"Matri, I'm fine."

Her mother looked at her admonishingly. It was her mother's way. She always thought of Maria as too thin, or too tired, or working too hard. Maria conceded that her mother needed to mother her. It was the least she could give her after what she'd done.

"No. You are not fine. I see it in your eyes."

Her mother placed her gun on the sideboard and led Maria into the kitchen. "You need your matri's food, tesoro. You can explain later."

Fire blinded Maria's vision. She closed her eyes, took in a deep breath, and drove the tears back to join the ache in her heart. "I'm sorry, matri," she said, her voice soft and weary.

Her mother turned from the pot on the stove. Kindness and unyielding strength merged in the look she gave Maria.

"You are alive, Maria, you are alive. What is there to be sorry for?" She gesticulated in the air as if to say what is done is done and we will speak no more of it.

Maria bit the inside of her lip and looked away. "I had to come back. Simone..." She hadn't told her mother about Simone. What did she know?

Her mother smiled. "Simone is the good girl, tesoro, sì?"

A faint smile suppressed the tears, even if the relief didn't show in her muted tone. "Sì, matri."

Her mother shoved a plate of steaming food on the table and pointed at it. Hungry or not, Maria would be expected to eat.

"Sit. Talk to me. What brought you back?"

Maria sat as requested. Her mother sat next to her and held her arm. Maria saw profound grief in her mother's eyes, tinged with joy.

"I just need to touch you, to be sure," her mother said.

Maria took her mother's hand, squeezed it tightly, and rested their joined hands on the table. She ate two mouthfuls of the food and put the fork down.

"Stefano has forgotten the rules, matri."

"A long time ago, tesoro. Nothing is new."

Maria took a deep breath. There was wisdom in the dark eyes that had already lived a lifetime, and the matter-of-fact tone her mother used. Her mother's mind had been equal to her father's. She was able to discern the battles worth fighting and those that would sort themselves out eventually. Clans could always be encouraged to self-destruct. But occasionally, her mother had a blind spot. "Yes, but now things are different."

She rubbed her fingers across the back of Maria's hand. "You are alive," she whispered, as if affirming to herself.

"Stefano ordered the hit on Father," Maria said and watched her mother's eyes fill with fire. "I am convinced of it."

"That no good son of a bastard bitch."

A sharp pain flared through Maria's hand. She eased her mother's nails from her skin.

"He's giving orders through Vitale, the detective who destroyed the evidence for them."

"You are sure of all this?"

Maria nodded. "As sure as I can be. Alessandro didn't have the balls to order a hit against Father. It must have come from Stefano, getting greedy, ambitious, or proving he wasn't impotent stuck behind bars. It makes no odds why. He doesn't trust Patrina and Beto is loyal to her, but he sees him as weak. He's replaced Alessandro with Vitale. Vitale comes with connections. Someone high ranking must have had the evidence against Vitale disappear."

"The bad get flushed out, eventually, tesoro. It's only a matter of time."

Maria stroked her mother's cheek. "Yes. Now I will flush out the bastards myself."

Her mother's eyes welled with tears. "No, tesoro. Please, don't go dying on me again. My heart cannot cope."

She wiped away the tears that marked her mother's face. "I never died, did I?" she said softly. She thought of Simone and felt her mother's loss. "I have too much to live for."

"I can help you." Her mother cleared her throat as she stood. "I insist."

Maria shook her head. "When the time is right." Which would be never. "I will speak to Patrina first. For now, I need you to stay put. I'll get someone to protect you."

"I don't need protection."

"Yes, you do. Talk to the mayor and keep him sweet. Make sure this incident at the site doesn't get it closed down. I can't—"

"You must not be seen."

Maria smiled. "Fortunately, it's hard to see a dead person even if they walk right in front of your nose. At some point they will know I'm here, but I intend to surprise them first. I have to take out Stefano, matri. Once and for all."

Her mother shook her head. Her cheeks had paled, and she exhaled deeply through a thin smile. "I prayed so hard for you, tesoro, so hard." She pointed her finger to the off-white ceiling. "You see, there is a God."

Who didn't save my father. Maria felt compassion soften her, and she smiled at her mother. "There must be," she said.

Her mother looked at the half-eaten food on the plate and frowned. "You're not going anywhere until you eat," she said.

"Matri, I have to go. I need to see Giovanni. Pesto will eat it for me, won't you?" Pesto's ears pricked up and he came running to her side. She stroked his back. "Please don't tell Catena I'm back. Not yet. She will worry and she needs to take care of the baby."

Her mother's eyes shone. "He is such a beautiful baby, tesoro. Dark curly hair and long eyelashes. He's a good eater. But he needs to meet his aunty."

It was her mother's way of telling her to stay alive and she intended to do exactly that.

*

She had watched the comings and goings at the Palermo General hospital for half an hour, leant against the scooter in the bike park directly opposite the main pedestrian entrance, her helmet on and feigning studying her mobile phone. She had ridden directly from her mother's, stuffed after the pasta lunch even though she had only eaten a few mouthfuls. She hadn't been followed and didn't recognise any faces. There was nothing suspicious. She pocketed the scrap of paper her mother had given her, reminding her that Giovanni was in room fourteen on the third floor of the spinal wing.

She removed her helmet as she strode through the automatic doors and glanced around the foyer. The ill-digested pasta turned in her stomach. Corridors split off like the spokes on a wheel. Two middle-aged men, an elderly man and woman, and single younger woman, visitors or patients, queued at the main reception desk. She noted green, white, and purple uniformed staff moving purposefully as they crossed the central point from one corridor to another. It was as she expected. A busy hospital foyer. Her heart still raced.

Voices drifted in and out of her consciousness, some urgent, some casual as she made her way to Giovanni's private room via the nurse's station. She introduced herself to them as Mariella Sanchez, his cousin from Italy. They took down her passport details and allowed her to pass. She stood outside his door and peered through the small, square pane of glass. Giovanni lay prone on the bed. His body was still, and he made the bed look too small.

A lead feeling expanded in her gut.

She opened the door. The lights on the monitor sharpened. She didn't care for the numbers or the details. Her concern was that Giovanni was alive and breathing. She carried the plastic chair to the side of his bed and sat as close as she could get. A sterile chemical odour lingered in the air with a gentle floral aroma coming from the flowers on his bedside table. Three get-well cards had been opened and set out around the flowers. She couldn't see who they were from, but the poignance of only three cards touched her. She hadn't sent him a card. A bag, quarter filled with near-orange liquid, hung from the rail attached to his bed. In addition to the tubes, his head was crowned in bandages and he was clamped inside a neck brace. His eyes were like a panda's burrowed in hollowness, and his cheeks were sallow. His lips were scarred with tiny cracks, drizzled with salt. His hands were shaped by purple bruising that wasn't caused by the needle that fed him.

She slipped her fingers beneath his palm and gently rested her thumb across his fingers. "Christ, Giovanni, what did they do to you?"

She kept her focus on his hand, willing him to communicate to her. His fingers remained flaccid and lifeless. She stifled a scream, pinched the bridge of her nose, and looked away. She waited until the burning in her throat receded before turning back and looking at him. A sharp pain jabbed her chest. "I'm so sorry. I'm so sorry. Forgive me."

She looked down when she felt a tiny movement. She glanced up at the machine, but the constant rhythm remained. She withdrew her hand slowly, stood, and stared at him.

"I will get the bastards who did this to you," she whispered.

She willed his eyelids to register awareness, to acknowledge that she was at his side fighting for his life as he was.

Did they flutter?

Her heart skipped a beat and she sat forward in the chair. She took his hand and willed him to hear her. "Giovanni. It's me. Can you hear me?"

He struggled to open his eyes and seemed to give up as he stopped for a moment. His lips twitched at the corners as if he was trying hard to smile. Then his lips parted. "Maria."

His voice was croaky, but it was like a melody to her. "Hey." She wiped the tears from cheeks that ached with the strain of her smile. "Hey, you look—"

"Like shit," he said. He opened his eyes and directed them at her as best he could with his head stuck inside the brace. "You look—"

"Alive."

He made a soft chuckling sound that became a restrained cough. "I'm not allowed to move."

"Sorry." Some colour had returned to his cheeks already. "How are you? What's the prognosis?"

"I'm surviving. I hate hospitals." He swallowed and licked his lips with slow deliberate movements. "I don't know whether I'll walk again, but I'm sure as hell going to try."

She squeezed his arm. "You'll walk again." She hoped.

"You're not here for me though."

"Well, you went and got yourself crushed while I was heading here, so yes, now I'm here for you too."

He rolled his eyes. "If I could shake my fucking head, I would. You have to take Simone and go."

"No, my friend. I'm going to take out Stefano and then go." Or maybe stay. She hadn't spoken to Simone yet about what they might do when they got through this. Much would depend on this man's recovery.

He closed his eyes for a moment and when he opened them, she sensed he understood even if he didn't agree with her. "How?"

She didn't have the answer. "You don't need to worry about that. You lay here and get better." She smiled. "I mean it. You need to heal."

"Vitale must have connections within the DIA, Maria. Or Stefano has bought someone at the mayor's office. Or both. DIA corruption is fucking rife."

Heat burned Maria's cheeks. She had asked one of the least corrupt officers in the DIA to assist her to commit murder. Maybe corruption was rife, but surely there was a difference between good corruption and bad? "The mayor is still on side with us?" She wouldn't have expected his loyalty to have shifted in the past six months, but when money was involved the right number could easily shift a man's allegiance.

"I think so. He's still indecisive as fuck, but I don't believe he's listening to Patrina. Though she has gone quiet. Things were going well before...Vitale. We need to stay close to the mayor while I'm holed up in here though." He licked his dry lips. "Vitale's family owns the warehouses on the zona industriale south. General storage: cars and car parts, and plant equipment. They ship containers around the world. It looks like a genuine business, at least on the surface. But that doesn't mean he's not running merchandise on the side. Could be weapons, drugs, booze."

"That's good to know. Thanks."

"Maria."

She held his gaze and understood the depth of emotion he felt.

"You can't trust him."

"I know."

"He's clever. He doesn't do the dirty work, but he has others willing to pull the trigger for him."

"I was being watched at the farmhouse."

He closed his eyes and his face looked strained. "I'm sorry."

"That's not your fault. I...we can't live looking over our shoulder."

He opened his eyes. "Stefano is using Vitale to take a stronger hold over Palermo."

She lowered her eyes. "I need to put a stop to them."

"How are you going to get to him, Maria?"

She looked up. "Do we know anyone on the inside?"

"No one who has access to him."

Her heart sank and anger rose quickly. "Fucking hell." He didn't move, but if he could have, she sensed he would have shrugged. They didn't have a plan.

25.

She parked on the main road just short of Hotel Fresco, opened the box on the back of the scooter, took out Roberto's old pizza delivery bag and slung it over her shoulder. Two taxis pulled up directly outside the front of the hotel. Three women and a man got out of the first taxi, collected their bags from the boot of the car, and lingered outside the revolving doors. They looked dressed for business. A man and woman alighted from the second taxi and stood on the pavement. The man handed the woman a piece of paper and she studied it. They looked more like tourists. Maria waited until the taxis had disappeared out of view and the guests had entered the hotel before approaching the doors. She looked around the inside before entering. Matteo, the hotel's manager that she had had dealings with previously when visiting Patrina at the penthouse suite, was thankfully distracted by the new arrivals. She strode through the foyer and stepped into the lift.

When the doors closed, she took a deep breath and leaned against the frame. She studied her reflection in the shiny metal. If it wasn't for the pizza delivery bag, she looked every bit like a gangster in the black leathers and crash helmet. Her heart raced as she imagined facing Patrina again. The last time she used this lift she had been heading out of Patrina's life for good. So much had happened since, and now she was here to persuade Patrina that the man at her side was big trouble. The floor numbers lit up too slowly. Eventually, the lift pinged its arrival and glided to a stop. She inhaled deeply and puffed out the air before walking toward the penthouse suite door.

She tapped four times, and it clicked open. She stepped into the room, pulled off her helmet, and inhaled warm air with notes of citrus fruit and alcohol.

"Well, the ghost appears," Patrina said and bowed.

There was humour in her tone, but Maria thought it misplaced. Patrina was drunk and when she was inebriated, she cared less, became careless, and couldn't be reasoned with. Already she was questioning her rationale for trying to involve her.

"You brought pizza, how thoughtful. I'm sorry, I've already had lunch with Contessa Marino. Turned into a liquid affair." The words slid clumsily from her tongue. She sipped from the cut crystal glass before she raised it toward Maria. "Would you like a drink?" She set off to the fridge before Maria could answer.

Maria pictured Patrina's lunch with the mayor's wife: fine wine flowing freely, an elaborate spread of bites and nibbles that would remain virtually untouched, and trivial conversation that would drive a sane mind quickly to madness. Giovanni was right. They needed to stay close to the mayor, especially given Patrina was lunching with his wife. She set the helmet on the table and removed the pizza bag and leather jacket. She deliberately left the holstered Smith and Wesson at her side, tucked under her left arm. Patrina would know she meant business when she saw it.

Patrina glanced at the gun as she returned and handed Maria a glass of wine.

Patrina had an odd look about her, not aided by her inebriated state, and she lurched forward as if she was either about to pull Maria into an embrace or fall over. Was she going to cry? Was that remorse? The instant Maria detected the vulnerability, it disappeared. "You look well, Patrina." She didn't actually. Her olive skin didn't hide the lines that aged her face, weathered irreparably by the ravages of time and worry, no doubt. Her eyes seemed smaller, set in marginally puffy cheeks. Her lips twitched hesitantly. At least she hadn't lost her sardonic manner.

"You look much better than the last time I saw you."

Maria probably couldn't have appeared any worse, though she had no recollection of how she looked that night. She had wavered in and out of consciousness and had been bleeding heavily. She placed her drink on the table. "Yes, I am much better."

Patrina swayed as she walked to the window. She placed her hand on the ledge. "I thought you were dead, bedda."

Maria tilted her head. "That was the idea."

Patrina sipped from the glass. "You broke my heart." She smiled though her eyes didn't. "I'm happy you're alive."

"Patrina. I need to stop Vitale before this goes too far. Giovanni...didn't deserve what happened."

Patrina's eyes suddenly darkened. "That was an accident. We sent a card of condolence."

Maria had noted the cards at the hospital. If that was one of the three cards at Giovanni's bedside, it was even sadder than she imagined. The term *we* stuck in her throat. "You can't control Vitale."

"You don't think so, bedda?"

"What does he want?"

Patrina's laugh sounded empty. "What do all men in Palermo want? Power and a woman they can parade at their side. But he's not like the rest."

Maria ran her fingers through her hair and held her hand at the back of her head. When she looked up, there was a clear distance between them that she knew would never be bridged. "Please, don't tell me you're fucking him."

Patrina lifted her chin and sipped her drink.

"Oh Christ. You really are. Here?" She indicated to the bed, not looking for a response. "He's more dangerous than you think."

"He reminds me of you, bedda." Patrina looked at Maria through eyes glassy from drink.

"You're a target, Patrina. Why can't you see that?"

Patrina sighed. "I am not. I can work with Tommaso and he is good for the business. He won't encroach on Lombardo turf, if that's what you're worried about."

"He already has. And when he digs deeper, which men like him always do, and he finds out about us, and the fact that you killed Alessandro, you are a dead woman. I need you to trust me. Help me to eliminate the problem. We can work together again."

Silence expanded in the space between them.

Patrina bit her lip as she lifted her chin and Maria got the sense that she was hiding something. Patrina looked out the window and Maria couldn't read her.

"You are planning to stay in Palermo, bedda?"

Maria shook her head. She wasn't planning that far ahead, but she would say whatever was needed to get Patrina to see sense. "Giovanni is in a bad way and I need to make sure the business is in safe hands before I do anything. You can help me."

"You walked out on your business, Maria. What changed?"

The words cut like a knife. Maria had run for her life. She had taken an opportunity leaving a clear plan in place for the Lombardo business. But Patrina was right. She had deserted her family and the business. She had been selfish, and the result was a lose-lose situation. She wouldn't make the same mistake again. "You, Patrina. You can't take care of your crew or your husband and that makes you as much of a problem to my business as they are to yours."

"You're threatening me, bedda?"

"No. I'm trying to get you to see sense. You had a good man in Beto and yet you jumped into bed with scum like Vitale."

Patrina turned back to Maria and laughed dismissively. "You have no idea how much I loved you, bedda. I still do love you."

Maria tensed. *If you love someone you don't treat them as badly as you treated me.*

"I trust Tommaso. He's smart and he thinks like you do. I understand him."

"That man is nothing like me."

"Pah. You don't know him. He didn't hide any evidence, bedda. That's why he was released. Maybe there was no evidence. Maybe your father's death was just an accident. I know it's hard to accept." She shrugged. Fire threaded Maria's veins. "The authorities washed their hands of him because that's what happens around here. It's part of their *new face* of the law that they want the public to see."

Maria stood with her hands on her hips, shaking her head, the pressure inside her head becoming unbearable. That wasn't what Massina had said about Vitale. Patrina couldn't seriously believe that Alessandro and Vitale weren't behind the death of her father. "You honestly think Vitale's an innocent victim in this?"

"He wants to make something of himself. Persuading Stefano to work with him was simply a way to get closer to me. He had to prove himself to Stefano and maybe stepped over the line. He and I work well together, and I'll make sure he knows the boundaries between our families. Believe me, if I could get rid of Stefano, I would consider the proposition seriously. But not Tommaso. You are wrong, bedda. He is like us."

Maria opened her mouth and closed it quickly. No, he wasn't like Maria, and neither was Patrina. And there was no *us*. There was no way she could share her thoughts and her plans with Patrina, even if Patrina wanted her husband dead.

Any plan involving Patrina would also involve Vitale. Trust Patrina. No, that she couldn't do.

"Tommaso is a good man, bedda."

Her stomach churned. She stood, immobilised by the illusion that Patrina had weaved for herself. Patrina had bought into Vitale's story and there was no changing her perspective. She spoke in a quiet voice, hoping one last time that a shift in tone might resonate differently. "Everything we fought for all these years will..." She stopped speaking to calm the rising frustration and took in a deep breath. "I nearly died once to rid this earth of the Amato plague, and I'm not going to get to that point again. I would rather have you with me than against me, but if you're with me, you need to see that Vitale isn't who you think he is."

"You will get yourself killed, bedda. His people are watching him all the time. He's untouchable. Just know that if you go after Tommaso, I will take it as a personal attack." Patrina lifted the glass to her lips and downed the last of her wine.

Maria frowned. "You need to be very careful, Patrina."

Patrina lifted her loose skirt high up her thigh to reveal a small, snub-nosed gun strapped to her leg. "Always, bedda. Always."

Maria couldn't think of a more appropriate place on Patrina's body to keep her protection. Sex had always been Patrina's power card, and she played with distinction, but the vain attempt at humour left her cold. "That isn't going to be enough."

Patrina gave a spirited laugh. "I think I know how to play the game, bedda."

Maria stared into her eyes. This would be the last time she walked out of the penthouse suite. "I'm asking you one last time. Are you with me, or against me?"

Patrina broke eye contact walked to the door and opened it. "I think we are done here, don't you?"

Maria put on her jacket. She felt the gun pressing hard against her ribs. She put on the helmet and felt the heat instantly. She stopped at the door. There was no remorse in Patrina's eyes. Whatever had passed between them was firmly in the past. A new set of cards had been dealt and Maria intended to win the next hand. "Goodbye, Patrina."

26.

"I can't punch any harder." Simone groaned, sweat beaded on her forehead, her arms like lead weights hanging from her shoulders. Her muscles burned, sapping her strength, and she gasped to fill her lungs.

"Put your shoulder into it more...like this."

Maria landed a rally of punches. It looked rhythmical and effortless, her shoulder coordinating with her arm to shift her full weight into the bag with every single blow. She left dents in the leather. The bag sprang swiftly back to life after Simone hit it. It was frustrating and exhausting. "My arms are too tired."

"That's because you're not punching from your shoulder."

"No, it's not. It's because my arms are dropping off my shoulders." Simone punched Maria on the arm.

"Ouch." Maria feigned pain, rubbed her arm with her gloved hand and started laughing. Simone punched her again and she threw her guard up. "So, you want a fight, eh?"

The sparkle in Maria's eyes, and the challenge she had thrown down, invigorated Simone in a flash. She raised her gloves to protect her face and jabbed at Maria.

Maria took the punch effortlessly on her gloves, skipped on the spot and jabbed a punch back at Simone.

Simone squealed as Maria's punch connected with her gloves. She tensed her arms and started moving her feet. This was fun.

"Now, hit me harder."

Simone swung and Maria dived out of the way. Simone kept moving and lost her balance. Maria kicked her gently in the bottom. "Hey."

"Kicking's allowed." Maria dodged another swipe, keeping her hands up, guarding the front of her face. "Keep your feet moving or you'll lose your balance again. You can't just lunge at someone."

Simone gritted her teeth. She narrowed her focus to Maria's gloves and tried to mirror Maria's foot movement. Shifting in small light steps, she dodged and weaved to get a better angle from which to strike a blow. Maria jabbed at her and she took the punches to her gloves without her arms giving way. Then Maria dropped her guard suddenly and Simone struck her.

"Ow, fuck." Maria held her hand up in defeat. She pressed her forearm to her nose and looked down at the blood.

"Oh shit." Simone swiftly closed the space between them, held Maria's head between her gloved hands and looked at the red mess smeared across her face. Blood trickled from her left nostril. "Shit. I'm sorry. I didn't mean to—"

"It's fine. I'm proud of you. That was one hell of a punch." She chuckled.

"You dropped your guard."

"You looked tired. I was about to ask if you wanted to stop."

"I'm so sorry." Simone kissed Maria on the forehead and held her close.

"It's fine. It was fun. You're stronger than you think."

Simone lifted Maria's chin and inspected her again. "It's stopped bleeding."

"You're good. We should spar more often."

"I've had the best teacher." Simone kissed Maria deeply, eliciting a moan from her.

The distinctive roar of the Maserati arriving in the driveway caught their attention. They both turned toward the noise.

Simone frowned. "Were you expecting Roberto?"

Maria shook her head.

Simone had the feeling of someone walking across her grave.

They walked across the veranda and around to the front of the house. She didn't think Maria could take more bad news. The hope and determination she had seen in Maria's eyes the night she arrived had faded over the last few days. There had been signs that Maria was regressing, struggling mentally with fighting what felt a lot like a losing battle. She was more restless, slept fitfully and looked increasingly more concerned. Lifting Maria's spirits was getting tougher. She understood Maria's frustrations. Perhaps, if Maria had anticipated that getting access to Stefano wasn't going to be simple, she would have thought twice about returning. Maybe it was an ill-conceived plan. You didn't just walk into the prison and eliminate one of Palermo's dons. Maria really had put all her hopes in Massina. If anyone was in a position to help, it was her. Patrina had behaved as Simone thought she would. She was unreliable and weak. It was disappointing, but predictable. Would Patrina go so far as to tell Vitale that Maria was in the country? They had to assume it was only a matter of time before she did, and they were still at square one with no clear idea of how to get close to Stefano.

"Donna Maria."

Roberto looked toward Maria with his head tilted downwards, highlighting dark shadows beneath his eyes. His mouth twitched and he didn't seem to be able to stand still. When he looked up, he studied Maria through a frown. Simone's heart sank.

"Come inside." Maria squinted as she glanced around and up to the cliffs to the east of the cove. As they entered through the beach side veranda, she glanced toward the western cliffs before closing the door behind them. She removed her gloves and put them on the table. "What is it, Roberto?"

"It's not good news, Donna Maria." Simone's throat clamped. She studied Maria's face and saw no response to the gravity in Roberto's tone.

"What's happened."

Roberto swallowed. "I met with Beto earlier."

Maria nodded.

Simone had always liked Beto. He wasn't like the others. He had always treated her with respect when she worked at Café Tassimo, and he too had suffered because of Alessandro's stupidity. He was cut from the same mould as Giovanni and would prefer to engage in legitimate business dealings rather than street fighting and gang warfare. He was a good second to Patrina, a safe pair of hands and loyal to her, though she feared Patrina didn't see him that way.

"He says Vitale has brought in two new faces who report directly to him. There may be more men, but these guys are professionals and they're active. They're not like the Puglisis. Davide Carusso and Leo Costa are their names. They have form, Maria. The Carusso clan is small, and it looks as though they are joining forces with the Amatos."

Maria lowered her head and he looked away. When she looked back at him his expression appeared darker.

"They're planning to make a move on the Riverside."

"When?"

"Beto didn't know."

Maria took a deep breath and nodded. "Beto wouldn't lie to us."

"No, Donna Maria. He doesn't like the new regime. He's been removed from Patrina's side. Vitale is now her right hand and he has been relegated to working for Davide."

"Okay."

"Shouldn't we go back to Massina for help?" Simone asked. Maria's stern gaze annoyed her, and she bit her lip. She wanted to help them find a solution.

"We need to deal with this ourselves. If we involve the DIA it could cause us more problems."

Roberto looked at Simone. She saw his concerns; they were her own. They didn't have enough men to protect the Riverside and the villa and Maria's mother. They were being stretched and that could leave them exposed on all fronts.

"There's more, Donna Maria."

Maria looked at Roberto with an unwavering gaze.

"We are losing rent. They are telling our tenants that we cannot protect them. That with Giovanni seriously injured in hospital they are vulnerable. They are matching our rates and our tenants are being forced to accept. There was a fire at the gaming shop last night, and the pizzeria on Cassia Stradde was robbed. Both had refused to take up the Amatos' offer."

Maria turned away and put her hands on her hips.

Simone wanted to hold Maria close and take away the pain, but a hug wouldn't change the situation. There had to be a better way than to fight. Surely, they could talk and strike a deal. There was enough business for everyone to benefit. "What are we going to do?"

"Take the men from here," Maria said. She turned and looked directly at Roberto. "Leave one man on the western cliff during the night, and make sure we have the Riverside adequately protected. Leave two men at my mother's house. I want her protected day and night. I want daily contact with our tenants to assure them of our honour. I want our men on the streets twenty-four, seven. Capisci?"

Simone's heart raced as the potential consequences of Maria's orders dawned.

Maria didn't look at her. "We have the CCTV to cover the front entrance. The cove is a riskier route to use because they would be seen, but we will get CCTV covering the cove from the back here too." She turned to Simone. "We have to protect our tenants, Simone, and the Riverside."

Simone nodded, recalling the last time the Riverside got hit. Antonio, their manager, had been badly injured. People might die this time. Innocent people. Maria's duty to them had to come first. Suddenly, studying the CCTV footage took on a higher level of importance. "I'll watch the main entrance and arrange for the additional cameras to be fitted," she said.

Maria looked away from them both. "I need to go for a run. Roberto, sort out the men, now."

"Of course, Donna Maria."

Maria gave a half-smile to Simone and headed out the door.

Simone looked at her brother. "Are you all right?"

He nodded. "Is Maria...?"

"She's fine." Simone looked over her shoulder, to the door onto the beach that Maria had just walked through. Maria didn't feel all right at all. She removed her gloves and put them next to Maria's. "Is there no other way of stopping this?"

He shrugged. "Not everything is within our control, sis. Sometimes we have to react and sometimes we can lead. Now we are reacting. When agreements break down, the rules change quickly."

She had been thinking, and Roberto was the only person she could ask. "How easy would it be for me to visit Stefano and talk to him?"

He shook his head and let out a short, clipped snort. "Are you mad?"

"Surely, if he knew it was his wife who killed Alessandro, he would think differently?"

Roberto's eyes widened. "Did she?"

"Yes. Patrina killed him. If I could get to Stefano and tell him, then he would go after his wife and not Maria."

Roberto was shaking his head. "No, sis. It doesn't work like that. He'll take the information, sure. We could pass that information through the grapevine even. And he'll take a hit out on Patrina as a result. But that won't stop him coming for Maria. If Stefano wants more power, he will do whatever it takes to get it. There's no negotiating with men like him. It's his way."

Simone lowered her head, irritated by the naivety of her thoughts now she'd articulated them. He was right. This was the man who had killed their parents and brother, and whilst he had gone to prison for doing so, it hadn't stopped him from causing further death and destruction. He had in effect killed Maria's father too and almost killed Giovanni. How the hell did you stop a man like that?

27.

She cowered at the thunderous crack. A ringing echoed in her ears. Pain, sharp and hot, shot through her chest. It was taxing to breathe. Voices came, a man and a woman. Another crack of thunder and another and then the voices stopped, and then the darkness came again. And there was silence, and breathing was too effortful, and she saw the image of herself on the boat below her.

Maria yanked the sheet from Simone as she bolted up in the bed. Her heart thundered against the inside of her chest. Her phone was ringing on the bedside table. She fumbled picking it up. "Yes."

"Donna Maria, there is a fire."

She flung her legs out of the bed. "Where?"

"To the east. Close to the perimeter. It looks contained. There was a flash of light."

"Okay."

Simone mumbled a sleepy complaint, tugged the covers back over herself and quieted. Maria's mind caught up with her senses and her heart pounded more heavily. She nudged Simone vigorously. "Simone, get up. Quickly." Simone groaned an objection. "Simone, now. Get up." She didn't want to shout. She didn't want to alert whoever it was on the outside of the villa. She couldn't see anything out the window but the shadows of the flora north of the villa. It was just short of two a.m. and although the dream had thrust her from sleep, maybe it hadn't all been a dream. The gunshot suddenly seemed very real.

Simone stirred. "What is it?"

"There's a fire on the estate. Get up, get dressed, and stay here. Take the gun and keep watch out the window. I just need to check what's going on."

Swiftly, she ripped off her sweat-drenched T-shirt and climbed into her tracksuit bottoms, trainers, and a clean top. She grabbed her phone and the Smith and Wesson and held the gun out in front of her as she moved. She opened the door slowly, assessed the living room in darkness, and stepped cautiously. She glanced up at the CCTV screen and saw the floodlit front gates. Then the screen went black.

"Shit." It was too dark to see anything except pitch-black out the window overlooking the cove. She headed out the door. Keeping her back to the villa she moved slowly toward the driveway.

The veranda door opened. She spun around, and pointed the gun at Simone, and spoke in an irritated whisper. "Fucking hell. I said, stay in the bedroom." She was too jumpy. She took a couple of deep breaths. "Go back."

"No. I'm not staying in there if you're out here."

She puffed out a sharp breath. There was no point in arguing. They didn't have time and she needed to find out what was on fire and whether there had been a breach of the perimeter. She turned her head back to the driveway and scanned the route as far as she could see. The fire was on her right-hand side, to the east, some distance away. It would take a while to reach the villa given the lack of any notable breeze and undergrowth that remained a little damp after the recent showers. It would more likely eat into the drier terrain up the eastern cliff.

She moved into the undergrowth, keeping the driveway on her right, and made her way slowly toward the front entrance. Simone followed her. She stopped halfway and waited, listening for new sounds. The gates hadn't been breached before the video blacked out, but that didn't mean they hadn't been subsequently. But whoever it was would approach in vehicles, not on foot. It was too far to walk, and they wouldn't announce their arrival by starting a fire. She was pretty sure the gates hadn't been breached and this was a warning, otherwise she would have spotted someone by now. "Stay here, Simone, I'm going to check the gates." Simone shook her head. "I mean it. Stay here. I will be careful. I don't think anyone has entered the grounds. Call Roberto and tell him to get men out here, now. And call the Vigili del Fuoco. Tell them we have a fire close to the perimeter of the estate that appears to be spreading eastwards."

Simone nodded and took Maria's phone.

Maria made her way swiftly through the undergrowth. The orange glow became visible. The smell of smoke became stronger, and tiny flickers of ash drifted like pollen in the air. She stopped and listened again. Still nothing other than the intermittent crackling of burning wood. She moved again and stopped when the gates came into view.

They were closed and shrouded in darkness.

She breathed a long sigh and slumped onto the ground. Her hands trembled and her heart thundered in her ears. She waited until the Maserati arrived before standing and making her way back to Simone.

Roberto stood in the living room, Angelo to his right and a man Maria didn't recognise at his left side. She didn't care to know who he was, just that he could do the job, and, in that respect, she had to trust Roberto.

Given the proximity of the fire to the boundary, the services surmised a firebomb had been used to start it. They had quickly brought the blaze under control. It had been one of several fires started that evening, the officer had said, and another indication of an escalation in mafia-related activities.

Maria paced the living room. "This is a warning."

Roberto stood to attention. "Yes, Donna Maria. It was my fault."

"Did you know this might happen?"

He shook his head.

"Then you have nothing to be ashamed about. Maybe this was a planned attack to show us they know our movements. Maybe a distraction to stretch the rescue services. Do you think Beto set you up?"

"No."

"I don't either. We need to move from here."

"Where to?" Simone asked.

Maria had considered going to her uncle's restaurant, but that would expose Lorenzo and Paola, and she couldn't do that to them. They had moved away from the mafia years ago and managed to stay away. There was only one place they could go.

"My mother's." Simone's eyes widened. "There's CCTV and we can coordinate our activities from there. And..." She stopped speaking as her stomach dropped. The urge to ensure her mother's safety was a fierce driver and the only way she could do that was to keep her mother closer.

"Your mother's house is easier to protect, Donna Maria."

She nodded then looked to Simone. "Go and pack some things. We need to go now." Simone went into the bedroom. Maria looked back to Roberto. "First light of day, see what you can find out from Beto about this?"

"Yes, Donna Maria."

She turned her attention to Angelo. "I want you to keep eyes on my sister's house." She trusted him and if she needed someone to keep Catena safe, she would rather it was he who did it.

Angelo frowned. "Donna Maria, what about Vittorio?"

Her brother-in-law's name still stuck in her throat when it came to his involvement in the business. He had been reckless, nearly got himself killed and could easily have taken Roberto down with him. He had been left with a partial paralysis for his poor judgement and as much as he might make a great father to his son, she still couldn't help but think of him as a liability in the business. "I can't involve him in this."

Angelo stood taller. "He should know about the threat, Donna Maria."

Maria gritted her teeth. He was right. How could Vittorio defend his wife and baby if he was unaware? She nodded. "Tell him that the Amatos are escalating. He should take his family out of the city for a while."

Angelo nodded. "I will make sure of it."

"Thank you."

Simone appeared from the bedroom with a suitcase. Maria noted the gun tucked inside her waistband. Warmth spread across her chest. Simone hadn't been scared earlier and she had been right to follow Maria out of the house. They were stronger together than apart. "We have to get moving."

"Do you need us to follow you?"

"No. Simone can take the Romeo and I'll take the scooter."

Maria paced the kitchen, her mother's concerned gaze on her every pensive move. "How, matri? How can I make this go away?"

The silence became dense and prickly.

"You need to leave, Maria. You will find a life together. Maybe in America or Australia. They are big countries and it would be easier to hide there."

Maria stopped and shook her head at her mother. "No. I don't want to hide."

Simone looked from Maria to Maria's mother. The early light of the day filtered in through the kitchen window as she sipped her coffee. The increase in temperature didn't do anything to alleviate the tension in the room.

"And now you are not safe, matri." Maria ran her fingers through her hair. *Fucking mafia.*

Her mother sighed. "We have been through these troubles many times before, tesoro. I have good security here, and now I have a handsome man watching me." She smiled.

Maria shrugged. "I had good security at the villa, matri, and look what happened. It's not enough now."

She joined her mother and Simone at the table, and they sat in silence drinking coffee. Maria turned to her mother. "Can you ask the mayor to help?"

Her mother remained silent for a moment longer. "I can try."

Maria felt the weight lift slightly from her shoulders. "Maybe he can speak to the commissioner? They dine at the same restaurants, frequent the same golf club."

"I would expect so. I will speak to his wife. She knows how to get him to listen."

"Massina said there are people at the DIA who would like to see the back of the Amato problem. There are bound to be officials within government circles who would like the problem to go away too. People who don't want to get their hands dirty. Especially after the fires across the city last night. We weren't the only ones targeted. There will be more disruption to come." She took in a deep breath and looked from Simone to her mother. "We will pay whatever it costs, matri." Her mother nodded. Maria's coffee tasted sweeter. The mayor was their best chance.

"And what if he can't help us?" Simone asked.

The sticky silence resumed.

Maria looked at Simone with a heavy heart. "Then we either stay and continue the fight, or we run."

Maria's mother squeezed Simone's arm as she studied her daughter from across the table. "You must both run, Maria. This is not your fight anymore."

Maria looked away for a moment then lowered her head and rested it in her hands. "That depends on Giovanni's ability to take care of the business."

"Business isn't everything, tesoro. Love is what matters."

Maria saw remorse in her mother's eyes, the same sadness that came to her when she thought about her father. Her mother was right. Love was all that mattered. In the end, it was love that had drawn her back to Sicily. Her love for Simone...and her love for her family, and Giovanni was a part of that family. "I cannot leave you again, matri. Not until this is finished."

Her mother shook her head. "You are too stubborn, tesoro."

"Yes, she is," Simone said, staring at Maria with glassy eyes and flushed cheeks. "That's why we love her, isn't it?" She smiled at Maria's mother.

Maria's mother patted Simone's arm. She stiffened her back and cleared her throat. "You found a good girl, tesoro. I am happy for you both."

Maria's heart registered her mother's acceptance of Simone. She turned to face Simone and wanted to kiss her. "Yes, I did. And I intend to keep her." As she watched Simone's cheeks darken, her heart fluttered. "Let's hope the mayor can pull strings for us." Simone nodded. Maria's mother rose swiftly and moved away from the table.

"I'm going to call him now and arrange to meet. We need to know."

"Yes, we do." Maria sat back in the chair, wanting to feel a sense of relief but unable to fully embrace it until she had an answer. As things stood, they were on the back foot. Their men were spread thinly and at some point, she would need to consider retaliation or risk losing face. If the mayor couldn't help, the war would be a bloody one, but she would lead, and she would do whatever necessary to take down the Amatos.

28.

Patrina looked up from page twenty-eight of the broadsheet newspaper, the column of small print that talked of a number of fires that had been started during the night. Three estates had been targeted, two of which belonged to prominent members of the authorities. The third, Maria's villa, caught her attention. The door to the penthouse suite opened. She stopped reading, folded the paper and put it on the table. Tommaso strode confidently toward her. "You look happy?" she said. His kiss was brief and tasted of coffee and sugar.

"Today is a very good day," he said. He sat at the table and poured himself a small coffee and filled the cup to the top with hot milk. He picked up a slice of salami, placed it in his mouth and chewed.

She watched him. In the absence of waiting staff, her husband would have expected her to cater to his demands. Tommaso never did. Often, he served her. "Did you see the news?"

He shook his head, took a piece of bread, and broke off the end. He dipped the chunk into his coffee and ate it. "What news?"

"The fires?"

"I haven't seen the papers. This is good salami. We should serve this at the café."

She didn't disagree. One of the things she liked about Tomasso was the fact that he had good taste. The lines in the newspaper came to her again. She tensed to stop the ache in her heart that hadn't lifted since Maria had walked out. *Goodbye, Patrina,* she had said. The finality sat like lead, as it had done when she had believed Maria had died. She may not agree with Maria about Tommaso, and she intended to prove Maria wrong, but she didn't enjoy the feeling that came with knowing Maria was alive and not in her life. When they had plotted to kill Alessandro, it had been so their families could get back to working more harmoniously together. She had dared to hope that might have led Maria back to her. She had been delusional, of course, and she didn't want to go against Maria now. But she had to ensure her own future. What else could she do? Maria had brought this upon herself.

"Who do you think is behind them?" she asked.

"The fires? I don't know."

"Strange they would target Maria's villa, don't you think?"

"Did they? Maybe because it is empty. It will be a petty gang. Kids wanting to stick two fingers up to the authorities."

How did he know the other two attacks were government officials' houses? She dismissed the thought. He must have seen or heard something and just forgotten. "What's that got to do with Maria?"

He looked at her and smiled. "I don't know. I'm just guessing because you asked me. I have no interest in that. I told you. I have more exciting news. Would you like to know?"

He looked engrossed in whatever it was he wanted to say. "Yes, of course." He leaned toward her. His eyes had that familiar glint in them. *Power.*

"Stefano is being moved."

Patrina's chest constricted. She remained silent, processing his words, and unable to formulate a coherent response.

"I thought you would be happy. He's being moved to Carcere Boniciro di Siracusa." His frown deepened.

"Yes..." Had Stefano paid someone? Where the hell had he got money like that from? They certainly didn't have it. She couldn't think of anyone who owed them that kind of favour and if there had been, she certainly wouldn't have asked them. Stefano was better placed in isolation, incarcerated in a cell for the rest of his life, as far as she was concerned. Boniciro was a soft touch prison by comparison. He would be able to increase his influence inside and outside from there, in a way that wasn't easily achieved from Palermo prison. "Why are they moving him?"

"This is where it gets interesting."

He had her attention.

"The request has come from the DIA to the prison governor, which means he's talking to the police."

Her inner voice was telling her no repeatedly. Stefano would never break the code of silence. She shook her head. "He wouldn't do that."

Tommaso shrugged. "I agree. The authorities must have their reasons. But you know what this means for us?"

She saw excitement in his lingering gaze. Her heart skipped a beat. If he was about to suggest what she thought he was, he was effectively putting his trust in her. She could have him killed if he pitched this wrongly and he would know that. "What?" Would he lay his cards out?

"Patrina, this is our chance."

His hand was warm and strong around hers. If he had any fear about taking out Stefano, he didn't show it. She liked that…liked that a lot. The thought permeated and started to take shape. They could take out Stefano and run the business together. It was the best opportunity and probably the only chance she would ever have to get to Stefano. She looked into Tommaso's eyes and saw her future with him. Days such as these, but with one difference that she had never experienced before. Freedom. "When?"

"Tomorrow. This is a protected move, so no one else knows." He kissed the back of her hand. "This is a great opportunity for us, Patrina. I can organise it, so you will be safe, and I will make sure nothing traces back to you."

She nodded. A mild sensation of guilt pricked her, and she mentally batted it away. She owed Stefano nothing. No matter how long they had been together, and even with all that they had shared, he didn't deserve her pity or her loyalty. She thought about Maria and the fact that it would solve the problem for them both. It would also prove to Maria that Tomasso had honourable intentions toward her and the Amato business. Her husband would get what he deserved the same way his nephew had, and there wouldn't be a tear shed in his name.

Tomasso was handsome; his goatee was trimmed and cut perfectly to shape his jaw, his eyes were bright and alive, and his smile was inviting. He looked impeccable at her side, as well as having an astute mind and ambition. She smiled at him and his cheeks darkened. "Yes. I want you to take the hit on my husband."

29.

The relief they had shared following the mayor's agreement to initiate a transfer for Stefano had been quickly overshadowed by Maria's increasing tension. In the last two days, since finding out the transfer details, Maria had become quieter and more distant, and Simone hadn't been able to reach her emotionally. It reminded Simone of the time she had turned up at Maria's villa, the night Maria went onto the boat with Alessandro and Patrina and never came back. The same night Maria made promises about a future they would have together, the night that had broken Simone's heart.

Simone had already sampled that future with Maria at the farmhouse and she was not inclined to let it go. If Maria was going to get her hands dirty, then so was she.

Maria hadn't glanced at her since Roberto and Angelo had arrived. Both men would have their own team for the hit, and she worried that not only would Maria get hurt, but there was a chance her brother could get injured or killed too. She would be left with no one in the world to care for, and no one who cared for her. *They will do it. They have to.* She swallowed hard past the lump in her throat, Maria's voice fading as she ran through the details of the plan.

"The van leaves Palermo at eleven-ten this evening and will travel out of the city on the A19, picking up the E932 straight to Siracusa. There will be a driver and guard in the front of the vehicle and two guards in the back with Stefano. They're scheduled to arrive at the Carcere Boniciro di Siracusa at one-forty-five a.m. There are two sets of road works currently on the A19 before the junction to Caltanissetta. We will create a new diversion at that junction of the E932 and the SS122 and bring the vehicle off the main road there." Maria pointed to the map on the table. "Capisci?"

Roberto and Angelo nodded.

"Angelo, you set up the diversion. Roberto, I want three men on the SS122 to stop the vehicle, another two either side of the road in support. I will be with you. The team will take out the guard detail and I will take responsibility for Stefano. If we could do this without killing the guards that would be my preference, but we can't. So, we will do whatever it takes. The families of the men who lose their lives will be adequately taken care of."

Roberto and Angelo nodded.

A chill passed down Simone's spine at hearing Maria talk about taking the lives of innocent men as effortlessly as tossing two dice onto a craps table. Judging by the sharpness of her features, the shadows under her eyes, and the way she carried herself with tension, this wasn't easy for Maria. It was necessary. Simone could see the signs, even if Maria's tone didn't betray her feelings. Her men wouldn't know what Maria didn't want them to. That didn't mean a great deal to Simone though. This was hurting Maria, and she felt every ounce of that pain.

"My team will travel back to Palermo after the hit via the 122 and the 121, staying west of the city. Angelo, your team are to take the coastal road. I am assured that the police will use the main roads once they realise the detail has been disrupted. We have a window of fifteen minutes, during which time all comms from the van will be down, so this job needs to be clean and swift."

"Yes, Donna Maria." Both men spoke in unison.

"What about me?" Simone asked. She had a distinct impression that Maria didn't want her involved, but she wasn't going to be ignored any longer.

"We'll talk later," Maria said without looking up from the map.

Simone's blood boiled. She gritted her teeth to stop from saying something she might regret. "I'm coming with you." Her brother was looking at her as if to say shut up. Angelo kept his focus on Maria.

Maria turned and looked at Simone through narrow eyes. Simone felt the sting in her chest. Maria pointed back at the map.

"I'll meet you in two hours at the service station, here. We'll move off from there together," she said to Roberto and Angelo. "Any questions?"

Both men shook their heads. She dismissed them with a nod of her head and turned toward the window as they left her mother's living room. With the click of the front door, she turned back to Simone.

Simone stood with her hands on her hips, her chest puffed out. "I'm coming with you," she said.

Maria shook her head. "Don't start this, please, Simone."

"Start what? We're a team. You said I did a great job the other night when we had the fire at the villa. You said I did the right thing by following you. You made a mistake then. You might make another one. I can help you. We are in this together."

Maria pressed her lips together then released a long breath. "This is not the same thing. I told you at the start, you need to follow my instructions. I want you to stay here with my mother."

"You want me to babysit your mother while you go off and potentially get yourself killed."

Maria shook her head. "That won't happen."

"You can't fucking tell me that. You were wrong last time. You could be wrong again." She knew she was right, and she knew Maria was right too. Her mind was blank one second and filled with thoughts the next, none of which made any sense. Her head felt tight with frustration. She wanted to be at Maria's side for this job and yet she didn't. She didn't want

Maria involved in the kill either. "Why can't one of your men take the hit?"

"Because this is my job. It's my responsibility. It's about respect, Simone. I don't expect you to understand—"

"Don't you fucking patronise me."

"Sorry, I didn't mean it that way. I must do this. I'm doing it for you and for me and for us and for every other poor bastard who has suffered because of that man. I need to know that it has been done properly. I can't run the risk of a fuck-up."

"You trust your men."

"This isn't about my trust in them. It's about me serving justice."

Simone shook her head in despair. Words eluded her. Maria looked thoughtful in the silence that separated them. Maria wasn't going to back down. Simone felt rigid with anger and fear. She wanted to hold Maria, but the distance between them seemed suddenly vast and growing quickly. She knew Maria's response was self-protection, and it sucked. Maria was looking at her, but all she could feel was cold detachment. She had seen the same look that fateful night too; she knew what was coming next.

"If anything happens to me, you leave here on the Octavia. It's at the port now, in the private moorings at the far side. There is a set of keys under the seat in the cabin. There is a gun in the locker in the living area, and one in the fishing box on the lower deck."

Simone couldn't speak, though she willed herself to acknowledge Maria's instructions.

"Tell me you will go, Simone. I need to know you'll claim your freedom. If something goes wrong, which I don't anticipate, they could still come after you here. If you leave, they will think twice, and that will be enough for you to get away."

Simone tried to speak. The words still wouldn't come. She cleared her throat. "Yes," she croaked.

"Good." Maria sighed. She closed the gap between them and tugged Simone into her arms. "It will be fine. We will get through this."

Simone pulled out of the hug. "I hope so, because I can't live without you."

Maria's eyes watered and her smile had a strain that Simone had seen before. There was always uncertainty and Maria had been trained to cope with the job, but Simone had a suspicion that this time Maria was more affected by the possibility of failure. The past did that...made the future more precious. Maria had been hurt before and that kind of trauma leaves a mark that runs deeper than any visible scar. The memory doesn't go away easily. "Are you all right?" She touched Maria's chest, the scar beneath the cloth of the T-shirt. "After this?"

Maria covered Simone's hand with hers. "I am. This will be a simple hit. I have good men around me. It's nothing like the last time."

Simone bit the inside of her lip as the fire engulfed her throat. The tears came too swiftly for her to stop them, and wet streaks formed on her cheeks, cool and infuriating. Her defiance faded with Maria's concerned gaze. Conceding to her desire to be held and comforted, she fell into Maria's arms. She closed her eyes. Maria's perfume resonated with her slow heavy heartbeat as she battled the insidious thought that this could be the last time that she held the woman she loved. Her mind went numb and she clung on tighter, unwilling to let Maria go. "I can't lose you again," she whispered. Maria's silence followed and the pain in her chest burrowed deeper.

30.

Stepping into Tommaso's inner sanctum knowing he was soon to take the hit on Stefano, Patrina felt dizzy with euphoria. The cooler air inside the building crept across her bare arms and the hairs on the back of her neck stood swiftly to attention. Her stomach buzzed with the thrill of celebrating with Tommaso in an hour or so, after he had disposed of Stefano. They would be free to stand at each other's side, to run the business together, and maybe even become husband and wife. She hadn't talked to him about marriage, but the thought had crossed her mind more than once since arranging the hit. With Stefano out of the picture, she had pondered her future and been surprised at the liberated feeling that had swept her away into a dream world that she couldn't have conceived of before. She stood outside the wooden door to his special room imagining the silk sheets on the bed softly caressing her skin and smiled.

Excitement, anchored in the occasions she had shared with him in this room, ignited a flame that moved like lightning to her core. She couldn't deny the effect he had on her. Maria had misjudged him, and he was about to prove his worth. It wasn't that she needed to prove anything to Maria. Even though they had parted because of their difference of opinions, it was heartening that Stefano's demise would enable Maria to also live freely. They would both get what they had strived for. Neither would live in the shadow of their past again after this night. A light airy feeling bubbled inside her and her hand trembled as she keyed the number into the pad. The latch stirred softly, and the door opened with a gentle hush.

The air inside the room carried a faintly sweet odour that emanated from the freshly laundered silk sheets. The bed looked pristine and inviting. She went to the cabinet, selected the brandy, and poured herself a large drink. A long slug slipped down her throat and a warm feeling caressed the butterflies in her stomach. She took another long slug and imagined Tommaso and the men surrounding the vehicle, and firing the bullet that would end Stefano's life. Then her thoughts shifted, and she became entranced by the burning heat in her throat. What if things went wrong and Tommaso got killed? Her stomach lurched.

She finished her drink and poured another, sat at the table, and imagined him opposite her, smiling at her, celebrating together. The ache in her chest became heavier. Her life would be nothing without him. *Please, don't die.*

*

Maria looked skyward as a slight drizzle started to fall. If the rain became heavy, it would slow the van and that could play to their advantage. Angelo had the roadblock in position on the junction of the A1, which would redirect the prison van. The driver would call in the deviation and he would be told to proceed. She hoped the assurances she had been given by the mayor played out that way. If they didn't, anything could happen. She had never put her faith in anyone outside her team before. Her mother had insisted that the mayor's wife would not let them down.

She had positioned a car on the opposite side of the road. The orange flashing light of the vehicle repair truck parked in front of it provided the only light on the road. The man with his head inside the engine of the car was one of their men. A construction lorry was waiting further down the road, along their escape route to the west, and it would approach the broken-down vehicle when the prison van approached from the other direction. This would force the prison van to move into the narrow layby to pass the chaos on the road. At this point, they would ambush the van. Roberto and three men waited under the cover of the trees at the side of the layby ready to stop the van and approach it from the front. Maria and two men waited at the entrance to the layby. They would force entry into the back of the van once it had been stopped.

She replayed the plan in her head, checked her phone for the time and looked up again at the grey blanket blocking the stars. *Come on, rain.* In ten minutes, this would all be over. In an hour she would be in bed with Simone. They would be free.

*

Patrina jolted at the sound of deep voices and snapped her head toward the door. More than one voice. Deep. Men. Two men. Laughing. Her heart thundered. Something felt wrong. She got to her feet, pulled her gun, and pointed it at the door. Her reaction was instinctive, and the intensity of the situation enveloped her instantly. The pounding behind her ribs reverberated in her throat. She stiffened her arms and curled her finger around the trigger, stopping at the point of greatest resistance.

The lock clicked and the door opened.

"Tommaso." She gasped and dropped her arms to her side. She went to take a pace toward him, but there was something unfamiliar and disconcerting in his stare.

She froze.

*

Maria waited until the car had passed and jogged the length of the layby toward Roberto. The prison van should have reached the junction by now. These routes were timed to the minute. Something was amiss. "Any news?"

He shook his head. "There's shit going down at the plaza. I've got people watching but told them not to engage. The Riverside is quiet."

"They're trying to draw us into the gutter. Where the fuck is that van?"

"Want me to get someone tracing the route? Maybe it broke down." He shrugged.

He was as unconvinced by that argument as she was. The notion that the mayor had set them up had crossed her mind, but it didn't ring true. Maybe she just couldn't bring herself to believe it. She had to trust her instincts. He may be weak, but he wasn't underhanded. Setting her up wouldn't serve anyone. Her phone pinged. *Angelo.*

Still nothing at this end.

Shit. "They're still not at the junction. I don't like this, one bit." She turned and walked back to the entrance of the layby. Her phone rang. She looked at the screen. Now she knew there was a problem.

"Massina."

"Maria. He's been busted."

"What?"

"The van was ambushed at the Cefalù junction. Where the hell are you?"

"Fuck." She paced the road, wringing her fingers through her hair. "We're further out. Fucking shit." Ice shot down her spine. "I need a favour."

"Maria, there was a shit storm going down here before this fucking mess. Stefano is on the loose, and I need to track him down."

"Please. I have to get Simone out of the city."

The silence became oppressive.

"Please, Massina. Can you go to my mother's and take Simone to the Octavia at the port? She knows what to do. I need to find Stefano."

"How are you going to find him?"

"Please. Just tell Simone, I'll meet her there as soon as I can. Tell her, we will leave Palermo. Arrest her if you have to. Just get her out of the way."

She should call Simone directly, but Simone would resist her instructions, and she didn't have the time for another debate. If Massina showed up, Simone would have to leave.

"What about your mother?"

"She's at my sister's house. I have men there and it will be Simone they go after first. They want to get to me."

"All right. But I will have to drop her at the port and run. I have shit to deal with."

"Thank you." The line went dead. Maria wiped the water from her eyes. *Now it decides to fucking rain.* "Roberto. There's a change of plan."

*

"Hello, Patrina."

Rigid with ice, she couldn't move or speak.

Holy fucking shit.

Stefano walked toward her, arms wide open, his smile bright and white, his eyes dark and sparkling like polished ebony.

"You won't need that now, will you?" He took the gun from her hand and placed it in his pocket.

He was the devil in living form, and she'd never felt more in need of her weapon. How the fuck was this happening?

"What, no loving greeting for your husband?"

He pulled her roughly into his firm arms and squeezed her too tightly. His hand massaged her breast, and his breath was hot against her neck and ear. She swallowed down distaste and fear. She had to breathe, had to think, had to make sense of this.

"Not quite the warm welcome I was expecting after all this time."

She willed herself to move, to embrace him and kiss his rugged, flushed cheek. Her thoughts wouldn't settle; they jumbled and tossed on the waves of increasing pressure in her mind. Then a nauseous feeling consumed all thought.

Tommaso watched her through a steady stare, and she wondered at the slight twitch at the corner of his mouth. He had helped Stefano escape. No, no, that couldn't be true. It was her time to die. Maria had been right. No, this wasn't what she thought it was. There must be a good reason for Tommaso to bring Stefano here. Perhaps he was going to do the job in front of her, or even give her the gun so that she could do it. She tried not to show her discomfort, presented a fragile smile over her husband's shoulder, and closed her eyes. Her insides quaked and her mind whirred with her recollection of the prison, imprinted strongly with the scent of urine, the chemical cleaning products used to wash the grey walls and floors, and the metal-on-metal clanging loudly in her ears. And then there was *him* pressing himself against her, his chest touching her breasts. Her stomach roiled. She refused to shed the tears that burned the back of her eyes and resigned herself to her fate.

Play the game, Patrina. She repeated the mantra, allowed herself to soften in his arms, and he released his grip sufficiently for her to ease back. She placed her hands on his strong, muscular biceps and looked into his eyes, wetting her lips so she could speak with affection. "You surprised me. My God, this is incredible. You look amazing."

His lips crashed onto hers. He breathed stale tobacco into her. His tongue hot and insistent, he took from her what he wanted. She eased out of his aggressive kiss. "How—?" He crashed his mouth to hers again. Pain shot through her lip and she winced. He pulled back.

And then he started laughing, and she saw the psychopath emerge in the whites of his eyes and his piercing glare.

Her blood curdled.

He glanced over his shoulder and lifted his chin to Vitale. "I fucking owe you, big time." He dipped his hand into his pocket and pulled out a mobile phone. He pressed the screen and held the phone up to Patrina.

She listened to Maria's voice…and then her own. She was going to die.

Vitale had bugged the penthouse suite and given the recording to Stefano.

She couldn't swallow, couldn't breathe and her legs felt as though they were going to give way. Her confession of love for Maria and the killing of Alessandro cycled with the spinning in her head and the ringing in her ears.

"You fucking double-crossing fucking whore bitch."

She didn't dare look in Tommaso's direction for fear of irritating Stefano further, if that was even possible. Her voice came in a whisper. "I can explain."

"Explain? There is no fucking explaining anything. It's fucking simple. You fucking betrayed me."

Stefano's eyes widened and his head twitched as he craned his neck toward her. He looked as if he might explode. She imagined her death. *Make it quick.* Then he straightened his body, put the phone in his pocket and started laughing. She watched his hand, her heart racing, expecting him to pull a gun on her. He stopped laughing as suddenly as he had started and smiled at her. He seemed to be enjoying himself.

"I'm going to kill you, you know that." He tilted his head and shrugged as if having a general conversation with her. He went to the table, poured a large brandy into the glass she had used and slugged it in one hit, then made a loud grunting sound as he swallowed. "That tastes like fucking nectar." He poured another and gesticulated with it in his hand as he spoke. "You see, Patrina, I always knew you worked for the fucking Lombardos. It's why I had to get rid of them. Calvino started to suck up to the authorities and clean up the Lombardos' act. He was getting in the way of progress. It's just business." He took another slug of his drink then twitched his head. "You never took care of my business, you lazy fucking bitch. Too busy fucking that fucking..." He gritted his teeth, seemingly unable to say Maria's name, his eye twitching violently.

Patrina's legs regained their strength. Her focus was sharper. Why hadn't he pulled the trigger already?

He shook his head. "Fucking shame. You see... Now, I have a big problem." He turned to Vitale and lifted his chin. "Brains, help me here."

"Yes, Don Stefano."

Patrina stiffened at Vitale's reverence to him. Brains was clearly the name Stefano used for Vitale. She'd blast the fucker's brains out if she could get near him with a gun. She watched Vitale give Stefano his undivided attention in a subservient manner that made her skin crawl. *Fucking bastard.*

"Help me with this problem, Brains."

"Of course, Don Stefano."

Stefano downed the rest of his drink. "Which one do I kill first? Do I make the fucking Lombardo suffer the most, the Di Salvo, or this whore?"

Vitale narrowed his eyes as if pondering the question.

"You'll never get to Maria," Patrina said.

"I have eyes on Simone, Don Stefano," Vitale said.

Rage flooded Patrina. She couldn't stop the words flying from her lips. "You fucking bastard, Vitale. And you're a lousy fuck. You know how small his dick is?" Patrina glared at her husband. If she was going down, which she was, then so was the bastard who had double-crossed her.

Stefano looked at Vitale's crotch and smiled as if pleased that he had something Vitale didn't have. He turned to Patrina and laughed. "You think I didn't give him permission to do whatever it took to find out the truth?"

A sharp sensation pierced her chest. She had been literally fucked, and in the worst way possible. Just one chance, and she would put a bullet through them both. Stefano planned to kill them all, and that meant she had a stay of execution. For how long before he changed his mind and pulled the trigger, she didn't know. But she needed to make every second count.

31.

There was only one person Maria could think of who would break Stefano out of prison and want him alive, only one person who could access restricted information such as the transit details for the prison move. Vitale must be behind it. And if that was the case, which she was certain it was, then she had to assume Patrina's involvement too. What the hell was Patrina doing? Vitale also had the perfect cover for Stefano. He could stay hidden at the warehouses until the initial chaos had calmed, after which he would surely leave Sicily. The police might eventually work out that Vitale was behind the bust and track him to the warehouses, but that would take days by which time Stefano would be long since gone.

She stood in the shadows, her focus shifting from warehouse to warehouse. Stefano had to be here. Angelo and two men to her right, gun in hand, also studied the warehouses for signs of occupation. Roberto, with a team of three, sheltered a few yards behind them. Roberto shifted his focus from the warehouses to Maria and back again.

The faint wailing of sirens came to her from the direction of the city. A streetlight overlooking the car park had been smashed, leaving one building shrouded in darkness. Rain thundered against the corrugated roofs. There was no movement, nothing that would indicate there was anyone on the inside, but that didn't mean anything. They would have to check inside each warehouse to be sure. She called Roberto and Angelo to her.

"We'll check the one in darkness first. That smashed light could be deliberate. Roberto, take your guys around the back. See if there's a window, any kind of access we can use."

"Carlos picks locks," Roberto said, pointing to a man who looked older than Maria.

"Good." She nodded to him. He dipped his head.

"Keep the noise down as long as possible. These places are giant echo chambers."

The men nodded. Roberto took his team to the rear of the warehouse under the cover of the other buildings on the site.

Maria moved toward the warehouse, crouched down in the cover of an electricity junction box, and scanned the surroundings. She indicated for her men to follow. Rustling noises became audible from the flora intended to add diversity to the area. She focused again on the building twenty metres away. Slowly, she edged toward the door, her heart racing. She tried the handle. *Damn.* It had been a long shot. She indicated for Carlos to start work on breaking the lock. Careful not to make a sound, she skirted around the outside. Nothing. The place was vast and there was no obvious way inside from what she could see. Whatever the hell Vitale did here, he sure didn't want anyone nosing around. She returned to the front door. "Any luck?"

"Tighter than a prison cell."

She drew a long breath and released it slowly, willing him to hurry up. A crack of thunder brought another downpour. *Fucking rain.*

She texted Roberto.

Anything?

She pocketed her phone, blinked to refocus, and listened.

*

"I'm sorry, I have to go now." Massina handed over Simone's suitcase and stepped off the Octavia.

Simone put the case on the deck. "I'll be fine." She didn't feel fine. She felt sick. "She's definitely coming, isn't she?"

"Yes. She won't be long, I'm sure. She was adamant that you both leave here as soon as she arrives."

Simone nodded. The sense of doom that had struck her when Massina had turned up at the door had lessened a fraction, but not enough for her to feel secure.

"Go in, before you drown." Massina seemed hesitant to turn away.

"Thank you."

"You're welcome, Simone."

The silence between them was filled with the patter of the rain against the deck, and Simone's concerns. The boat rocked with a gust of wind.

"She knows what she's doing," Massina said.

Simone swallowed. So, it seemed, did Vitale. At least Massina had told her everything she thought had happened. What Massina hadn't said, because she didn't know the answer, was what Maria was doing now. Trying to track down Stefano, yes. But surely that was futile. The man could be hiding anywhere. He would have a plan. "I know," she said.

She watched Massina drive off and the sinking feeling in her stomach became deeper and more disturbing. She found the keys under the seat as Maria had said, picked up the case, and went to the door of the main living area. She stepped into the living space and closed the door behind her. It was half past one. She couldn't sleep until she knew Maria was safe. She took her suitcase down to the lower deck and lay on the bed staring at the cabin roof above her head. She was trembling. She stood. Moving felt better than lying around doing nothing. She would make a drink and keep herself occupied until Maria arrived. She climbed the steps back into the living space.

She froze.

The cold metal dug into her temple. She glanced to her right to see the man dressed in black. He had moved swiftly and silently from behind the top of the steps. Fear vibrated in every cell in her body. She turned slowly and looked defiantly at the dark centre of the barrel. They must have been followed. "What the fuck do you want with me?"

The man laughed, a light but throaty sound suggesting he smoked heavily.

"The answer to that question should be obvious."

His accent was strong, though he also sounded more sophisticated than the Amato men she'd known while working at Café Tassimo. Now, she was the bait. It was Maria they really wanted, and they were using her to get to Maria.

The man smiled at her. "My name is Tommaso Vitale."

The bent DIA detective. She let the urge to slap the smug look off his face pass. He could shoot her before she reached him. He lowered the gun. "Get back down there." He pushed her down the steps into the lower cabin.

She stood in the bedroom facing him, swept strands of wet hair from her face, then crossed her arms. "Why are you here?"

"You are smarter than that, Simone."

Her name rolled off his tongue as an old friend's would.

"Save yourself and tell me, where is Maria?"

"She's not here." She turned away and then heard footsteps on the deck above her head.

"You are waiting for her?"

"I wasn't. I'm going fishing."

He laughed. "I can see Maria's attraction. You're feisty and loyal. Those are good qualities in a woman."

The door to the cabin opened and Patrina jerked toward Simone. Wet hair straddled her face, the bags under her eyes were deeper and heavier, and she had a look that said she had come face to face with death. Vitale bundled Patrina onto the bed.

"What's going on?" Simone caught Patrina's eye just as Stefano appeared in the doorway. Her heart moved into her throat and words deserted her. It was clear that whatever relationship Patrina thought she had with Vitale, she didn't, and it looked as though Stefano knew every secret Patrina had tried to hide from him. His eyes formed slits, his jaw moved with the grinding of his teeth and he looked around the room skittishly. They were going to die. Her mind went blank.

Vitale's voice deepened. "Where the fuck is Maria?"

"I don't know," she whispered.

Stefano stepped closer to Simone. Simone cowered. He sniffed at her and grinned. "She likes them sweet. Where's that fucking whore bitch who fucked my wife?"

Simone stifled a gasp. "Honestly, Stefano, I don't know." She hoped the use of his first name might reach something deeper inside him. It didn't. The loud crack came a split second before the sting. Her cheek flamed, her jaw felt broken, and her eyes watered. She screamed out and fell onto the bed. Tears streamed down her face and she prayed that Maria would stay away from the Octavia.

"You two stay here." Stefano said. "Brains, check her and then search the boat. There will be gear stashed. Find it."

Shit, the guns Maria talked about. Simone sat up swiftly and shouted. "You can play your games all you like, but Maria will kill you both. You're a fucking pathetic excuse for men." She ducked her head into her hands and adopted the foetal position as another blow struck her ribs and then another landed on the middle of her back. She screamed out as pain ripped like fire through her.

"Shut the fuck up, or I'll have to fucking kill you before your girlfriend gets here."

Simone stifled the sobs. As the door closed, she felt Patrina's hand on her shoulder. She flinched away and gritted her teeth as another sharp pain seized her. "Get the fuck off me."

*

Roberto steered the car into the road leading to the abandoned tech park. Hazard tape marked off the area of the incident still under investigation. Taped-off areas further restricted movement around the site. He drove through a temporary barrier and parked close to the half-constructed building with doorways sealed by red and yellow criss-crossed tape.

"It's a long shot, I know. If he's not here, we'll call it a night." Maria got out of the car, pulled her collar up around her neck, and made her way to the taped entrance. Roberto moved a pace behind her, gun in hand. The remainder of the two teams had split up and were searching the other parts of the construction site. Patrina's perfume had been present at the warehouse and there had been a strong scent of male cologne. A glass half filled with cognac remained untouched on the table. The Amatos had been there recently and they weren't hanging around. This was the only other obvious place she could think that Stefano might go. It was out of commission and wasn't being monitored by the police. Her rationale wasn't the strongest, but other than a house to house search, it was all she had. She was desperate. If he wasn't here, their plan would need to be rethought. Time was running out.

Inside the building, running water echoed where rain fell through the unfinished roof and pooled on the concrete floor. Damp air chilled her. She stopped and listened beyond the echoing sounds.

"I don't think there's anyone here," Roberto said.

She wiped her face and stepped cautiously, further into the darkness. They went through another hole in a wall that should have become a doorway, perhaps leading to a beautifully furnished high-tech facility, or a library, or a canteen. The floor was dry and the air slightly warmer.

There was nothing to suggest they had been here.

They moved swiftly from space to space, navigating collapsed beams and brick rubble, half-constructed walls, and metal girders that should straddle the doorways and windows. They moved through another hole and the unfinished block wall opened into a larger space, with pillars that might be used to section the room. A crashing sound from somewhere in front of her made her heart race. She stopped and tried to listen beyond the thundering of her heart and took a deep breath. "Something's fallen from the roof?"

"Sounded like it. It's not safe."

She turned to Roberto and nodded. "Let's get out."

They moved swiftly back to the car, retracing their route into the building.

"What next?" Roberto asked.

Maria stared out the passenger window at the destruction that should have been her father's legacy. She looked at her phone. It was two-forty and there was no response from Simone. Just a text from Massina to say that she was settled on the boat. Simone must be asleep. "We're done for the night." She turned to him. "Can you drop me at the port? We'll stay out at sea for a few hours. See what you can find out from Beto. I want eyes everywhere."

Roberto dropped Maria at the main road. The Octavia was moored a short walk along the port. She watched the Maserati's rear lights disappear, irritation brewing inside her. Where the hell was Stefano and how was she going to get to him now? This was a fuck-up of the worst kind. She had promised Simone they would leave. They had come so far, and now they would still be running. Simone had said they would always be running. Maybe she was right. *Fucking mafia.*

The Octavia sat in darkness. The metal chains that formed a low boundary around each deck of the craft chimed hauntingly on the wind. Police lights flashed from the top of the vehicles stationed at the far end of the main shipping area of the port, where the bulk of the moorings were located. The police would be patrolling. There was some comfort in that.

She stepped onto the deck and through the door to the main living space. A chill shot down her spine. It was too late to reach for the gun at her side. Too late to react and respond to what might happen next.

The click stopped her heart.

The loaded gun dug into her back. *Fuck.* "Vitale, I assume?"

32.

Stefano stepped out of the darkness at the far end of the living room, behind the stairs to the lower deck, and walked toward Maria. "I knew you would come." He grinned, opened her jacket, and removed the gun at her side. "Nice piece." He tucked it into his trouser waistband to join the three other weapons he had acquired.

Maria recognised the two guns from the Octavia and snub nose that Patrina always carried. There was still the harpoon gun attached to the outside of the lower deck, but that wasn't loaded and how the hell would she get to it? "You want me, Stefano. Take me, but let Simone go. She means nothing to you."

He laughed. "Wrong. Wrong. Wrong." He shook his head with each word.

Maria bit her tongue.

"See, if the bitch means something to you, then she means everything to me. Get it? It's really very easy to get. I should not need to explain this to you, Maria. See, you should already get it, cuz you fucked my fucking wife, remember."

Maria let the accusation ride over her. "Where is Simone?"

"Boring. Boring."

He paced toward the stairs to the lower deck and then back to her. He seemed to have acquired a nervous twitch since she last saw him, and it revealed the emotional state that accompanied his crazed mind. She needed to remain calm, though calm was hard to find under these circumstances. If she could bide her time, appeal to Stefano's ego, maybe it would be enough. Just one chance was all she needed, but to do what? *Discipline is the most important quality, Maria.* Her father's tone was softly reassuring. *Look into their eyes, Maria. Deep into their soul. You will sense the truth there.* Stefano was running a short fuse. Time was in short supply. They would have a better chance if they were on the outside of the boat rather than holed up inside. They could jump and would quickly become invisible in the darkness.

"So, it's like this, Maria. You bitches are going to die."

"Where is Simone, Stefano? She has nothing to do with this. You want to kill me, I get that. But why Simone? She is innocent and you have bigger fish to catch." This might be a waste of time but talking could lead to distraction and that might create an opportunity. He clearly had a plan, or he would have killed her and Simone already. Patrina might already be dead. "You're growing the business. You don't need this shit, surely?"

The whites of Stefano's eyes became whiter. He leaned toward her and she smelt alcohol. He stared at her with his head on a tilt and then backed away.

He prodded his finger at her as he spoke. "Guilty. Guilty. Guilty."

Maria tried to swallow as she stared back at him. She had nothing with which to wet her lips. Her tongue felt too big for her mouth, and sticky.

Stefano lifted his chin, sending a message to Vitale. The pressure in Maria's back lifted and Vitale went down the stairs to the lower deck. Maria waited, her heart running a slow leaden beat. She had to keep control. No matter what, she had to stay alert. Simone appeared at the top of the stairs. She had blood smeared at her mouth and her cheek looked badly bruised. The air bled from Maria's lungs and she fought the urge to run to her and hold her. She stood taller and stiffened her posture. Simone would understand that she couldn't give anything away, not even to her. Patrina appeared. Maria tensed. Patrina glanced down at the floor. Maria turned to Stefano. As far as she could tell, it was the Vitale and Amato show. Two against three. Stefano was arrogant and deluded, though he held all the weapons. *Think, Maria. Think.*

"Sit the fuck down."

Stefano pointed to the leather-backed metal chairs around the glass-topped table on the starboard side of the room. The windows overlooked the lower deck of the cruiser and the central port with the lights on the police cars still flashing. The sea was as dark as the sky. It would be four hours or more until daylight broke, if they made it alive to see the light of day.

"I need some air." Simone said and received a thump to her face from the back of Stefano's right elbow. Blood oozed from her lip. She whimpered.

Maria jolted and stopped. She turned the rage inwards and felt it form a tight ball in her stomach.

"Fucking hell. How fucking difficult is it for you fucking bitches to follow a fucking instruction. Fucking. Sit. Down."

Maria took the seat at the end of the glass table facing toward the front of the boat. Simone sat at the other end and Patrina sat between them with her back to the windows and the port beyond.

"Brains, get this fucking boat moving. We're going on a trip."

Vitale exited through the door Maria had entered and passed along the outside of the deck. A moment later the engines whirred, and the craft eased forward slowly.

"Where are you taking us?" Simone asked.

Stefano's lips curled up, but it wasn't a smile. "I thought we could do breakfast at sea." He laughed. Maria stared at him. "You'll be the breakfast for the fish."

Maria glanced briefly at Simone and was pleased to see that his statement hadn't moved her.

The lights at the main port were fading quickly. Rain sounded against the roof and streamed down the windows, and the boat started to move on the waves the further out to sea they went. Maria felt the darkness encroaching inside her mind, the void sucking her in. *Stay present, Maria, stay present.* She closed her eyes and shook her head to disperse the feeling. The sounds were changing, becoming muffled and indistinguishable. *No, please don't do this.* The pressure on her chest threatened to crush her and it was becoming harder to breathe. No, she screamed silently. *No.* She opened her eyes. A flash of light expanded in her chest. Stefano's features were strongly defined. She could hear him swallow and smell his sweat. The long hand on the clock on the wall moved subtly with every click. There was a strong smell of diesel and salt. She had never felt more alive.

"I'm going to be sick," Simone said, holding her stomach. "I really need some air."

Stefano moved to the table and looked out the window. He moved to the port side of the boat, keeping one eye on the women, and glanced out the window there. "You'll have to fucking—" Simone retched. He groaned. "Get the fuck outside." He ushered them through the door and onto the back of the lower deck.

Maria sat on the starboard bench with Simone to her right. To Simone's right the deck stretched a path to the front of the boat and steps leading to the middle and upper decks. It would be a route to the Captain's cabin, to where Vitale was steering the craft. Patrina sat on the rear bench, to Maria's left. Stefano paced the space between them, facing the women, moving his focus from one to the other. The boat heaved on a wave, and then so did Simone.

"It's not their fault, Stefano."

Stefano glared at his wife. "Did I ask your opinion?"

Patrina shook her head. Her back jarred as the boat took another dive. She cursed under her breath. If only she could get to the fire extinguisher on the inside of the door they had just walked through.

"What do you want, Stefano?" Maria asked. "Money? I can give you wealth."

"Stop fucking talking, bitch. Alessandro is trying to speak to me. This is important." He held the top of his head in his hands, his focus still shifting from one woman to the other.

Patrina caught Maria's eye. They were both thinking the same thing. How to escape?

"Patrina first, then Simone, then Maria." Stefano smirked. "That's my boy."

"He wasn't your boy, Stefano," Patrina said.

Stefano rose up in height and strode across the deck. "You fucking dare."

"He was your nephew."

Stefano struck her across the face. She turned swiftly to face him again. "You know fucking nothing."

Patrina righted herself on the seat and watched Stefano playing out his tortured mind, determined not to show him the pain that he had inflicted. And then the penny dropped. "Fucking bastard son. You fucked your brother's wife?" Well that explained the fact that he had treated Alessandro like his own from the time he was born. She had just thought of him as a doting mafia uncle. He wouldn't be the first. A nephew was family and family were sacred.

He pulled the gun from his waist and pointed it at Patrina. "I'm telling you. Shut. The. Fuck. Up. I am trying to talk to Alessandro."

"I don't give a shit. Kill me. You're going to anyway. What are you waiting for?" She knew one of the things he was waiting for was to be far enough out to sea for any shots fired not to be heard.

Maria shook her head and mouthed *'no'* to Patrina. Patrina eased back on the bench and glared at her husband.

They had to do something before he stopped the boat. She glanced at Maria. Maria glanced back at her. She knew that look. It said, how do we get out of this?

"I will shoot you if I have to. But Alessandro wants you to drown and this is his decision…" He glared at Maria. "And you, bitch, are going to watch them die before I kill you."

"You bastard." Simone spat the words at him. Her stomach churned.

She had watched Patrina communicating silently with Maria. They were trying to work out how to escape but without the chance to talk it was close to impossible. If they tried to jump Stefano, someone would get shot and that had better not be Maria. Leaping overboard they could get lost in the darkness and swim, which would be good, but without a float and in the choppy sea this far from shore they would likely drown before they got back to the port. "I need the bathroom."

He laughed. "Nice try. Piss yourself."

She did. There was something soothing about the warm feeling and then it became part of the chill and the rain that had soaked her. She leaned back with relief, and that's when she spotted the flare attached to the outside of the cabin. It was out of arm's reach, just beyond the first aid box. She glanced again and quickly looked back to Stefano. "Do you mind, I'm taking a piss," she said.

He laughed. "You're funny." He laughed louder.

"Fuck off."

"Oooo, got a feisty and a sweet one there," he said, making his point to Maria. "How do you do it?"

"Do what, Stefano?"

"Get women to love you."

"You jealous, Stefano?"

He laughed raucously.

The lights at the port looked like stars from this distance, flickering in and out of sight. The horizon merged with the sea, black on black. They were surrounded by darkness made up of shades of grey, except for the illumination at the front of the boat. At least the rain had eased a fraction.

Stefano nudged his chin forward, and stared at Maria, tilting his head from side to side. "You will suffer the most."

"Leave her alone," Simone said.

He glared at Simone. He looked like a mentally disturbed hen, one bird whose thick, vulgar neck Simone would be happy to wring. A fake laugh, one built on an uncontrollable mix of fear and anxiety, bubbled in her chest. He plucked his phone from his pocket and pressed the screen.

He put the phone to his ear. "Stop the boat."

Simone's heart thundered and she looked up at the clouds. The effect of the waves rocking the boat ceased to affect her. Time stood still. Her breath caught, then gave way to trembling that gripped her uncontrollably. The engine quieted, and the boat took on a gentle bobbing motion.

She waited, noted the narrowing of Stefano's eyes and the broadening of his smile that suggested he knew he was on the verge of success. He brushed down his shirt as if he was about to attend an important meeting and ran his hand across his tightly shaved scalp. He clapped his hands and then rubbed them together.

"You first," he said, looking directly at Simone. He threw a rope to Maria. "Tie her feet together. Good and tight."

Please, God, help us. Please, God.

This was it. She was going to die.

33.

Maria's hands shook, and the rope was wet and stiff from the waxy coating that hadn't yet been worn from the new weave. She couldn't look at Simone as she threaded the knot. She had failed her. She stopped tying and ran her fingers along Simone's calf for the last time. "I love you," she whispered. When she looked into Simone's eyes, she could barely see through the tears. Simone's smile did little to ease the ache in her chest. She rubbed her eyes with the back of her hand and carried on tying, leaving the rope as loose as she could. Simone was indicating something to her with her eyes. Something that Maria couldn't see, to Simone's right, where the edge of the lower deck cut a path to the front of the boat.

"Brains, check that fucking rope. And tie her hands to her feet. She'll go down like a rock."

Maria stepped to Simone's right as Vitale pushed past her. She took a pace back, giving her a better view to the front of the boat. What was Simone trying to say? She glanced at Vitale as he tied Simone's hands, then glanced down the deck. Simone's whimpering ripped through her heart.

"Stop fucking whining. Drowning's an easy way to go. You're lucky." He glanced at Patrina.

Maria looked up and saw it—the flare gun clipped to the deck wall. Her heart raced and a smile grew inside her. She glanced across at Patrina.

"What you staring at her for? She's not going to save you."

She didn't know if Patrina had smiled at her just to rile her husband, but Maria certainly had done it to get a reaction from him.

"You fucking whore bitches are still at it. What the fuck are you doing with that rope?"

"Ready, Don Stefano."

Simone pulled in vain against Vitale as he finished tying her hands to her feet.

"Stand the bitch up."

Vitale pulled Simone to her feet. Her body was bent-double. Her heels touched the upright of the bench-seat she had been sat on. Another wave hit the side of the boat behind her. She prayed.

"Now, this is the bit I've been wanting to see. You." Stefano pointed at Maria.

Maria took a step back so she could clearly see the flare gun. It was out of arm's reach, but she had a plan. "Yes."

"You push her over the side."

Maria looked at Simone, crouched and shaking, and then back at Stefano.

"Wait." Patrina stood.

Stefano turned swiftly, pulled a gun, and pointed it at her. "Back off, bitch. You're going in next."

"Stefano." He kept his gaze on Patrina. "This is insane."

Maria inched closer to the flare gun.

"What do you care? The bitch stole your fucking lover. How fucked up is that?" He laughed and twitched.

Maria caught Patrina's eye and indicated for her to back off. She sat down and Stefano returned the gun to his waist. He rubbed his hand across his scalp. "Now throw the fucking bitch over the side." He was looking at Maria.

Maria hesitated.

"Right, Brains, you fucking do it. I haven't got all night. I need a fucking drink. We got to get out of here before it's fucking daylight. Get on with it."

Vitale grabbed Simone's arm. She thrashed against him and toppled forward onto the deck and onto her side and crunched herself into a tight ball. Vitale bent down and took a grip on the rope. He yanked her up, tugged her to the side, and levered her using the seat and his knee. He shoved her overboard.

The splash couldn't be heard above Maria screaming and pointing at Patrina. "Watch out, Patrina."

Patrina stood up and Stefano pulled his gun on her again. Vitale turned toward the husband and wife. It was the split-second Maria needed. She kicked Vitale hard in the back, throwing him forward and he sprawled onto the deck. She grabbed the flare gun from the wall, pointed it at Stefano and pulled the trigger. A trail of blinding white light flew in a direct line into Stefano's chest and tossed him like a ball. The gun spun from his hand and hit the deck. Patrina dived to grab it. Stefano's scream died instantly as his body flew backwards and over the portside of the boat. Vitale scrambled quickly across the deck after him and jumped, but not before Patrina fired off a volley of shots. He screamed out before the water silenced him.

Maria jumped into the sea.

Working in blindness, she dived down at the spot she thought Simone had hit the sea. The boat was bobbing on the waves though; Simone could be hard to find. She had to be close. She had to be. She thrashed her arms and legs, turning circles under the water, submerging slowly, covering as big a reach as she could. The voice in her head screamed at her to find Simone quickly. Her lungs were bursting. She turned a deeper circle, reaching out, grabbing the water, and praying.

A new sensation at her fingertip fired her to push harder. She drove down with her hands and grabbed again. Simone's hair. She tugged and heaved and reached for a stronger hold. Her lungs were screaming, and a sharp pain was trying to force her to inhale. *Fight, Simone. Help me.* She kicked hard with her legs, pulled with her free hand, and dragged Simone's lifeless body toward the surface.

She kicked harder, willing the surface to appear. Another kick, another push with her arm, and her head broke through the water. She gasped for air and choked on salty water as she tugged Simone up to the surface. Simone's limp body was working against her. She clutched Simone's head and lifted her until her mouth was out of the water. She was heavy, with her hands and feet tied together making it an almost impossible task. Simone was also unresponsive. Maria was losing her. She screamed to Patrina. "Help me." She held Simone as firmly as she could, kicking hard to stay above the water, and dragged her as close to the boat as she could get.

Patrina threw in a lifebuoy ring. Maria caught hold of it and relieved herself of the strain, gasping for breath. She screamed out with frustration, fighting exhaustion as she forced Simone onto the edge of float the only way possible, face down. Her head was out of the water, but she didn't look as though she was breathing. "Come on, baby. Please don't die on me." Her words got swept away. Hot tears stung her eyes. "Get a rope."

Patrina threw in a rope. Maria tied it around Simone and the float. Patrina took the strain. "We'll never get her over the side. We need to go to the back." The rear of the boat had a lower ledge. There was a ladder from the water to the deck and they would be able to lift Simone up more easily from there. Patrina held the rope taut from the top and Maria guided Simone and the float. Together, they lifted Simone onto the deck.

Maria wrapped her arms around Simone's limp body and turned her onto her back. Her knees were bent up to her chest. "Undo the ropes." She tilted her head back and breathed short fast breaths into her mouth, then thrust the palms of her hands down on Simone's chest, just above her heart, in the rhythm of a pulse to the count of fifteen. Water seeped from Simone's mouth as she pulsated her chest. "Come on, baby, please." Patrina released the ropes and straightened Simone's legs. Maria breathed another set of breaths and applied the pressure to Simone's chest again. Firmer and with an increasing sense of panic, she counted out loud. "Four, five, six—"

Water gushed from Simone's mouth, lifting her head from the deck. More water spilled from her and trailed down the side of her face and then she spluttered and started to cough.

Maria fell back onto her knees and tears flowed down her cheeks. She screamed out in relief, lifted Simone into her arms and rocked her as she sobbed.

34.

"Unlike the last time, I am delighted to be able to do this, Maria Lombardo." Massina smiled and held out her hand.

Maria shook it and sensed Massina's unwillingness to let go as she lingered on the threshold of the villa.

"Promise me this is the last time? I'd like to fill out that paperwork so I can't have you dying on me again."

"I promise you, I have no intention of going through this ever again."

Stefano Amato's body had been picked up by one of the police boats searching the area after Patrina made the call at just after four-twenty. The police report would read that Don Stefano's death was presumed to be an act of retribution as a result of him breaking the code of omerta. An investigation would be undertaken to find out the gang or gangs responsible for his death, although the resources given to that task would be too stretched to give it any proper attention. The mayor would give his heart-felt condolences to Lady Patrina and then the matter would be quickly put to bed. The fact that they hadn't located the body of Tommaso Vitale would be kept out of the news. Having Vitale's name associated with this latest event would do more damage to the DIA's reputation. The city had suffered enough that night, thanks to the instructions given by Vitale to create a diversion for Stefano's escape, and in the coming week the DIA would be expecting questions to be asked about the DIA's competence. They didn't have the answers, but time would bring a natural reduction in criminal activities and normal order would soon be restored to the city. There would be one less don to worry about and the authorities would breathe a sigh of relief.

Massina took a step toward her car then looked back over her shoulder. "Take care, Maria."

"I will." Maria shut the door and walked through to the living room. Patrina was staring out the veranda door into the darkness. "Help yourself to a drink. There's cognac in the cupboard." She didn't respond. "I'm going to check on Simone." Still no response.

She walked into the bedroom. Simone looked up at her through half-closed eyelids. Maria went to the bed and sat facing her. "Hey, baby," she whispered. She lifted a loose strand of hair from Simone's face and tucked it behind her ear.

Simone smiled. "You've never called me baby before."

She had, in the sea, at the point she thought Simone was going to die. But Simone wouldn't remember that and that was a good thing. Simone didn't need to know how close to death she had come. "It's how I feel about you... Not in a small screaming child kind of sense."

Simone chuckled. She squeezed Maria's hand. "I like it," she said, and her eyes closed.

The gentle sigh of Simone's breathing was music to Maria's ears. She leaned closer and kissed Simone's forehead. It was cool against her lips and she smelt of linen from the clean sheets and soap. It felt like returning home, comforting and reassuring. Maria eased back and tucked the cover around Simone's shoulders. She traced her fingertip lightly along Simone's eyebrow, followed the line of her temple, then her jaw, and then gently touched her mouth. Her skin was pale except for the red-black bruises around her right eye and cheek, and her lips were dry. The cut on her top lip was swollen and angry. The wounds would heal. Maria suppressed the urge to kiss her, every millimetre of her. She craved the feeling of Simone's precious warm breath against her mouth, their bodies touching along their length, and caressing Simone's breast in the palm of her hand. That time would come. Firstly, Simone needed to recover, and they both needed sleep.

She had never felt more scared than when seeing Simone unresponsive. Her heart had splintered, and her world had caved in, and in that moment in the water that had lasted an eternity she too would have allowed herself to drown with Simone. Something deep inside Maria had stopped her giving up on them both. Faith. Love. She didn't know. It was like a miracle that had come true. Now, she couldn't take her eyes off Simone. She felt so perfect to touch and so incredible to watch. Maria's heart raced and soft vibrations expanded from her chest and tingled her skin.

Lost in the preciousness of the moment and not wanting it to ever end, she had forgotten Patrina in the other room. Slowly, reluctantly, she stood and made her way to the door. She stopped and looked back; the drive to stay and observe Simone breathing was overwhelmingly powerful and it took all her willpower to not climb into bed next her. She resisted stepping out of the room, closed her eyes and savoured the moment. Reminded again of Patrina's presence in the villa, she took a long deep breath, opened her eyes, and exited the bedroom.

Patrina turned her head to Maria as she approached. "How is she?"

"Sleeping."

Patrina hadn't moved in the time Maria had sat with Simone. Maria went into the kitchen, took out a bottle of cognac and poured them both a drink. They stood in silence watching the sun bleed along the horizon. The clouds had disappeared, and the sea lapped gently at the beach. The contrast couldn't be more different from the rain of just hours earlier.

Patrina put her drink down and turned to Maria. "I'm sorry, bedda."

She was trembling. Maria held her arms open and Patrina leaned into them.

"I was so stupid."

Maria wasn't going to argue that point. "It's never easy, knowing who to trust." Patrina sniffled against her chest. "It's done, Patrina. It's over."

"Do you think *he's* really gone?"

She was referring to Vitale. "Whether you shot him or not, I wouldn't gamble on him making a five-kilometre swim back to shore in the pitch black." She had struggled for the minutes it had taken to retrieve Simone from the cold water and she was stronger and more capable than Vitale. Vitale would never have survived.

Patrina eased out of Maria's embrace. She was still trembling. "I hope so. I hate him more than I've hated anyone, even Stefano."

"He was nothing without Stefano behind him. Smart, yes. An opportunist who enjoyed exploiting a weakness for his own gain, yes. But he was a nothing."

Patrina shook her head. "What was I thinking? What scares me is that I believed he cared about me."

Maria sipped her drink. "He was a master manipulator, Patrina. Don't be too hard on yourself." She really wanted to tell Patrina that she didn't need a man like that at her side and that she could run the business just fine without one. But that would have been too much so soon. Patrina looked beaten and Maria knew what that felt like. "I'm sorry about Alessandro."

Patrina took a long breath, picked up her drink and took a sip. "I've been blind, haven't I?"

Maria thought about the nightmares and the episodes she had had, and denied, while at the farmhouse. She had nearly lost it on the boat, and even though she managed to hold herself together, she still had work to do to deal with the ongoing impact of her past. They all had a past, a history that defined their future. "I think sometimes it's easy to dismiss what we don't want to acknowledge. The familiar is more enticing to us than the potential that change might bring. It's comfortable, even though it's not necessarily healthy or the right thing to do. It's a tough choice because there's always a risk. The fear that we might be worse off if we change things."

"I think I always suspected Alessandro was his, deep down."

"The apple never falls too far from the tree, eh?"

Patrina huffed. "Stefano wasn't like that when we first met."

Maria hadn't known Stefano back then. "This life changes people, Patrina. Look at you and me. We're not who we once were."

Patrina stroked Maria's face. "Are we better people, bedda?"

Maria hoped so. "I would like to think so."

Patrina forced a smile. "I'm tired, bedda."

Maria nodded. Patrina was referring to being worn down by the business. It got to everyone at some point, in one way or another. Maybe you either go crazy or you find a way out. "Beto is a good man to have at your side. You work well together and legitimate business is always a way forward."

Patrina huffed. "As legitimate as this business gets. If we don't look after our clients, bedda, someone else will come and do it for us. That much never changes."

Patrina was right. Maria finished her drink. This wasn't Maria's world. It never had been. But now she could be out of it while still enjoying her family here in Sicily. "Our businesses can still support each other, Patrina. We will both be stronger that way."

Patrina's eyes sparkled as she smiled. "You are planning to stay?"

Maria thought about the farmhouse and the hens that were still being looked after by Madame Verdéaux, and the locals she had got to know who eagerly awaited the reopening of the restaurant so they could resume their social routines—card games, conversation, and sipping pastis while sat at the tables that adorned the street at the front of the restaurant. She would miss her daily walk to the boulangerie and their amazing pastries. She shook her head and smiled. "No. We won't be staying. We have a home in the Pyrenees to go back to."

Patrina nodded. "I'm pleased for you, bedda."

Maria saw loneliness. She had seen it many times before. It wasn't anything she could help Patrina with. Patrina needed to create her own life now that she didn't have Stefano undermining her. "What will you do?"

"I'll talk to Beto."

Red and orange streaks now marked the end of the sea and they watched the gold crescent rise and transform swiftly into a white ball. The sky had become a lighter shade of blue and light shimmered on the surface of the dark blue sea. It was a spectacular sight, and never more so than this morning. They had survived.

"I think it's time to sell the hotel, bedda."

Maria continued to stare out the window. Hotel Fresco had been Patrina's baby for as long as she could remember. The penthouse suite had been their haven and although things hadn't ended well between them, she had fond memories of their time together there too. This was a huge decision and not one Patrina would take lightly. "Wow."

Patrina sighed. "As you say, the familiar is more enticing. I think it's time for a change."

Maria smiled. "I think you're right."

Both women turned to the sound of the bedroom door opening. Simone's smile turned to a yawn. "I think I'm too tired to sleep."

Maria held out her arm and Simone snuggled into her body.

Patrina put her glass on the breakfast bar. "It's time I left you in peace." She picked up her phone and called Beto to collect her. "You may not be able to sleep, but I will."

"Well, I do need to pay a visit to my sister." Maria grimaced. Her sister, Catena, would not forgive her that easily for disappearing out of her life, coming back without a word, and then nearly getting killed again. She wasn't looking forward to the initial hello, but aside from that she couldn't wait to hold Flavio for the first time. If they hadn't arranged a Christening service for her nephew already, then she would look forward to helping her sister. They were in no rush to return to France.

"And your mother," Simone said.

Maria smiled at Simone. "She will expect us to have lunch with her, you know." In truth, she looked forward to being able to enjoy a relaxed meal with her mother. It had been a long time since they had dined together.

"And dinner. She won't want to let you out of her sight again."

"And dinner... And we can bring Pesto back with us. He's going to love being back at the beach." Simone squeezed her waist. "And he's going to love the farmhouse."

"Yes, he will," Simone said.

"I hope Giovanni recovers quickly," Patrina said. She lowered her gaze.

Maria pursed her lips as she nodded. She hoped so too. She wanted him back up and running the business as soon as possible, and without wishing to sound callous, the main reason was that she wanted to go home. "Yes."

"Do you think he'll accept a visit from me? I owe him an apology."

"You weren't responsible for what happened to him, Patrina."

Patrina held her hand up, palm facing Maria, and shook her head. "It was my fault. If I had taken better control of the business, it wouldn't have happened."

"It might have been a genuine accident," Maria said even though she thought it too convenient to be a coincidence. Patrina smiled at her as if reading her mind.

Maria tilted her head and smiled. "Shall I let him know you're going to call in on him?"

"Please... Thank you."

The buzzer to the front gates sounded. Maria went to the keypad in the kitchen and pressed the button to open them. Patrina walked to the front door and opened it as Beto arrived in the driveway.

"Come over for a drink, before you go back...both of you. To the house."

Maria nodded. She hadn't been to Patrina's house for as long as they had been together.

"Patrina, wait."

Patrina turned her attention to Simone who was walking toward her.

Simone wrapped her arms around Patrina and hugged her. "Thank you for helping us."

Patrina nodded, turned away and closed the door behind her.

Maria felt taller and stronger in Simone's aura. Simone came to her and she kissed her tenderly on the lips, leaving a tingling sensation that spread like fire across her skin. She couldn't love Simone more if they lived for another thousand years. There was nothing they couldn't achieve together. And now they had a future to build. Anything their hearts desired. She was not inclined to sleep, but her mind was becoming sluggish and her muscles were tired from the exertion. She looked into Simone's eyes and saw her own exhaustion reflected there. "Will you come and lay down with me for a while?" Simone took her hand and led her into the bedroom.

Her back ached and then the softness of the mattress eased the tension and she felt her weight sinking slowly. She eased her arm around Simone and held her close. Simone hooked her leg across Maria's and put her arm around Maria's waist. Maria stroked Simone's forearm then lifted her hand and placed it on her chest, above her heart. She cupped Simone's hand to her and held her tighter. Butterflies took flight in her stomach as the question she wanted to ask slipped from her mind to the tip of her tongue. Simone's hand suddenly felt hot against her racing heartbeat. This was a different kind of nerves—pleasant and exciting. She took a deep breath. "Do you still want to marry me?"

Simone turned her head and kissed Maria's neck. "Yes, I do," she whispered.

Simone's breath was warmer and more soothing than the sun caressing Maria's face, and the effect of the sensation on her skin ran deeper than she knew was possible. She was gradually losing the sense of where her own body ended, and Simone's began, and it was like floating in a bubble of bliss. Simone's breathing was shallow and delicate, and Maria drifted with the feeling of them breathing and moving as one. Simone's weight becoming heavier, Maria's eyes closed.

I love you. The words drifted in her imagination and in a state that was neither reality nor a dream she wondered whether she had said them out loud. She didn't recall hearing them. It didn't matter. Nothing mattered. There would be other times. Many times. Simone was asleep in her arms and they were safe, *together*. She vowed she would say the words again when they woke. Just to be sure…that… She drifted deeper… Simone needs to know… *I will always love you.*

* The End *

Discover *Madeleine* by Emma Nichols

Chapter 1

Génissiat, France 1947

Claudette gazed skywards, her eyes weary, the light fading as she ambled towards *Restaurant Vietti*. The rain clouds had passed in a brief moment, leaving a spongy feel to the lightly dampened path, the wetness insufficient for the soil to stick to the well-worn boots that weighed heavily with every pace.

The day had seemed endless and the work, as always, arduous, but even more so on this, her first day. She had vowed to pace herself, not to feel that she needed to prove herself, but railway work was a man's work — she'd heard it said often enough — and she found herself doing more, working longer, demonstrating her strength to the eyes boring into her back. The sniggering had stopped soon enough, though the subsequent silence in her presence and whenever she moved past a chattering group of men, told her all she needed to know. She wasn't welcome, didn't fit in. Never would. She had skipped lunch, her stomach groaning, overhearing the men describe in great detail the sumptuous meal they had stopped to consume. They were cruel, rigid in their beliefs, and bigoted. Yes, very narrow-minded. She nodded her head, affirming her thoughts, and inhaled deeply, her pace slowing to a stop. She had hoped the war would have changed things, but it hadn't. If anything it had made matters worse – men reasserting themselves into a world they left behind, one that had changed in their absence but without their approval.

The pervasive scent of ferns springing to life, the musty earth, and a subtle sweet-floral smell drew her from her musings. The rain did that, brought nature to life. She breathed in the fresh fragrance, gazed at the sky again. Dusk was approaching earlier these days, with the transition into autumn, but the sun still held warmth, and it would be another two hours before it dived behind the mountains. She removed her jacket, slung it over her shoulder and continued to amble.

Something was reassuring about the near silence inside the wooded parkland, and she wondered if her Papa had walked this path before her. A smile crept into a yawn, and she rubbed her eyes. He was right; this was a beautiful part of France. She rolled her shoulders, eased the tension held in tired muscles and wondered, momentarily, where the tightness had gone. She squinted into the sky expectantly, but it looked the same. Being in nature always seemed to affect her in this way, give her cause to question the essence of life, but there was something intangible here too, soothing and calming. Ethereal. A large boulder resting under the canopy of an old oak tree caught her attention, and her feet followed her eyes to the edge of a lake. The water was motionless, a black mirror settled into a bed of ferns and foliage. She dipped her boot, humoured by the ripple that danced across the surface, obscuring her reflection. Folding her jacket neatly, she pressed it against the boulder, sat and leaned her head back, her eyes closing, her mind stilling. Aware of a distant dog barking, children's laughter, and birdsong, she sighed as she drifted. Settling her body against the smooth hard surface, her lips parted slightly, and her breathing slowed.

'Help! Help! Help!'

Claudette jumped to her feet before her eyes opened fully, her ears locating the panicked cries, her heart pounding in her chest. An urgent groan escaped her as she squinted across the lake.

A young child, a girl, grappling frantically at the side of a small boat seemed to be struggling, unable to reach the boy's hand. The girl's head dropped under the water, re-surfaced. The high-pitched screams echoed across the water. The boy leaned over the boat, reached out again, trying to find the small hand, shouting instructions. Fingers slipped through fingers, and the girl submerged then resurfaced again.

Wading, diving, Claudette punched her arms through the water, adrenalin driving her the short distance at a swift pace. Lifting the girl with ease, the boy shaking, wide-eyed and silent, she heaved the small body into the boat. The girl was staring at her, and she tried to smile reassuringly. Then the girl started to sob uncontrollably. 'It's okay,' Claudette said, her heart racing. She had no idea how to handle children. None whatsoever. 'You're okay. It's okay. I'm going to get in the boat,' she said, nodding at the girl and then the boy, seeking an affirmation. The boy stared, the girl continued to sob. She climbed in. 'Where is the oar?'

The boy pointed to the stick resting on the bank.

Merde! She lowered herself back into the water and moved behind the boat. Arms pushing and legs kicking, she eased the craft to the bank and stepped out of the water. Reaching her arms out, the young girl climbed into them, and

Claudette lifted her to the ground, thankful that the sobs had ceased. She dropped to her knees, assessing the girl.

The boy jumped out of the boat and stood, his eyes downcast, scuffing at the loose soil at his feet. She gazed up; he looked pale.

The girl threw herself at Claudette and wrapped her arms around her neck in a vice-like grip. Claudette froze at the unexpected contact then softened, enfolding the child in a reassuring embrace. 'You're safe now,' she said. The girl clung on tightly.

The boy kicked at the soil.

'My name is Claudette, what's yours?' she said, addressing the boy.

'Albert,' he mumbled, his gaze still firmly directed at his feet.

The girl's grip eased, and wide eyes studied Claudette's face intently. 'I'm Natty. I'm six, and he's ten,' she said. Claudette's lips curled, and Natty beamed a smile.

'We'd better get you home,' Claudette said. 'You're soaking wet.'

Natty twiddled with Claudette's now off-white shirt in her fingers. 'You're all wet too,' she said.

Claudette laughed. 'Yes, I am.'

Albert stared at her. 'I'm sorry,' he said.

Claudette stood, placed her hand on his shoulder and squeezed. 'Where do you live?' she asked. She smiled, hoping to draw him from his concerns.

He gazed down the path. 'The restaurant,' he said, pointing down the tree-lined route from the lake. He still wasn't smiling.

'Ah, right. Well, that's good because I'm really very hungry,' she said. She beamed a grin at him, and his mouth twitched.

Natalie grinned back at her. 'I'm hungry too,' she said, her hand finding its way into Claudette's.

Claudette frowned at the unfamiliar sensation against her palm. The fragility she would have expected with something so small and delicate also held the quality of strength and determination she associated with something far more robust. She held on firmly. 'Right, lead on,' she said.

Albert led.

'She's going to be cross,' he said as they walked.

'Who is?' Claudette said.

'Maman.'

'Ah, yes.' Claudette nodded and reached out her hand. He seemed to relax with the comforting touch. 'Do you come to the lake often?' she said.

He kicked a stone across the ground as he walked. 'Maman said we're not allowed to go in the boat,' he said, his voice broken.

'Ah, I see,' she said, squeezing both their hands, falling effortlessly into step with Natty's shorter pace.

'I'm cold.' Natty said.

Claudette stopped, studied the straggly fair hair and chattering teeth. She glanced over her shoulder. Merde! 'I left my jacket on the rock,' she said.

'I'll go and get it,' Albert said.

'It's the other side of the lake.'

He shrugged, released her hand, and ran back along the path, heading for the track leading around the water's edge.

'We'll wait here for you.' Her words followed him, and he raised his hand in acknowledgement before dipping out of sight.

'I'...m c...o...l...d,' Natty said again, her eyes watering, her lips a shade closer to blue.

Claudette crouched, pulled her into her chest and kissed the top of her head. The tiny arms wrapped around her, gentle sobs snuffled into her chest. 'You're okay,' she said, lost for anything more reassuring to say.

Natty stopped snuffling suddenly and pulled out of the embrace. She stared at Claude intently. 'Are you a man?' she said.

Claudette released a short puff of air in a splutter. 'No. Claudette is a girl's name. Though I prefer to be called Claude,' she said.

'Maman calls me Natty. My real name's Natalie.'

'That's a pretty name.'

Inquisitive eyes scanned Claude. 'You've got no breasts,' Natty said, staring directly at her chest.

Claudette chuckled, aware of the rough damp cloth that had been rubbing against sensitive skin. 'My shirt hides them,' she said, wondering if that was the right response to give to a six-year-old.

'Maman's got big breasts.'

'Oh!' Claudette gulped, her throat constricted, and a brief coughing fit challenged her breathing.

Natty stared wide-eyed, studying her further. 'Why is your hair short?'

'Because I like it that way.' Claudette looked down the track to the lake, willing Albert's return.

'It's like a man.'

'Yes.'

'Why?'

'Why what?'

'Why do you have it like a man?' Natty reached up and pulled at the short hair around Claudette's ear.

Claudette retracted. 'Do you always ask a lot of questions?'

Natty nodded. 'Maman says it's good to ask questions.'

'Ah, right. And what does your papa say about that?' The smile on Claudette's face was met with nonchalance and a shrug.

'He's dead.' Natty said. She turned her head towards the path and started waving.

Claudette took a moment to follow Natty's gaze. She stood, took a deep breath and released it slowly, relieved that Albert was running towards them with a beaming grin on his face.

'Here,' he said, puffing and holding out the jacket. His smile thinned his lips and revealed brilliant white teeth. He would be a handsome man in a few years.

'Thank you.'

Claudette glanced at Natty. 'Do you want to wear it?'

Natty grinned, and the tip of her nose and cheeks glowed. She held out her arms enthusiastically. 'Can you put it on me?'

Claudette guided the short arms into the long sleeves, wrapped the jacket around the slender frame and buttoned it up. Natty looked down at the cloth hanging from her body. Claudette tried to roll a sleeve up, but it slipped down immediately. She shrugged. 'Shall we go home?'

Natty reached up, and Claudette clasped the sleeve-covered hand, fully aware that the other sleeve was dragging in the dirt as they ambled along the path.

Chapter 2

'Mon Dieu!'

'Maman,' Albert said, his shoulders slumping. He avoided her fierce glare as they approached the house and Madeleine closed down on his personal space.

'Albert, what on earth happened?'

He winced.

The woman's eyes darted to her daughter, who stood stiffly, attention on her brother. The woman reached out and pulled Natty into her arms. 'Are you hurt?'

Natty shook her head. 'I just fell in the water,' she said, in a voice that was noticeably quieter than when she had fired questions at Claudette.

'What have I told you about playing next to the lake?' she said to her son, thrashing an arm towards him. 'Allez! Go to your room. Maintenant. Now!'

Albert's eyes caught Claudette's briefly, with a look that said, please don't tell her about the boat, and then he turned towards the restaurant and ran.

Claudette stared. The passion emanating from this slender woman, in a wrap-around dress that perfectly accentuated her figure, caused her muscles to tighten and she found herself standing to attention next to Natty. She cleared her throat, forced her shoulders to relax and held out a hand. 'I'm Claudette,' she said.

The woman's eyes eventually shifted from her daughter to the outstretched hand and then settled on Claudette's smile. 'Bonjour, Claudette. I am Madeleine,' she said, shaking hands.

The grip was firm and warm. Claudette cleared her throat again, acutely aware of the tingling sensation that had caused the hairs on her arms to rise and her skin to prickle. Words escaped her, and all that came out of her mouth was a mumbled groan. She stared. She couldn't help herself.

'Madeleine Vietti,' Madeleine said.

The words pulled Claudette from her stunned inarticulate state, and she rubbed clammy hands down her trousers. 'Sorry, I, umm.' Madeleine's eyes were assessing her, and her racing heart was making words even harder to find.

'You are soaking wet,' she said.

Claudette hadn't expected Madeleine to reach out and touch the shirt on her arm, or the electric response that shot through her body, or the groan that she fought to suppress. 'Umm.' She looked down. Her shirt had dried a little, but her trousers hung heavily from her hips, and when she wriggled her toes she could feel the pools of warm water that bathed her feet.

'We need to get you out of those clothes,' Madeleine said.

'Umm, I'm fine, thank you. Natty got very cold.' Claudette could feel heat rising to her cheeks.

Madeleine stilled, her hand resting on Claudette's arm, her eyes fixed on Claudette's face, and then a smile formed that softened her features. 'Yes, Natty too,' she said, removing her hand and raking her fingers through her hair.

Claudette swallowed, absorbed by Madeleine's movement that seemed suddenly self-conscious, and smiled. She touched the burning spot Madeleine had left on her arm.

Want more? Madeleine is available to order from Amazon and all great book shops….

AMAZON REVIEWS

"Surely, it must be impossible to read Madeleine and not fall a little in love with her. An outstanding novel - 5 stars"

"Emma Nichols' lesbian historical romance, MADELEINE, is a pure delight."

"A sublimely beautiful love story between two women set against the backdrop of post-World War 2 France."

"Gripping love story perfect reading for a cosy winter night."

"I read this book in less than a day... I didn't sleep all night. Just perfect."

"Madeleine - What an amazing book, read it you won't be disappointed - 5 star read."

About Emma Nichols

Emma Nichols lives in Buckinghamshire with her wife and two children. She served for 12 years in the British Army, studied Psychology, and published several non-fiction books under another name, before dipping her toes into the world of lesbian fiction.

You can contact Emma through her website and social media:

www.emmanicholsauthor.com

Facebook: @EmmaNicholsAuthor
Twitter: @ENichols_Author
Instagram: @enichols_author

And do please leave a review if you enjoyed this book. Reviews really help independent authors to promote their work. Thank you.

Discover other titles by Emma Nichols

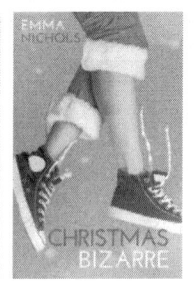

Thanks for reading and supporting my work!

Discover other great books by Indie Authors

Call to Me by Helena Harte
Sometimes the call you least expect is the one you need the most.

Addie Mae by Addison M. Conley
At the beginning of a bitter divorce, Maddy meets mysterious Jessie Stevens. They bond over scuba diving, and as their friendship grows, so does the attraction. (Release scheduled for October 2020)

Sliding Doors by Karen Klyne
Sometimes your best life is someone else's.

Nights of Lily Ann: Redemption of Carly by L L Shelton
Lily Ann makes women's desires come true as a lesbian escort, but can she help Carly, who is in search of a normal life after becoming blind.

The Women and the Storm by Kitty McIntosh
Being the only witch in a small Scottish town is not easy.

Isabel's Healing by Maggie McIntyre
A devastating car accident leaves Bel broken, but when a young assistant steps into her life, could Bel learn to live again?

Stealing a Thief's Heart by C L Cattano
Two women, a great escape, and a quest for a soulmate.

Maddie Meets Kara: Remember Me by D R Coghlan
Who is her enemy? Who is her friend? And what really happened that night?

What's Your Story?

Global Wordsmiths, CIC, provides an all-encompassing service for all writers, ranging from basic proofreading and cover design to development editing, typesetting, and eBook services. A major part of our work is charity and community focused, delivering writing projects to under-served and under-represented groups across Nottinghamshire, giving voice to the voiceless and visibility to the unseen. To learn more about what we offer, visit: www.globalwords.co.uk.

A selection of books by Global Words Press:

- Desire, Love, Identity: with the National Justice Museum
- Aventuras en México: Farmilo Primary School
- Life's Whispers: Journeys to the Hospice
- Times Past: with The Workhouse, National Trust
- World At War: Farmilo Primary School
- Times Past: Young at Heart with AGE UK
- In Different Shoes: Stories of Trans Lives
- Patriotic Voices: Stories of Service
- From Surviving to Thriving: Reclaiming Our Voices
- Don't Look Back, You're Not Going That Way

Self-published authors working with Global Wordsmiths:

- John Parsons
- Emma Nichols
- Dee Griffiths and Ali Holah
- Helena Harte
- Karen Klyne
- Ray Martin
- Valden Bush
- Simon Smalley

Printed in Great Britain
by Amazon